MW01135426

Healing Scars

Audrey Ravine

A Military Romance

DEDICATION

As always, my books are dedicated to my family. I have been so blessed to have a husband that supports everything I do. Without you I wouldn't be able to be who I am. You and the kids are my world! I love you!

PROLOGUE

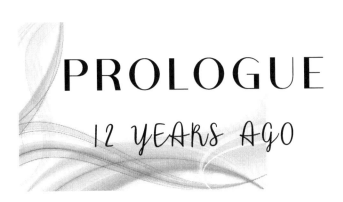

12 YEARS AGO

Crash!

I cringe looking at the mass of bodies squeezed into a monumentally sized dog pile across from me on the forty-yard line. Kent loves this game, for some God forsaken reason. Since I love him, it is customary for me to love the game. However, I hate football. I hate football with a burning passion and can't wait for the damn games to be over with.

Kent and I have been together for three years, roughly sixty football games from sophomore year to now. I'm going out of my mind with boredom. What is it about this game that gets everyone all in a tizzy. I don't see it. Seriously, all I see is my boyfriend getting gross and sweaty on the field throwing a ball to other gross and sweaty dudes. All before yet another gross dude brings him to the ground in a sweaty semblance of a bear hug.

I mean, come on. This sport is *absurd*.

Just as Kent is about to throw, I feel my phone vibrate in my pocket. "Thank God," I say under my breath, grateful for the distraction.

Mom: What time is Kent bringing you home?

My mom, the ever-present worrier. Swiping the screen to open the phone, a bump from behind causes me to just about double over. Catching myself with my hands on my knees I look behind at the celebrating freshman that made me drop my phone. Even though he seems genuinely sorry, I can't find the compassion at the moment.

"Where the hell is my phone?" Looking around I can't find it anywhere. "Lee, do you see my phone?" I ask my friend, and fellow football girlfriend, sitting next to me. We're both moving bags and food trying to unearth my missing phone.

After a solid three minutes of looking, "Oh wait, there it is." Lee points to the slit in the bleachers at the ground below.

"Perfect." I sigh, standing. "I'll be right back." Walking down the stairs to the space below our seats.

"Come here phone. I know I just saw you." I coax my missing phone to show itself. I literally just saw it from my seat on the bleachers. "What the hell?" I say, throwing a rock. Unable to rein in my frustration. Not only am I at the dumbest sports game on the planet, but now I have to find my phone in a pile of freakin' pebbles and trash.

"Looking for this, Ty?" That voice. That nickname. For being a girl named Tyler, Zac is the only one to ever call me Ty quite like that. Like it's salvation leaving his lips. As I turn my head, all I see is that crooked smirk. The smirk that looks equal parts mischievous and sexy. The smirk that I see in my dreams and long to turn into a full-blown smile that -I already know- will weaken my knees. The smirk that is attached to the most aggravatingly gorgeous man I've ever met. A man with hazel eyes so caramelly they look golden is currently holding back the entertainment he gets out of teasing me. Why does he bother me so much?

"Yes, I am. Thank you." I reach for it and see the cigarette in Zac's other hand. "You do realize smoking is bad for you and everyone around you, right?" I say, as his eyes lock with mine and he brings the cigarette to his overly plump lips and takes a drag.

I can't be here looking at him, I think and drop my head. Only not looking in his eyes is even more dangerous. Peeking out from the side of his sleeve there's a glimpse of a tattoo. His corded arms somehow look right with the artwork. Zac sees me staring and looks down at the work and lifts his sleeve.

"Is that new?" I ask, before my brain can catch up with my mouth.

"No." He steps closer. "But there are some new ones." He takes another step closer. "Care to see?" He steps even closer and pulls at the hem of his T-shirt. My eyes are fixated on the small amount of smooth skin showing. Zac's pants are low on his hips and the trace of a deep "V" and abs show with a sprinkling of hair below his belly button.

I can feel my cheeks redden. The heat rising from my core giving me away in front of Zachariah. I've made it all year without Zac or Kent catching my wayward glances. It has to be the heat in our small Georgia town that's making my body rise in temperature.

Zac steps closer still and lifts his shirt enough that the six compact muscles of his stomach flex against the thin fabric of his shirt hem. His hazel eyes sparkle with mischief as he sees the pink spread from my cheeks to my chest and down my arms.

"I have to go," I say, snatching my phone. I turn to head back to my friends and watch the abysmal game on the field. "Oof." A super lady-like grunt escapes my chest as I trip on the gravel from spinning too quickly. Before I completely lose my balance, large hands grip my hips and keep me upright.

Standing to my full height, Zac is so close I can feel his heat against my back. His hard form a breath away from touching my skin. I have to physically and mentally catch myself before I lean back into him. We stand there for a never ending minute, his musk and cigarette wafting around me. For the amount of shit I give him for smoking, the mixture of cologne, smoke, and something inherently Zac is causing my insides to tighten with need.

I have a boyfriend.

I have a boyfriend.

I have a boyfriend. Kent, who is right now on that field getting sweaty and bruised to show off to me. I need to get back up to the stands to watch him play. Then when he's done, I can release all this pent-up estrogen on him.

The best laid plans, I think as Zac leans forward and brushes his lips against my ear. "Let me know if you want to see where the rest are." His raspy voice drops an octave as his breath warms my ear causing my heart to pause. My head tilts and it drops against his shoulder until I finally come to my senses.

"Um." I stand up and create space between Zac and I. "I'll be sure to let Kent know you're offering an art gallery for us." Without looking at him again, I round the corner out of his sight. I take a minute to catch my breath before I trek the rest of the way to my seat.

There's no way to play off the blushing of my cheeks. Lee would know in a heartbeat something happened. And something did happen. Zac does this to me every time. There's something about his bad boy tendencies that intrigues me. Every time he's around, I find myself forgetting about Kent and everything he and I have planned for next year.

We've already been accepted to the same college. I need to steer clear of Zac. I need to keep my eye on the future, which is currently on the field playing for the state title. As I turn to brave my friends a hand rests against my shoulder.

"Oh my G-," I gasp turning to see who has a hold on me.

"Hey, hey," my dad's calming baritone vibrates through me bringing a sense of calm. "Where's the fire, Tybear?"

"You scared me, I dropped my phone and was just coming back from getting it," I say, looking toward the entrance to under the bleachers I just came from. Before my eyes can dart back to my dad, Zac comes into view.

"Mr. Thomas, fancy meetin' you here," Zac says, clearly enjoying the fact that my dad is upset that I've been caught with the town bad boy.

"Zachariah, you been smokin' back there, son?" My father's condemning tone isn't lost on either of us.

"No, Sir. I hear they're bad for you," Zac says, his golden-flecked hazel eyes locked with mine. I wish I could stop the tornado of emotions, but everytime I see him they seem to get stronger. Graduation can't come soon enough. I don't know how much more I can take before I give in and let him destroy the relationship I've had since I was a preteen. "I'll see you at school on Monday, Ty." He takes a step closer to me as if he's going to hug me, but my father clears his throat. Not missing a beat Zac places his palm against my cheek for just a second, before looking to my dad. "You have a good night, Mr. Thomas."

"You too, Zac." My dad watches Zac's lithe figure slink away into the shadows of the parking lot before turning back to me. "Tyler, you're smarter than that." He points in the vague direction of the street.

"Daddy, it wasn't what you think. I just dropped my phone between the bleachers and when I went down to pick it up he was already there."

"Alright, darlin', but that boy is no good. I see the way he looks at you. I know there's cracklin' of something brewing between you two, but he's not what you need. I don't much like Kent, but he's good to you and he's goin' places. That's what you need. I don't want you settlin' in this town. You're better than that." Of course, this isn't the first time my dad has drawn conclusions from the town drunks son. Just because he grew up with the man doesn't mean that is the man he is destined to turn into. It's no use arguing. I've been there and done that. I've tried to convince my dad that Zachariah isn't who he thinks he is, but even when he sees my side of things the conversation ends with, 'well, I still don't want him around you.'

"Yes, Daddy," I say, counting grains of dirt on the ground. "Daddy, what are you doin' here? Isn't it date night?"

"It is, but you didn't answer your momma's text and she got worried. We were just finishin' dinner, so she asked me to stop by here and check on you. I've checked, now I'm gonna take your momma home and draw her a bath. You run along now." My dad loves my mom something fierce. I want that kind of love. I hope Kent is the one that will give it to me.

I hug my dad goodbye and head to the bleachers with my friends to finish watching the game. This is what I have to look forward to for the next four years of school. Maybe more if he makes it to the NFL. Ugh, what a way to spend a cold evening. As I watch the game unfold, I keep thinking about what my dad said. He's seen the connection Zac and I have. Have I been that obvious? Do other people know how he makes me feel? Surely not, right?

Of course not. My dad is just being overly watchful of his daughter. Although, he doesn't much care for Kent sometimes; he clearly agrees with the town that any option is a better option than Zachariah. Sure, his dad may be the town drunk. And he may miss more classes than he attends, but he's passing everything. He's a bright kid. He has a sweet personality if you're willing to look past all the sarcastic bullpoop he tries to feed everyone.

But, my dad is right. It's already been established. I'm going to college with Kent and we're going to have the life he always talks about-him in the NFL and me barefoot and pregnant with the love of my life's children. Yes, that is going to be my life!

CHAPTER ONE

Tyler

Divorce is expensive. Forsaking the life you built over two decades with someone you were supposed to grow old with. It was the hardest decision I've ever had to make. I never thought I'd be here. I never thought the man I fell in love with my sophomore year of high school would be this hostile man who looks at me with nothing but contempt.

Sitting on the bench outside the judge's chambers, I can't help but reflect on how we got here. How did we get so off track? Off track to the point that I'm genuinely concerned that this man I once loved might actually fulfill one of his many drunken threats against me. One of the threats that just became too numerous and too close for comfort to ignore any longer.

If it were just me, I'd probably overlook the drunken outbursts. It's not just me anymore, though. It hasn't been just me for almost ten years. Wyatt, our beautiful girl, is finally old enough to ask questions. I see the fear in her eyes whenever Kent comes home after "hanging out" with his buddies. I mean they're cops, you'd think they'd realize he is not a stable person when he's drunk. What the hell are they all thinking sending him home to his wife and daughter in such a state of inebriation that he waves his service revolver around like a trophy.

Does that make him more of a man? To terrify his family just to keep his control? My final straw. His last outburst was my breaking point and I can't- in good conscience- allow my daughter to be around such a hateful, resentful man.

"The judge will allow fifteen more minutes for Kent to arrive and then we will have to proceed without him," Janice, my lawyer, says taking a seat next to me and covering my hand with hers offering me much needed comfort.

She knows this has been hard for me. This has been a long time coming and Kent has been a shadow of the person he once was for a while now. Though, it's still hard admitting defeat. Admitting that this commitment I made in front of God, our family, and our friends is unsalvageable. "Thank you," I say to her. I don't let my eyes reach hers. I can't bring myself to look at the sympathy in her eyes. The pity I see in those same friends and family now. I need to be strong. I need to stand my ground. Is it bad that I wouldn't be upset if Kent didn't show up for this?

"I'm here, I'm here." Kent jogs up to us, alcohol emanating from his pores. He's one of three things. A. still drunk from last night. B. currently plastered so he can deal with this mess. Or C. hungover beyond caring that he reeks of beer and body odor.

"Great, let's get on in there," Janice says, helping me up.

"As for custody..." The judge looks over the paperwork in front of her. Probably at the custody agreement my lawyer and I have worked up. I know Kent will be upset, but what does he really expect? "Mrs. Williams, you are asking for sole custody with supervised visitation until Mr. Williams finishes an approved alcohol and anger management course for a year. Is that correct?" She looks at me.

I look at Janice then look back at the judge. "Yes, that's correct, Your Honor," I say, hoping I sound more confident than I am. I can feel Kent's eyes on me and I try my hardest not to look his way.

Judge Herrera opens her mouth to speak when Kent interrupts, "you bitch." I look over and he's practically steaming with anger. "You think you can take away my daughter? You good for nothing little shit. I should have kicked your ass out when I had the chance. See if you'd still stand up to me with my foot up your ass."

Judge Herrera bangs her gavel repeatedly trying to quiet Kent down. "Mr. Clay, you need to remind your client he needs to remain quiet or he'll be held in contempt," she says, as Kents lawyer tries to calm him down. "In light of that outburst, I'm going to grant Mrs. Tyler Williams sole custody without visitation until Mr. Kent Williams has completed six months of alcohol and anger management classes. At that point, supervised visitation will be organized until the full year of classes has been completed by Mr. Williams."

The judge looks down to sign her name to the new agreement.

"You whore," Kent calls from behind his lawyers back. Poor Mr. Clay, he had no idea the handful Kent would be when he took him on as a client. Mr. Clay is trying to pull Kent away when he breaks his lawyers grip and marches up to the Judge. "It's just like a whore to side with a bitch. You women are all the same. You side with each other no matter what. Pussies stick together, huh?" Kent looks at me with so much venom in his eyes I physically cringe from the look alone. "Women should never be put in places of authority. You'll only use that power to cut men down. It's not our fault you weren't born with a penis."

"Order, order," the judge shouts over Kent's outburst while banging her gavel. "Bailiff please escort Mr. Williams to holding. Mr. Clay, I'm holding your client in contempt of court. You will be able to speak with him after his arraignment."

I stand there next to Janice in shock. Stunned into silence. Kent really showed his true colors today. As sad as it is to see my marriage fall apart- as hurt as I may be- I can't say I'm upset watching the bailiff put handcuffs on my state trooper husband. Ex-husband.

Wyatt and I will be fine. Most of our things are already packed from living with my friend for the past few weeks. The truck is ordered for tomorrow and we will finally be out of the cross hairs of that man. The man who swore before me and anyone who would listen that he would love me and our child with everything he had. I guess that was only until he felt it wasn't convenient anymore.

No matter. Tomorrow Wyatt and I are moving back

to my hometown in Georgia. My parents are still there to help and we're going to move on. We're going to be fine.

We are fine.

We have to be.

CHAPTER TWO

Tyler

"Wyatt, baby, look. We're getting close." I jostle my sleeping child's shoulder to wake her before we get to the heart of the town. From our distance, you can see the top of the University of North Georgia buildings and its bringing back all the familiar feelings of being home. I start to point things out to Wyatt as we make it to the town square. The old town feeling of the buildings like the Gold Museum and all the fixtures that I grew up with are finally going to be a part of Wyatt's life.

Kent never liked coming back here. He said we were too big for this town and we were meant for more. He always made our parents trek it to Virginia whenever they wanted to visit. I never thought it was fair. I missed home and it would cause countless fights between Kent and I. Unfortunately, those little disagreements were the least of our problems.

Forty minutes later, Wyatt and I sit on the hood of the rental truck waiting for my parents to arrive. My mom agreed to occupy my nosey nine-year-old and Dad offered to help unload as much as he could then get one of the neighbors to help with anything he couldn't lift.

My dad may be old, but he's one of the most in shape over fifty-year-old's I've ever seen. That man goes to the gym more than people half his age. Not that my mom's complaining. She's the first to tell anyone she meets about her "hunk of a husband," her words not mine.

God, I've missed them.

Finally, my parents round the corner into our cul de sac. Hopping down and helping Wyatt to her feet I hear a car pulling into the driveway behind us. I turn to look at my neighbor, but Wyatt's squeal calls my attention. I watch her take a flying leap into my dad's arms and it melts my heart. I always feared that the distance, and Kent's unwillingness to come visit, would strain their relationship. I'm glad to see my fears were unwarranted.

"Baby Girl," my mom coos to me, wrapping me in a hug. My parents were always the young parents, but seeing my mother and father start to show their age is saddening. It hurts that it has been almost 18 months since I last saw them.

My mother releases me, long enough for me to catch my breath before my dad pulls me in. "Tybear," he says against my temple. The rumble of his chest as he says the nickname he's had for me since I was a child breaks the seal. Tears fall against his shoulder. We stand there in our embrace as he transfers his strength to me. I pull back to see my mother has taken Wyatt into the backyard of our new house and started to play. Leave it to my mom to read the moment and make sure my daughter never sees me breakdown.

Thankful for her distraction, I look at my dad. "Where did it all go wrong?" I ask him. I've always been a daddy's girl and looking to him for answers has been his second job since I learned how to talk. He never really cared for Kent. He always put up with him for my sake, but he hoped and assumed Kent would be a passing fancy and never develop into anything. Then, when I got pregnant freshman year of college he knew we were all stuck with him.

"Honey, you are stronger than this, you'll see," he says, then looks back at where my mom and daughter disappeared. "You have to be. You got that little girl out there lookin' to you on how to handle all of this. She may know her dad wasn't the greatest man, but he is still her daddy and she's havin' to come to terms with the man he really is versus the fantasy dad she always thought him up to be. You need to show her that life goes on and you can survive anythin'," he says, holding onto my shoulders.

"Thanks, Dad," I say, wiping my eyes before anymore tears fall. "Now, let's get me unloaded." I turn and shift back into 'Protective Momma Mode.' My go-to self-preservation mechanism for getting through this.

"I'm just going to bring this last box then I need a break," I call out to my dad, who's been so nonstop that I can't keep up with him. It's been two hours and we are down to the last few things, but I'm struggling.

Walking down the ramp backwards, I fear I may have overestimated my strength on this box. It's not particularly heavy, but rather oddly shaped and my grip is weakening. The box starts to wobble and I can feel my muscles giving out. Trying to readjust my grip yet again, before I lose the box when my heel hits the uneven divot in the ramp I warned was going to be the death of me, and start to fall backward.

"Woah," I hear faintly, but with the adrenaline rushing through my body it sounds fuzzy and distant. Although, it can't be too distant, I feel a hand on my hip and the box feels a million times lighter within seconds. Thank God, my dad caught me! I lean my weight against him until I feel comfortable on my legs to stand straight with the box.

"I got it," I say, turning and lowering the box to the ramp between my dad and I. Although, it's not my dad. Those Vans are not my dad's. Those thick, corded muscular calves disappearing into light cargo shorts are not my dad's. The man in front of me, the man who had his hand on my hip is most definitely not my dad. The broad shoulders and tapered waist of the man in front of me are perfectly proportioned and muscular, pulling his light Polo to its limits. His dark hair is buzzed short, allowing caramel eyes to pool and draw all the attention. I'm lost in those eyes when I realize I literally just leaned against a total stranger. A very large, very attractive total stranger.

Great!

After two hours of moving in the southern heat I know I smell like the back side of a rhino and probably look a lot worse. Of all the days to, quite literally, back it up against a hot stranger it had to be today. I'm a mess from driving for nine hours then moving for two. I must have been a real bitch in a former life cause my luck is just nonexistent.

"I'm sorry. I thought you were my Dad," I say, reaching up to shake his hand. "I'm Tyler, I know it's a weird name for a girl, but that's what it is." Now I'm rambling. This just keeps getting better and better. The strange man reaches for my hand and his long fingers clasp around mine. I'm not sure what it is, but there's a surge of electricity that shoots from my fingers all the way to my core. I feel the blush on my cheeks break through and try to look anywhere but his- somehow knowing- eyes. I can't get lost in those again. Although, following our connected hands up his arm to the thick muscles of his forearms, I might be in even more trouble. His corded arms are hard to look away from.

The hand that is connected to mine is attached to a thick gallery of dark, tattooed artwork. The black line-work and gray-shading following the curves and divots of his arm muscles are mesmerizing. My eyes trace the captivating work up to the end of his shirt sleeve. The edge of the tattoo there seems so familiar, yet I can't place it. Maybe it's a famous artist's work that is represented in ink on this stranger's skin.

"I've always thought it strange, but it suits you, Ty." The velvety rumble of his voice and my name falling from his lips causes me to meet his eyes once more. It can't be. That voice, it's so familiar. I look into his eyes and see the mirth clear as day. Looking back at the tattoo I found so familiar then into this man's eyes once more I realize, this is no stranger at all.

"Zachariah?" I question. There's no way the Zac I went to high school with is as put together as this man standing in front of me.

I take a step back to have another look at the man in front of me. This time really looking at the whole picture. The man in front of me, while attractive and in shape is wearing a light blue-collared golf Polo that makes his eyes a creamy golden caramel color. One arm encircled with black and gray tattoos while the other has the newest Apple watch around the wrist. His khaki shorts are tight and fitted in all the right places. Showcasing thighs that make my insides tighten and my thighs to squeeze together. His feet are in comfortable maroon Vans that scream out of place, but on him almost work perfectly. This man in front of me in no way has anything in common with the person I'm remembering from high school. Well, except the tattoos, maybe.

"Man, no one's called me by my full name in years. It's good to see you again, Ty." Again, the way he says my name leaves me craving him to say it again- repeatedly. Holy shit, it really is Zac!

CHAPTER THREE

ZAC

Today was a long ass day. Although, lately I feel like they're all long. My back has been killing me and I almost dropped a damn overweight lab on the floor this morning. I know I need to get my back checked out again, I'm just worried about the outcome. The idea of another surgery causes chills to overtake my body and goosebumps to line my muscled arms. After everything I've been through, not much else scares me. Yet, the fear of what could be wrong with my back terrifies the shit out of me.

Walking to the kitchen for another handful of painkillers, I notice the moving truck in front of the house next door. Was that there when I got home from the office? Was I really so self-absorbed I missed the damn moving truck in front of the house that has sat empty for almost three years? Shit, I guess I was. Watching through my kitchen window I see a blonde bombshell. I mean this chick is so out of place in this town it's not even funny.

Sure, we have cute girls. All the co-eds from the University of North Georgia are only fifteen minutes away. Ergo, my buddies and I always run into hot chicks at the bars in town. Yet, none of them hold a candle to this chick bending down repeatedly in front of my eyes. Her tiny waist and slender hips. Tits and ass begging to be licked and legs that go on for days. Normally I'm an ass man, but if you're going to present me with an ass I can sink my teeth into as well as a chest that's begging to be palmed you're not going to hear any quarrels from me. And let me tell you, this chick has both in spades.

Resting my hip against the counter, I watch my new neighbor bend and strain to move her things from the truck into her house. If my back weren't shit today I'd offer to help, but seeing that I'm about to pop some more pain killers I should probably sit this one out. Besides she looks like she's got help, I notice the buff, bald guy helping her move in. A ping of fire courses through me and I'm not really sure why my body is having such an intense reaction to the well-endowed stranger's help. Looking closer, I can't help noticing that the bald guy looks familiar.

"Shit, that's Mr. Thomas," I say to myself, after a few minutes of staring at the older man. "What is Mr. Thomas doing helpin' a young girl move in?" I question. Did he divorce his wife? Does he have a mistress? Damn, this just got super real super quick.

I lean forward, ignoring the pain emanating from my back and look closer at the young girl. Just as I'm about to write her off she turns and I see those unmistakable blue-gray eyes. Eyes of which there has never been a match- in my opinion. Eyes that have trapped me since I moved to Georgia my sophomore year. Eyes that I'd swear turn purple only for me. Beautifully expressive eyes that belong to none other than Tyler Thomas.

Tyler was good looking in school, but she's only blossomed with age. Her body has gone from cute to total knockout. Before I can catch up with my feet I'm already headed out the front door to offer help. Back pain be damned. Walking closer the entire front yard smells like cherry blossoms. Ty always smelled so sweet it's refreshing. Falling under the same spell that brought me to my knees as a high schooler. The only girl to ever make me fall-ever.

Getting closer I see her start to struggle down the ramp with a box that's way too big for her. Where the hell is her dad? Jogging the last yard toward her, I catch her right before she's about to go down. I reach around her grabbing the box and taking most of the weight while my other hand hooks around her hip to steady her. She doesn't pull away and I can't believe I have the one that got away literally falling into my arms. Not only is she in my arms, but she's starting to lean back into me. I tighten my hand on her hip to stop myself from moving it higher along her waist.

Ty adjusts her footing and bends to drop the box. "I got it," she says, raising to her full height to meet my gaze when something flits across her eyes. "I'm sorry. I thought you were my dad," she says holding out her hand. "I'm Tyler, I know it's a weird name for a girl, but that's what it is."

She's introducing herself. Does she really not recognize me? Was I that forgettable? I'm not sure how I feel about this, but I can't help myself from fucking with her, just a little. After all, if I want her to remember me what else would I do but give her a hard time. Just like I did in high school. "I've always thought it strange, but it suits you, Ty."

The second I say her shortened nickname, a trace of recognition crosses over her beautiful features. She looks me dead in the eyes and I try to contain the pleasure I get from messing with her. Ty's eyes dart to the tattoo peeking out from under my sleeve and I enjoy watching the last puzzle pieces fall into place as she looks back at me.

"Zachariah?"

Hearing my full name on her lips, even as a question, is almost more than I can take. I feel my cock twitch in my shorts and I try to readjust by changing my footing. "Man, no one's called me by my full name in years. It's good to see you again, Ty," I say, and her mouth goes slack. I guess even after she asked the question she didn't actually think it could be me. Well, take a good long look, because it's all me, baby.

I've always wondered what happened to Tyler after high school. I knew she followed that tool, Kent Williams, but I just assumed she eventually saw him for who he really was and dropped him before he ruined her life. Looks like I was right- I'm glad to see- since there's no trace of Kent here.

"I'm sorry, Zac. I just can't believe it's really you. I heard you moved away or something," she says, and it's refreshing that she doesn't know the story of how I ended up back on the outskirts of Dahlonega, Georgia.

"Or something. Although, it seems we've both found our way back. Do you need any help?" I ask, as her dad comes out for more boxes. "Hey, Mr. Thomas, how's little Miss Rosey doin'?" I ask, remembering his wife's Yorke just came in for shots not too long ago.

"She's doin' great thanks to you. And call me Caleb," he says. Tyler looks between her father and I like she's missed a key part of the puzzle. "Grab a box, son," he says, slapping me on the shoulder. Mr. Thomas may be the same age as my parents, but that man could give me a run for my money. Even on my best day.

"Oh, no, Dad. I'm sure Zac has plenty of things-" Tyler starts, but I'd never pass up the opportunity to watch her exert herself from hard work. Wow, I'm really appreciating my mental filter right now.

"Nonsense. I'm right behind you, Mr. Tho- Caleb," I say, grabbing a box and winking at Tyler as I walk past towards the house.

Forty-five minutes' pass as we trek back and forth, bringing the last of the boxes and furniture into the house. It's only as we're finishing that I realize it's a mighty large house with quite a bit of stuff for one person. As much as I hope Tyler has lived a happy and fulfilled life with someone to love her and she love in return, I'm not sure I can live with seeing that right next door-every day. Shit, I lived through that in high school and that damn near killed me. I can't do it again- I won't.

"So, I was thinking about ordering pizza and grabbing some beer. Either of you interested?" Tyler asks, pulling me out of my retrospection. She's been away from Dahlonega for so long her accent is completely gone. The more she talks the more I hear the North in her. She's been picking up the 'g' her dad and I have been dropping all day.

"Sorry, Tybear, I'm gunna have to get your momma

home so she can get to bed. She's got an early day tomorrow," her dad says, pulling her into a hug.

"Oh, alright." She pauses, "Zac?" Tyler looks at me, but doesn't meet my eyes. I know she's hoping I'll to say I'm busy, but when have I ever done what she'd like?

"Pizza and beer sounds like the perfect ending to a movin' day." I say, trying to hide the smirk that wants to slide across my face.

"Ok, let me just get Wyatt and make sure pizza's ok," she says, turning. My smile fades and I start to think I'm going to be the third wheel. But, shit, if Wyatt was here the whole time where the hell was he while we were unloading the truck. Some jackass he is. Screw him. I'm seething that Tyler would be with such a pansy ass kind of man that I don't notice Tyler's reentered the room with someone.

Although, it's not a he at all. Instead, standing before me is a young girl- maybe eleven max- looking at me with questioning eyes. "Wyatt, this is Zac. He's our neighbor to the right. I also went to high school with him forever ago," she says to the little girl. "Zac, this is my daughter, Wyatt."

I look between the girl and Tyler and I'm taken back by the unmistakable resemblance. Although, instead of Tyler's wispy blonde hair the girl has a cool sandy blonde thing going for her and crystal-clear blue eyes that look almost white around her irises. I've never seen eyes so clear in my life. The girl is undoubtedly going to be a gorgeous woman when she's older. Granted, with a mom like Tyler, she didn't have much of a choice.

"Hi, Wyatt. You look so much like your momma it's crazy," I say, crouching to greet her at her level, just like I would at work. Little kids are like scared animals, right?

"Thanks. Everyone always says I look like my dad. I'm glad I'm finally starting to look like my mom," Wyatt says, and I find myself in awe of her maturity and the way she handles herself around new adults.

"Well, I've never seen your dad, but even if I had, I'd know without a doubt you got your beauty from your momma." I look back at Tyler who has an unreadable expression on her face. The comment seems to appease Wyatt, though, so I stand back to my full height. "Did I say somethin' wrong?" I ask Tyler under my breath.

"No, it's just been an interesting few months is all. So, Wyatt, pizza?" Tyler asks, and Wyatt jumps around with excitement.

Knock, knock, knock.

"I'll get it." Wyatt jumps off the couch, running full speed to the door.

"Hell, do you ever feed that child?" I ask Tyler. She shoots death rays at me and I can't help the smile that splits my face. She's always been so easy to rile up.

"You know what, no more questions from you." Questions my ass. She's been dodging all my questions all afternoon. All I know is that she's moved here with her only daughter and she wants to start a bakery. I feel like I have jackshit to show for the almost two hours we've been moving and catching up. Granted, I haven't been all that forthcoming either. "What is it you do for a living? Professional pain in my ass?"

"Actually, I'm a vet. I have a practice just down the

road." I know I shouldn't, but I take a little pleasure in the wide-eyed look of surprise on Tyler's face. The high school prick that I was would never have dreamed of being a successful anything, let alone a vet. Then again, with what came after high school, I was left with few other options that didn't lead to becoming a veterinarian. Her daddy stopped me shortly after I got back and told me how proud he was of what I'd made of myself. Told me he misjudged a young man and wanted me to know he was wrong. It wasn't just him though, it was the whole town. It was nice of him to own up to it, though.

"So that's how you know my parents' dog," Tyler says, pulling me from my thoughts.

"It is." It wasn't a question, but I answer her anyway. Talking to Tyler is like pulling teeth. She's never been this closed off before. I realize I haven't spoken to her since high school, but the girl she used to be, the girl I would wake up every day to see, seems to be lost. I find myself wanting to comfort her, remind her of the girl she was back then. I just need to come up with a plan to make sure we spend a lot more time together. Even as neighbors, that might be harder than it seems from the way she's acting.

"Momma, can we eat on the coffee table since Zac set up the TV?" Wyatt asks. She was very insistent that I focus the majority of my attention on getting the TV and cable hooked up for her. She's a precocious little thing. Wyatt reminds me so much of her mother, actually, I can easily imagine Tyler was just like her at that age.

"Sure, that's fine," Tyler says, rummaging through a box to find the plates. "Here, take a plate and there's cans of soda and beer in the fridge," she says, handing both Wyatt and I a plate.

"Are you not eatin'?" I ask, noticing the absence of a third plate.

"I'll just pick at Wyatt's. My nerves are shot from the drive and the move." I nod understanding that moving is a hassle.

We continue to eat and watch movies. Wyatt and I on the floor in front of our plates at the coffee table and Tyler curled on the couch. She's looking out the window- seemingly lost in thought. She must feel my eyes on her, because a minute later she turns to me and gives a tight- lipped smile. Again, as I look at her, I get the feeling of how lost she's become from the person I once knew. It saddens me to see that her life hasn't been that of joy and ease.

"So how do you plan on buyin' this bakery of yours?" I ask, pulling her out of her inner thoughts.

"Oh," her reaction makes it seem like she forgot we had been getting to know each other again. Almost as if I scared her, she recovers well though. "I started an online bakery a few years ago. I rented out a kitchen and sent everything out for overnight delivery or catered. It was mostly for large parties or weddings. Things like that. Over the past year, it's really caught on and I've been thinking of buying a storefront for a while. Figure being back home, there's no better place to take that leap," she says, the determination in her eyes as she talks about her business plan is reassuring. I see a flicker of that fire that once burned so brightly. I wish there was something I could do to ensure her dream becomes a success.

"Hey, you know what? What if you made specialty

dog treats? There's a huge market for those these days," I say, realizing that's a perfect solution to both our problems. I'll have a reason to spend more time with her and she'll have a lot of income coming into her shop.

She takes a few minutes thinking about the idea, before looking at me. Her blue-gray eyes glowing purple with her excitement. She loves the idea, I can tell. "If I did, would you agree to sell them at the practice?" she asks, trying to downplay her joy from my suggestion.

"Well, we'd have to test them out. See if dogs even like 'em. Assumin' you don't kill any of our taste testers, I'll think about it." I turn my head from the pizza just in time to catch a throw pillow aimed for my face.

"You jerk. My cooking is not going to kill anyone-or any dog!" Tyler practically screeches.

"Hey, hey, I'm just sayin'." I hold my hands out in front of me in defeat. "So, when is this bakery of yours opening?" I ask, trying to pull more information out of her and it seems the bakery is the only safe topic at the moment.

"I have an appointment on Monday to meet with a realtor about renting a property." Tyler is visibly vibrating with excitement. She's so fucking cute.

CHAPTER FOUR

Tyler

"Have a good day, bug," I call out, waving as Wyatt hops out of the car at the kiss-and-ride drop-off at her elementary school. God, she's growing so fast. I still remember her first day of kindergarten. Kent couldn't be bothered to go with us, but she was so brave. She walked into that classroom like she owned the place. Kent said I was an idiot for walking her in. That she would be fine- that I was simply babying her. I should have known that was the beginning of the end for us. Unfortunately, it took me four more years to finally put my foot down and say enough was enough.

Looking back at all those years of abuse, I don't understand why I put up with it. I guess I always told myself since he wasn't physically hurting me it wasn't a big deal. Maybe a part of me always assumed we'd find our way back to the loving couple were in high school. I'm not sure why I even wanted it back. In high school, things had always surrounded him and football. Things I wanted and liked to do took a back seat during our whole relationship. Some things never change, I guess.

Hell, I even had to keep my online bakery a secret from him for almost a year. When he found out I'd been spending "his" money to rent a kitchen when we had one of our own for a "pipe dream", he was furious. He threw things and yelled calling me a "dumb bitch" or "stupid waste of space." Then I started pulling in a profit and all of a sudden my starting an online business was a stroke of genius. Although, when he found out I'd been keeping a good portion of the profit in an account in my name he went ballistic. I don't think I'd even been as scared as I was that day fearing he'd cross the line from verbal to physical violence.

"Mrs. Williams?" Pulling me out of my nightmarish memory, I turn to see the realtor standing next to the bench I was sitting on. We were in front of the first location of our tour.

"Yes, I'm sorry. I was lost in thought," I say, standing and holding out my hand to the realtor. "Please, call me Tyler."

We shake and her friendly face calms my racing heart after mentally reliving Kent's abuse. "It's great to finally put a face to the name. I'm excited to show you the three properties and hope one of them meets your needs." She seems hopeful. I nod not knowing how to respond to her kindness. "Well, let's get started. This property has been many things. The last of which was a mini-mart," she says, unlocking the door. Her voice drowns out as I walk around the space trying to imagine what it would look like as my dream bakery. The space is very open and that's great, but I'd have to retrofit it completely. There's no kitchen or display case. There's nothing that could easily be transitioned into a bakery and all that means is more expenses above the purchase price.

No, thank you.

"This is it!" I say, vibrating with the possibilities. Looking around the corner store of a popular shopping center, I see everything I've ever wanted. It used to be an ice cream shop so the display cases are perfect. It's also just shy of a full kitchen in the back, meaning I won't need to completely construct a kitchen from scratch. I can see it all in front of me. I can see my name on the sign outside. I can see the cases and front windows filled with my handiwork. I can't believe my dream is actually- finally- going to be a reality.

"I saved the best for last. I knew this would be a winner," the realtor states. "I'll go to the office and start the acquisition. Should we meet tomorrow at the office to finalize the paperwork?" she asks, escorting me out.

"Yes, I can be there at 8:30 after I drop my daughter off at school," I say, vibrating with anxious energy.

"That sounds great. I'll make sure to have everything ready. We'll move on this quickly. This shopping center is moving fast and we need to get on this property now if we don't want to lose it."

"Fast is perfect. I'll bring the closing costs and down payment tomorrow. Just email me the totals," I say. Doing the quick math in my head I know I'll have more than enough for both plus the cosmetic costs of creating my dream bakery.

"Alright then, Mrs-" I tilt my head at her and she catches herself. "Tyler. I'll see you tomorrow and we'll make you a property owner." The realtor walks to her car, but I stay back staring at the storefront that will soon have "Ty's Pies" written across the front. I can't take it. As I watch the realtor's car disappear into the distance, I jump up and down dancing in front of the first thing other than my daughter that will truly be mine. I will own this store. Then, Wyatt and I will live the life I always knew we should.

"You've got some nice moves there, Ty." The velvety smooth voice causes goosebumps along my arms and a chill up my spin. I freeze in mid-hip swing.

Maybe I'm imagining it. A Freudian-esque voice I'm subconsciously hearing after the time we spent together last night. Maybe he's not really there. In fact, he can't be there. I'm going to turn around and see that it was a figment of my imagination and the voice I heard was all in my head.

Unfortunately, that is not the case. I turn to see Zac standing there in all his suited glory. As good as he looked last night- in his polo and comfortable cargo shorts- he looks ten times better now. He's wearing dark blue dress pants with laced, tan dress shoes. His pants, perfectly tailored to his muscular legs. I've never noticed thighs before as anything more than ordinary, but in those pants, on that man, they're sure as hell not ordinary.

Moving past his matching tan belt, my mouth dries at the slim cut white oxford shirt showcasing the intense "v" of his trapezium and bulky shoulder muscles. If it weren't for the tattoo on his right arm showing through the rolled-up sleeves he'd look every bit the professional veterinarian.

God, those forearms, though. Since when have I found *forearms* attractive? I'm not really sure, but looking at the corded muscles of his right forearm traced with black and gray line-work there causes my core to tighten and a hot spike to run up my spine in ways it hasn't in years.

Zac is most definitely there. If I wasn't sure by his voice, than looking at his caramelly- hazel eyes and that smirk with his overly plump lips would have made it crystal clear. He's enjoying my slow appraisal of his new body- part by smoldering part. He's changed so much since high school; he was always in shape, but slightly slender. Now he looks like he's doubled in size since those days walking the halls. His athletic build has intensified and the bulk of his muscles are in all the right places. I need to get a grip. I can feel my stomach tighten and my center dampen with need. It's been way too long since I've felt a need this strong. The intense need I have endured over the short time I've being back home. The time spent with Zac.

"Oh, umm," I fight to string words together. Thinking of what my body would feel like under his sculpted one. "Why are you here?" Too late, I realize I'm being rude and the words are already out, but what the hell. I mean I'm in a random shopping center in the middle of the day. He has a practice to run, why would he be here to witness my gleeful celebration?

"Well, bein' that you asked so nicely," Zac pauses, smirking at my being visibly flustered. He knows he's getting to me, the ass. "My office is just there." He steps closer so we have the same view and points to the vet clinic on the other side of the plaza. One that I hadn't noticed initially. "And considerin' it is noon, I thought I'd get me some lunch on my hour break between patients." He's speaking to me as if he's talking to an ornery child. I guess I deserve that.

Right now, I feel like an ornery child. "Oh." What else can I say? He witnessed me dancing like an idiot, smiled at my rude greeting, and then, I had him explain his actions to me. "I'm sorry. You just surprised me. You don't have to answer to me," I say, feeling the blush creep up my chest to redden my cheeks. "Enjoy your lunch."

"I intend to. In fact, there's this great Chinese place I was walkin' to. Would you like to join me?" I can't stop my heart from jumping. Yes, I want to join him. I want to just stare at him, but is that the wise choice here? Should I be spending time with another guy, even if he is a high school friend, while the ink on my divorce paperwork is still practically drying? What the hell, if nothing else, my ex always had an issue with Zac. I'll go just to stick it to Kent.

At least that's what I'll tell myself, anyway.

"Sure, Chinese sounds amazing."

We walk in comfortable silence the five blocks to the Chinese restaurant. Escorted to a table where we sit across from each other and Zac crosses his arms in front of him on the table. His right arm is closest to me and I can't drag my eyes away from the intense array of movement along his uncovered skin.

"It looks like you've been busy since I last saw you." I gesture to his arm. I figure tattoos are a safe topic.

"To be fair, Tyler, it's been about twelve years since we've seen each other," Zac says, pulling his sleeve up a fraction higher to allow me to see more of the collage. Sitting this close without Wyatt around to pass judgement, I really look at the pieces and see all the care that went into making the tattoo cohesive. There's a dog- maybe a German Shepard- an hourglass, and a compass. All of which arranged with a flattened globe as the background- complete with latitude and longitude lines. That's all I can make out before his sleeve covers the rest. Although, I know there's an archangel on his upper arm from high school.

I find myself wanting to see if he has any others and where. Maybe a little to interested in where. Suddenly, his invitation from high school under the bleachers at one of Kent's games fills my head. "They're gorgeous. A dog I'm assuming from your profession?" I ask, trying to ignore the zing in my spine from the memory of that game. Zac just nods and looks away, which seems an odd response to my innocent observation.

"Do you have any?" Zac asks, and I remember the tattoo I wanted when Wyatt was first born. That was a fight and a half, resulting in my locking myself in my room for two days. Kent made it clear that the only women who get tattoos are "whores."

"No, but I wanted one after I had Wyatt. I just never had the opportunity," I say, bending the truth a little.

"What about Wyatt's father? Did he have any?" Zac asks, and I know he's fishing. I don't feel like talking about Kent, but there's no way around not giving him a breadcrumb.

"No, he wasn't the tattoo enthusiast you seem to be." I can tell Zac wants more, but there's not much more I feel like spilling. "Plus, he's not in the picture anymore anyway." There, that's enough, he won't get anymore.

It seems like I don't have to give anymore either, the waiter comes to take our order just as my words sink in. Zac has a pleased smirk on his face and I can only assume it's because I told him I'm no longer involved with Kent.

I need a subject change. Now. Zac turns to me after handing his menu over and opens his mouth, but I don't want to hear what he's going to say. I'm going to lead this discussion back to neutral ground. "So, if I take you up on that idea of dog treats, will you agree to sell them at the clinic?" I ask, and one of his eyebrows raise at the idea. God, why does that make him look even hotter? His chiseled jaw- lined with just the right amount of scruff- ticks and I feel like he's holding back a triumphant smile. He knows it was his idea and he knows he just won something. Won what? I'm not so sure, but the victory is seeping through him.

"Sure," he pauses. "I'd love to get into bed with you," and there it is. The Zachariah Jacobson I always knew he was.

"Leave it to you, Jacobson," I say, shaking my head at his absurdity. Although, I can't help the tingle in my lower belly as his eyes never waiver from mine. Luckily, we're saved by our soup starters.

"Hey, some buddies and I are gettin' together this Friday for drinks. Care to join us?" Zac asks, digging into his egg drop soup like it might disappear.

"I'm not sure. We just moved in and there's so much stuff that still needs to be done." I know it's a lame excuse, but I don't think drinking and Zac should be a combined activity.

"Maybe next time," Zac says, looking down at his food.

"Yeah, maybe." I don't think that's ever going to happen. I'm not so sure time alone or around alcohol is a great idea with someone who makes me tingle the way he does.

CHAPTER FIVE
ZAC

The music is in full swing, deafening my normal hearing. As I walk into the bar all I can think is, "man, I feel like I'm gettin' old." Moving through the crowded dance floor I'm stunned at the reminder that only a few years ago this atmosphere would have been too much. The loud music, lights, and bodies everywhere would have caused me to drop to my knees in a cold sweat. I've come a long way in a short time compared to a lot of my buddies that are still dealing with the effects of our time overseas. All in all, I'd say I was pretty far along in my healing, in the grand scheme of things. I pull myself out of the pit of memories I'm falling into in time to see my buds waving me over towards the bar.

"Sup, we thought you got lost on your way here for a minute," Jay says, of course, not letting it slide that I'm more than an hour late to the bar. I took my time getting ready. Not that I care about what I look like, but that's what I told myself. If I'm being honest, it was because I was hoping Tyler would change her mind and come knocking on my door to join me.

She never knocked.

I have barely seen her- just in passing- the whole week and it's killing me. I'm literally ten yards away from her, but it might as well be miles. She's all I've been able to think about. The way she looks. The vulnerability in her actions. Memories from high school coming back and rearing their ugly heads. Man, was I a little shit back then. Although, she was always able to see through all that. She was always the one to get the real me. The me that I tried to forget through my 'rebel without a cause' ways.

"Hey, you there?"

"Yeah, sorry. Got held up." I say, rolling it off.

"Yeah, it couldn't have been much since Jane's been here as long as we have." Max points to the opposite corner of the bar. I look over and there she is, trying to pretend she wasn't just looking at our group.

I don't know what it is about Jane. She's not my type at all. She's cute and all, but her dark hair and almost black eyes don't do the trick. Granted that doesn't stop me from sticking my dick in her when nothing else pans out. Whatever, judge away. She's a friend, a nurse I met at the hospital after one of my many sessions. "Yeah, we're not a thing," I say, suddenly glad Tyler didn't come with me.

"That's not what it looked like as you were shoving your tongue down her throat as the Uber drove off." *Shit, I can't argue with that.* What do I say, that wasn't me? My friends are right, I do hook up with Jane. A lot.

What? Don't look at me like that. She's hot. Angular

cheekbones, long slender legs that squeeze around my hips as I pound into her. Her tits a real too. Those things bounce just right as I drill her from any angle. The best part though? She understands that she and I are not a thing. She knows that if we're in the same place it's not a guarantee I'm leaving with her. If I find someone else who meets my fancy, then I'm going home with them that night. The same goes for her. She doesn't need me. She's a straight ten. She could have anyone in here she wants. If it happens to be me and I'm not into anyone else, then its go time.

Whatever, give me those judging eyes all you want. This is me. I've had a rough life so far and if I want to be with someone for a night- hell, if I want to be with someone for an hour- then it's my prerogative. It's not like I'm leading Jane on either. She knows she and I aren't exclusive. She knows I can't be with her as anything more than we are. Shit, I probably can't be with anyone, not really.

Just as that thought enters my mind, Tyler's face fills my mind's eye. She's not really here. I know that, but thinking about not being with her is hell now that she's back in town. When she wasn't here it was easy to find something- someone- to occupy my time. Even if I never realized it, I always measured every girl up to her. In high school, she was all I saw. Now that she's back I'm not sure I should even try. I'm damaged in so many ways, I wouldn't want to hurt her. And she's got a kid now. What would I do with a kid? On the other hand, I'm not sure I can be without her.

"Hey," a breathy voice pulls me from my deep thoughts. "Where have you been all night?" Jane asks, sitting on my lap. I guess she didn't like the other options in here tonight. I haven't had a good look, but I'm not cold enough to push her off me. I'm still a guy and she still has her bare legs draped over me.

"Just got held up. How are you, Jane?" I ask, resting my hand on her hip. I need to forget about Tyler for a little. Jane will be the perfect distraction. Jane and Jack. I nod toward the bartender and hold up two fingers. A minute later, a double Jack and Coke appears in front of me. There we go, that'll help clear my head.

Twenty minutes later, I'm three drinks in and feeling no pain. Jane is still on my lap, but she's taken to grinding to the music. At this rate, we'll be leaving in no time. Well, that or we'll be having a blast in one of the bathroom stalls.

"Baby, you better be careful before you start somethin' you're not ready to finish here," I growl into Jane's ear.

Jane turns her head toward me and leans back into my chest. "Who says I'm not willing to finish here?" she asks, running her hand between her thighs and pressing against my growing erection.

"And that's my cue boys." I stand, turning to my friends. "Someone's gettin' a little handsy," I say, spanking Jane's ass to move her towards the door. "I'll see you guys next week."

"Come on," I say to the keys that refuse to get in their hole. I didn't think I was that fucked up when I left the bar, but my keys are making me slightly regret every shot of Jack I consumed.

"Open the door or I'm getting on my knees right here on your doorstep," Jane purrs, her teeth scraping across my earlobe. Rolling my eyes in pleasure, I need to focus. If I don't get this damn door open, I'm kicking it in. Jane is not joking; she will gladly suck me off on my doorstep for anyone to see.

"Thank fuck!" I grunt, as the door accepts my key and we stumble into my foyer. "Come here." I push Jane up against the back of my door and pin her there with my body. "Is this what you want, baby?" Grinding my tented pants into her, she moans her approval.

Bending at the waist, I crush my lips against hers and take from her what I want. Her soft moans ring out in the still air of my empty house. She grants me access and I slip my tongue into her silky mouth, deepening the kiss. Jane rips at my shirt and I break the kiss to pull fabric from my body.

Attacking her neck, I pull the straps of her dress down and drag the skin-tight material down her body. Skimming my hands up her legs, I grab her ass and lift her against my body. Walking to the couch, it occurs to me we're probably not making it to my bed. She's grinding into me and my cock is begging for release. I put Jane down and pull back only to see Tyler's face.

Fuck! What is that?

Jane comes close and pulls my earlobe into her mouth. "Fuck me, Zac," she says, and I can't believe I'm thinking of anyone else with Jane stark naked and begging for it in front of me.

Shaking my head, I try and rid myself of all things Tyler. "Fuck," I growl and turn Jane so I can't see her face. Yeah, yeah, I know, you're judging me again. I shouldn't be thinking of Tyler when I shove my dick in someone else, but if I pull away from Jane now I'm a prick. This is a lose, lose situation for me.

"Bend over, baby," I say, pushing down on Jane's upper back, forcing her to bend over the armrest of my sofa. Leaving her at the perfect height for me to ram into her. A lot of thought went into my furniture before I purchased anything. Call me a pig, but if any guys tell you he wasn't thinking surfaces to have sex on when he bought furniture, I'm telling you I call bullshit, right now.

I unbutton my pants and pull a condom from my wallet before dropping my dark jeans and boxer briefs. Once sheathed I bend over Jane, my whole chest covering her back. "You ready for me, baby?" I growl into her ear, reaching around her to tracing circles around her clit. I follow her lower lips to her sopping wet entrance. "You little slut, you're so wet for me. Aren't you?" Jane moans her response, smashing her ass against my dick. "You want me to fuck your slutty cunt?" I groan, nipping at the shell of her ear.

"Yes, fuck me!" Jane screams and I enter her in one hammering thrust. "Ahhh," she yelps from my rough treatment of her body.

Setting a punishing rhythm, Jane's thighs start to tremble against the couch arm. The room growing muggy with the scent of our connection. The flesh of my hips slapping against her ass at a harder and harder rate. "You like that?" I ask, bringing my cupped hand down on her ass cheek.

"Mmm," Jane moans into a couch cushion.

"Say it. It feels good, doesn't it?" I stop thrusting, instead I grind into her from behind gripping her hips with all my strength. Getting as deep into Jane's slit as I can.

"Yes, Yes. I like it. Spank me. Treat me like your fuck

doll," Jane groans, as I resume thrusting into her. She backs her ass into me, meeting me with every thrust. The sound of our slapping skin slowing taking over my senses.

"Fuck," I breathe between my teeth, bending over her body to nip at her shoulder. I won't last much longer. Reaching around her hips, I press my middle finger against her clit. Slowly applying more and more pressure. "Let go, baby," I growl, into her ear; tonguing the shell.

"Ahhh," Jane goes off. Her tight pussy milking my cock. Pulling me into the warm heat with everything she's got. I leave my finger against her clit, prolonging her climax and after three more rough thrusts, I'm shooting my life juice into the condom that separates me from her wet walls.

"Mmm," Jane rumbles, catching her breath.

"Yeah," I say, pulling out and tying off the condom. "You know where the bathroom is. I'll see you in the mornin'." Turning my back, I walk towards my room and close the door behind me. You can call me an ass or whatever you want, I'm not that worried. I haven't been able to sleep with anyone, and I mean just sleep, since I got back. Make of that what you will. I guess I'm not as far along in my healing as I thought.

The nightmares have gotten better over the last few years, but there are always the rough nights that scare the shit out of me. Waking in a puddle of sweat. The cold sweat becoming so much that I'm physically trembling. After all the shrinks I've seen, I'm still struggling. No one should be subject to seeing me like that. Plus, Jane isn't really the cuddling type. So, call me whatever you want, this is the way it is. The way I am. Maybe, Tyler's better off without my pursuing her.

Now I know I'm a piece of shit. I literally just had my dick in Jane and here I lay thinking about Tyler. I know it's wrong, but as I lay here drifting off to an exhausted sleep, she and her little girl are the only things I can think about.

"Jacobson, get your ass out of there now." I can hear my name being called, but with all the debris and flames around me I can't seem to make out the words. "Jacobson, where are you?" I know that voice. I've heard it yelling my name so many times before. Why can't I remember who it belongs to? "Jacobson," the voice drones on, but I can no longer think about the words the disembodied voice is saying.

My head is throbbing and it hurts to open my eyes. Shit, it hurts to even think. Moving my arm, I try to rest on my elbow and assess the situation. What just happened? Why is there so much shit around? Where are the flames coming from? Why can't I see over them? I look down, but I'm still flat on the ground.

Did I forget to move? Looking down at my hand on my stomach, I try to move again. I need to sit up to judge my surroundings. My right hand is still on my gun trigger and my left remains unmoving on my abdomen. Why can't I move?

Clenching my ab, I try to sit up, but can feel nothing. I feel no muscle contraction. I feel no tingling sensation of life in my body. Looking around what surrounding I can see, I know I'm still in hostile territory. I know my men are looking for me. I know I need to get my ass up.

Then it hit me like a ton of bricks. Where the fuck is Mac?

Sitting upright in the bed, the dawn is just starting to break over the horizon. Sweat runs down my spine and

I lift my hands to remind myself I'm not back there. I'm not caught in the flames unable to move. It was a dream and I'm ok.

I am ok.

Getting up I head for the bathroom to shower the terrors from my past off of me. Resting my hands against the wall of my shower, I lower my head and let the memory fade away with the cascading water down my back. It's been a good two months since I found my way back to that warehouse where it all went down years ago.

Absentmindedly, my right hand drops to my rib cage. The tattoo memorializing the incident seared into my brain on display there. Everything happened so fast that night. One minute Mac was standing by my side and the next I'm flat on my back unable to move a muscle from my shoulders down. As if needing to feel my body isn't frozen again- laying, stuck on the ground- I bring my hands over my head to rid myself of the emotions that drown my subconscious ever since that night.

Walking past the guest room, I can see- a still naked-Jane strewn across the blankets. Last night was fun, but I'm not sure Jane is doing it for me anymore. I mean, hell, I had to be practically half shitfaced before I brought her back here. She'll wake up shortly and I'll have to come up with another excuse for why we can't spend the day together.

Maybe she's not as easy as I was telling myself last night. If she was really easy, she wouldn't be here occupying my guest room while I stand in the hallway in basketball shorts toweling my hair dry. I need coffee. That will make thinking of an excuse easier.

Resting against my kitchen counter watching the coffee pot percolate is like watching paint dry. I've been meaning to replace it for almost a year, but can't seem to find the time to be bothered to buy a new one. After fifteen minutes, the drip stops and the almighty ding alerts me that my liquid sanity is finished. I can hear Jane stirring from the back room and I'm praying she gives me a little longer in peace before she disturbs me.

Walking over towards the kitchen table I catch movement out of the window above my sink. Stepping in front of the faucet, I stare at the cause of my distraction. Tyler is dancing in her kitchen holding a wooden spoon in front of her face like a microphone. God, she looks good. She's wearing short plaid sleep shorts and a tight matching tank top. Her long blond hair is piled on the top of her head like she threw it there after a deep sleep.

Suddenly, Tyler stops dancing and turns to sing to someone. My hands clench around my coffee mug as I move in for another sip. She's already had someone stay the night? I'm pissed and I can feel my heart rate climbing until I see Wyatt jump into view holding a spatula to sing to her mother. As cute as Wyatt is dancing around and singing, I can't keep my eyes off of Tyler and her ass cheeks playing peek a boo with the bottom of her shorts. The more she moves and shakes her ass to the beat the more of her delicious globes I can see.

My hunger must have been in the air, because almost immediately Tyler turns towards me to dance back to back with Wyatt, causing her to catch me staring through the window. She stops dancing as elaborately

47

and smiles her shy smile for me. I tip my coffee mug at her and she pushes a stray hair behind her ear and waves. Just then, I feel hands wrap around my ribs and fingernails scrape down the front of my naked chest.

Tyler blanches and I can see her visibly uncomfortable. Fuckin' Jane. I look down at her candy apple red nails resting against the top of my basketball shorts, thumbing my happy trail. When I look back at Tyler she's closed the blinds and I'm cut off from her. I can feel the disconnect deep in my chest as I turn to Jane.

"This isn't goin' to work anymore, Jane."

CHAPTER SIX

Tyler

The blinds may be closed, but I can still see those neatly manicured nails scraping down Zac's chest. Touching his tanned skin, pulled tight over rippling muscles. I can feel my face heat with embarrassment. How could I think he was flirting the other day. He asked me to go out with his friends because he genuinely wanted me to have people to hang out with. That *must* be it. Because of course he has a girlfriend. Why wouldn't he? He's fucking gorgeous, any girl would be a fool not to snatch that up and lay claim.

Turning back to Wyatt, dancing and singing, totally unaware of the heat radiating from my body. I'm not even sure if the heat is coming from my embarrassment or my sheer attraction to the man Zac has become. Hell- if I'm being honest with myself- I've always been attracted to Zac. There's a very fine line, though, between finding someone attractive and acting on it. I was always with Kent, so, I never really thought too much on how Zac made me feel. Well, with the exception of a few stolen moments when it was just the two of us throughout senior year. Moments in time that left my body singing and my mind reeling from the intensity I felt with the nearness of Zac. Intensity my body has never felt around anyone else, not even Kent.

As much as I pledged my love and body to Kent, he was never able to make me feel, even at our most intimate, a fraction of what Zac made me feel by just his proximity. Although, seared into my brain now are the ruby red nails wrapped around his "v" cut waist. Taking a downward journey towards the hem of his low cut athletic shorts.

What does it matter anyway? Once again- looking at my oblivious daughters' face- I realize I have more important things on my plate than who's dating an old high school acquaintance.

Ring, Ring, Ring.

Turning down the music and answering the phone that has interrupted my internal dialogue, my lawyers name flashing on the screen. A deep-rooted fear takes over my body. With trembling fingers, I slide the lock to the right and bring the phone to my ear. "Hey, Janice. What's up?" I ask, faking a joyfully innocent tone, when all I want to do is brace myself for the inevitable terror she's capable of spilling in reference to my ex-husband.

"Hey, how's Georgia?" Janice asks, the light and airy tone to her voice, cools my nerves, but only slightly.

"It's great. I've missed it here. It's nice being close to my parents and catching up with old friends." Visions of Zac's shirtless body flood my mind and I have to physically shake my head to make the manifestation causing my dampening panties to disappear.

"That's fantastic. I'm so glad you decided to make the move." Janice pauses, and I brace for impact. "So, the reason I'm calling is because I wanted to let you know that I just heard Kent has missed several sessions with both his AA group and the anger management counselor. The latest of which was last night.

"That being said, we are back at square one and you don't need to worry about Kent coming up for visitation, supervised or otherwise, anytime soon. The year starts when he begins both groups and ends only after a full year of sessions. If any session is missed for anything other than hospitalization- with the reason for hospitalization being out of his control- the year begins anew."

The idea of Kent not being able to see his own daughter breaks my heart on some subconscious level. However, the idea of keeping a disgruntled, drunken gun handler away from MY daughter keeps that feeling buried so far down in my psyche that I refuse to even acknowledge it.

"Oh, ok." I pause. Unsure how happy or upset I should be about this information. "Thank you, Janice. I really appreciate you keeping me updated." We say our farewells and hang up.

Luckily, Wyatt has taken over as lead singer. She stands on her chair at the kitchen table, eyes closed, belting Katy Perry into a wooden spoon. Girl's got moves. Especially given the small platform. Watching her move without the weight of the world on her shoulders brings my heart a much needed breath of calm.

Then my mind flits to Zac again and I can't help feeling

like I'm caught in the eye of the storm. My attraction to Zac, Kent's unruliness, and Wyatt's calm circling around me. Threatening to blow my life to shreds with the slightest change of the wind. How could I have ever thought anything could happen between Zac and I. Shit, anyone and I. My life is surrounded by the glow of Wyatt and the shadow of Kent.

I can't deal with all this nervous unrest. I need a break from myself. I need to do something for myself. Reaching for the kitchen island I produce the contract for the property that will be "Ty's Pie's" and sign on the dotted line. There, it's done. I'll drop these off today. Something for me, check. Now what to do about clearing my head?

"Wyatt, after breakfast do you want to head to the splash park?" I ask, remembering the newly renovated, open area park with a splash ground. A rubber rain deck covered area with little water nozzles that spray water upward.

"Yes!" Wyatt screams, all thought of her performance erased. "I've been wanting to go. They have an area set up just for us so we don't have to worry about little kids. At least that's what my friend Cindy said. She went last weekend with her older brother." Wyatt is practically jumping up and down with excited energy. If only I could be so easily entertained.

Seven hours later, a very smelly and very tired Wyatt and I turn onto our street. Thoroughly water splashed out. I think my hands and feet will be prunie for the next week. Although, watching and playing with Wyatt and her friends from school did clear my head. So, I guess all in all it was worth my wrinkly extremities. Riding high from the calm the splash ground brought me, I roll down the windows and enjoy the last block of my drive with the breeze flowing through my hair.

"What is that?" I whisper under my breath. I reach to turn the radio down to try and figure out where that music is coming from. As I drive closer and closer to my house the music gets louder and louder. "What the hell?" I hiss, pulling into my driveway. "Well, so much for calm." Wyatt gives me a confused look. "Nothing." I say, drawing my attention away from the driveway next to mine.

Squirming in the driver's seat, I'm having trouble taking my eyes off the glistening Adonis standing less than twenty yards from me. Rounding the corner into my driveway, I see Zac washing his jeep. Shirtless, donned only in athletic shorts. Zac bends and plunges the sponge into the sudsy water sitting in a bucket at his bare feet. Moving up his arm, I see the tattoos move and come to life with each flex of his muscles. My eyes feast on the tanned, sweat soaked skin as I ascend with the tattoo up to his shoulder. Here the tattoo seems to breath a life of its own as it weaves around his right shoulder onto his toned, tight pectoral muscle. What does a vet need with all those muscles? I mean come on. Give a lady a chance here.

As my eyes continue to peruse his glistening body I see another tattoo on the opposite rib cage. Along his left hip there are combat boots side by side with a rifle standing tall between them, moving up his ribs. I can't see what's written on them, but there are clearly a pair of dog tags hanging from the handle of the gun. I wonder if he knew someone in the military. Or maybe it was a parent. Maybe it was a girlfriend before the buxom brunette from this morning. I never really saw anything except her hands, but I can only assume she was beautiful to have caught Zac in her clutches.

God, it takes all my concentration to make it into my driveway and stopping without hitting anything. Why does he have to be washing his car now? Why does he have to be washing his car at all? Hasn't he heard of a damn car wash facility? Or a shirt? This is the second time in less than twelve hours that I have seen him without half his clothing. Without a shirt to cover his rippling abs as they bend and twist, moving the soapy sponge along the hood of his jeep. Without a shirt to cover his hulking back. Why do I find the massive size of his back so comforting? I can feel myself start to dampen between my legs. Great, just what I need to pair with my pruned body.

I need to get my ass inside before I do something to make our friendship awkward. One last peek, I think to myself as I turn to watch Zac reach for the hose. The hose is on the opposite side as the bucket and he twists so that his back is directly facing me. The sun beams down on his wet skin and, I might be mistaken, but there appears to be close to a dozen faded pink lines across Zac's spine. Is that another tattoo? I stare for a little longer than I should trying to decipher a pattern or shape to the lines, but nothing comes to mind. I can't figure out what he was trying to portray on his back and decide to file it away and ask him later. You know, when he's got clothes on, and all.

"Come on sweet girl," I say, nudging my sleepy child. "Let's get you inside and showered. I'll make dinner, you just get cleaned."

Wyatt trudges out of the car and up the front walk to the house. I step out of the car and repeat a silent mantra. 'Don't look, don't look, don't look.' I keep saying this and it almost works. I make it to the first step in front of my porch when he pulls my attention.

"Hey, neighbor," Zac calls from his driveway.

Turning, I look into his eyes hoping he didn't see me ogling him from my car. "Hey." I pause, "I think you missed a spot."

"Very funny."

CHAPTER SEVEN

ZAC

She's got jokes, huh. Alright, I see how it is. Well, let's see you joke your way out of this, Tyler. Holding her eyes for just a second longer then dropping them to the sponge and letting it slip from my hand back to the bucket. When I look back, Tyler seems to have followed the sponge, but has gotten distracted on her way back to my eyes. Just like she had when she pulled up.

Tyler stands frozen looking at the "v" of my hips disappearing into my basketball shorts. There you go, Tyler. Where are your jokes now? Standing still to let her feast on my abs, her tiny tongue peeks out to lick her plump bottom lip before pulling it between her teeth and biting down. Damn, that's sexy. I can feel my cock twitch in my shorts and have to look away or this flimsy material will be tented in no time.

Breathe, I tell myself. When I think I've got myself under control, I look back at Tyler and see a crimson glow creep across her chest and neck, all the way up to her cheeks. How she can go from being a sexy seductress one minute to an adorable temptress within such a short time I'll never know. But whatever it is, it's working for her. It's working for me.

"Hey, about this morning," I start, but Tyler holds up her hands to stop me. I need her to know it wasn't what it looks like. Well, it may have been, but it won't be anymore. Jane isn't my girlfriend. Hell, she's not even a friend. If it weren't for her being at the same bars I end up at on nights when no one else turns my head, I'd never even strike up a conversation with her. Again, think I'm a dick all you want, but it is what it is.

"No, don't worry about it. I shouldn't have been looking into your kitchen," she says, still holding a hand up to keep me from talking. "Really, what you and your girlfriend do in the privacy of your own home is none of my business."

"But that's just the thing. Jane isn't.." Again, Tyler cuts me off before I can get out the fact that Jane isn't my girlfriend.

"Zac, it's ok. You don't have to explain," she says, then continues. "I've got to get inside to make Wyatt dinner. We had a long day and she's probably going to have an early night. It was good seeing you. Have fun finishing your car."She turns to head for her house leaving me flustered.

What the hell? How can I set her straight if she won't

even let me talk?

With her receding form heading up the stair towards her front door, I finally take in what she's wearing. Her long legs are on full display in a pair of short cut-off Daisy Dukes. Everything is covered entirely, but I can see the swell of her ass through the material and my mind is creating visions of how it must look underneath.

In my head, she's probably wearing a pair of lacy, cheeky panties with the bottom swell of each cheek exposed. Toned and tight flesh hanging out of the crescent shape of the material asking to be tasted. I'm practically salivating, thinking of what her sweet skin would taste like. My palms tingling with the idea of what Tyler's smooth skin would feel like under my skillful hands.

Then she stops. I look up to find Tyler half turned to look at me with a knowing smirk on her face. Busted. I return my gaze to her eyes and wait for her to look away. To my surprise she doesn't. Tyler doesn't shy away from my eyes, instead she turns to fully face me.

"Have you gotten all of your tattoos done at the same place?" The question surprises me and I drop my gaze to my sleeved arm that's resting on the hood of my jeep.

"Uh, yeah. Why? Thinking about lodging a complaint?" I joke.

"No, I've just wanted one for a while, but never knew where to get one." Tyler pauses, "well, that and Wyatt's dad would have flipped." She's already told me this, but hearing it for a second time still doesn't make it seem real. Hearing her talk about someone having the ability to approve or disapprove of something doesn't sound like the Tyler I've put on a pedestal all these years since high school.

"I could call my guy." I mentally calculate the odds of Trey being free anytime in the foreseeable future. Then again, he owes me a favor. I could have him open the shop early to do a piece for Tyler. "If you're interested."

"Yes, that would be great! Thanks, Zac." Maybe the fun-loving Tyler isn't so lost in there after all. Her excitement over getting a tattoo is buzzing in the air around us.

"I could drive you up. That way if you don't want to drive back after getting it done you don't have to worry how you'll get back to Wyatt." I know I'm reaching, but, at some point, I'll do just about anything to get some alone time with Tyler.

"Um, sure. That works. What time should we leave?" Tyler pushes a fallen wisp of the most beautiful blonde hair I've ever seen- the long hair I'm dying to run my fingers though to see just how soft it really is- behind her ear. So much so that I have to fist my hand against the jeep hood to keep from reaching for her.

"Well, probably have to leave by nine. That way he has time to draw up what you want. Plus, it's an hour drive."

"Sounds great. Thank you, again, Zac." With one last smile, Tyler disappears into the house. Leaving me here washing my car and thinking about how I'm going to convince Trey to open his shop early for us tomorrow.

CHAPTER EIGHT

Tyler

"Mom," Wyatt calls, from upstairs. "Is dinner ready?"

"Almost," I can feel my mouth moving, but my brain is fixated on the movement outside my kitchen window.

Hidden from this angle, I can watch Zac moving from the hood of his Jeep to the side closest to my house and then the back. Leaning over the sink to catch his movements as much as I can. The way his body moves, the muscles that flex with each bend and twist and stretch has me captivated. I can't pry my eyes away from his sweat glistened body. The added moisture seems to only be there to send my body into longing, causing my eyes to fixate on pools of dew in every divot and depression of his musculature.

I feel my body reacting to his. The way my core tightens invitingly. The way my panties are rendered immaterial, as my own arousal rolls down my inner thigh. Zac's own thighs bending and flexing to wash under his back bumper. The grace and agility of his movements painting the picture of how he might dominate in bed.

God, I need to stop this. I'm a breath away from an orgasm and I haven't even touched myself. Not to mention, the man I am currently daydreaming about has a girlfriend. I've been reduced to a hormonal puddle of high school lust. And I'm going to be stuck in a small confined space with the man causing my lust to skyrocket for an hour each way tomorrow. Great, this should be *easy as pie.*

Yeah, right. I can smell myself here in the kitchen with all the aromatic spices I've used on the chicken doing nothing to disguise it. He'll pick up on my arousal in no time at this rate. I need to get myself under control or tomorrow could get really awkward- really quickly.

"Mom, is it ready?" Tearing my eyes away from Zac's body to look at my daughter, I nod my head.

Moving to the stove, I plate Wyatt's dinner, but leave my chicken cooling on the counter. I've lost my appetite. Plus, I need to call my parents about watching Wyatt tomorrow. I need to finish the rudimentary tattoo design of what I've wanted since Wyatt was born, as well. First, I need to see if Wyatt is ok with me getting a tattoo.

"Hey, bug, what would you think about me getting a tattoo?" I ask, without any preamble or context.

"That would be cool, but what would you get? Please don't say a tramp stamp butterfly. You are way too old for a tramp stamp." Wyatt pauses, "and a butterfly for that matter."

"Wow, Wyatt, you really know how to wound a woman. I'm not that old, I might remind you. And since when do you think it's ok for you to use the word tramp?" I ask, mom voice kicking in at the last question.

"Dad, used it all the time. I didn't think it was a big deal." My heart falls and I see all the small ways that allowing Kent to remain in our lives for as long as I did has affected my baby girl. It kills me thinking about the things Kent would say off hand. He had no consideration for how his words would plagued my little girl.

"Yes, well, just because your Dad does something, or says something doesn't mean that it's ok for a nine-year-old to say. Or a lady at any age to say- for that matter. Do you hear me talking like that? I'm not raising a sailor and I expect better than that from you. You know better." I'm trying not to lay into her too much, but the way Kent acted around her has caused her to be confused as to where the line is sometimes.

Although, I can probably take some of the blame for that. Kent never let me reprimand Wyatt when she did something like this. He thought it was funny and I wasn't allowed to go against him. I could have- should have- gotten both Wyatt and I away from him a long time ago. A part of me kept thinking I'd get my husband back. Not that Kent was a great catch before Wyatt was born, but at least then I thought he loved me. At least then, he tried to compromise. He at least pretended he cared about my feelings and the feelings of those around him. Since college, and his not being drafted into the NFL, Kent has become hard and selfish.

Granted, when I look back, Kent always had those tendencies. It was my fault that I overlooked the signs. Everyone, even Zac, tried to pull me away from Kent. Maybe that stubbornness was what gave me the courage to be who I was in high school. As much as it made me who I was back then it also caused me to stick it out in high school with Kent when I should have called it quits.

"I'm sorry, Mom. I won't say it again." The look of remorse on Wyatt's face hurt my heart. I know she didn't mean anything by it.

Take a breath, Tyler, it's ok, I tell myself. "I know, Baby Girl." I say, soothing her remorse with my tone. "So about this tattoo, I was thinking of getting a mother and baby elephant with an old-time pocket watch. Like the one my Grandpa gave me. The one you used to play with when you were little." I pause, waiting for her to remember. "I was going to get the time you were born on the face of the watch and your name and birthdate there too. Somewhere. What do you think" I ask, nervous to see if Wyatt will approve. The whole tattoo screams Wyatt. She loves elephants and she used to play with my Papa's pocket watch. It was her favorite toy when she was a toddler.

"Mom, that sounds awesome!" She jumps out of her chair, food forgotten, and throws her arms around my neck. Nearly knocking me over with the force of her hug. My shoulders sag now that there's no need for the anxiety of her approval.

"Oh, I'm so glad you like it. I think I'm going to get it tomorrow." I say, motioning for Wyatt to sit down and finish her dinner.

"Can I come?" Yeah, right. Bring my nine-year-old to a tattoo parlor.

"I think you're going to spend the day with Pop Pop and Nana."

"You can't go alone, Mom. Who will hold your hand?"

The sincerity in her eyes melts my heart. My daughter, always thinking about others.

"Actually, I'll be going with Zac. You've seen his tattoo's, so I figured who better to take me than an expert." Though, this is the first time I think that I'll be able to touch Zac with a reason. Being able to reach for his hand and extract the strength from him causes another surge of moisture from my core.

"Six hours," I breath, looking at the alarm clock on my nightstand. I have a whole freakin' six hours until I have to be ready for Zac to collect me. Six hours until I need to look good for a guy I'm lusting after, who- might I add- has a girlfriend. Six hours that I should sleep, instead, I've been laying here for two hours with sleep still evading me. Why? Why now? What do I have to do to get some sleep.

After dinner, my parents gladly agreed to watch Wyatt for me tomorrow. Granted, they have no clue the real reason I'm hanging out with Zac. Although, they seemed oddly excited about the prospect of my spending the day with him. All of which, things I'm choosing to not think about at the moment.

Zac is not what I need to think about. Yet, even now, as I lay in my bed, I can remember the feel of his eyes on me as I walked away from him this afternoon. The way he watches my every move. Almost like he's cataloging it, in case he never sees it again. Never sees me again. I guess it's only fair. I did disappear without a trace after high school. All Kent's doing. Now I'm back though. Now I'm back and lying in bed thinking about a gorgeously unattainable and buff Adonis.

Closing my eyes I can see his shirtless form moving in front of me. Moving for me. The way his thick arms connect to an even bigger- hairless- chest. The kind of chest that makes you envision the amount of weight he must be able to lift. The tapered rib cage and toned six pack. Oblique's that form the disappearing "v" into the hem of his low hung shorts.

I can feel my heart rate increase under my palm. My nipples tingling with the thoughts of what Zac might look like with the shorts around his ankles. Mouth watering, I swallow my loneliness and move my hand over my body. Slowly caressing my pair of tight buds straining against my thin tank before my hand moves along my rib cage. Past my hips to rest on my stomach, just above the hem of my sleep shorts. Fingers toying with the edge of the frilly material. Daring my brain to allow access.

One more thought of Zac, dampened with sweat from the heat of the day. Rivulets sliding down his back. Caught between the thick muscles encasing his spine on either side. The last vision behind my eyelids does it. That thought breaks my threshold for sanity and my fingers slip below the shorts waistband and into my panties. My core tightening.

Toying with the idea of Zac being the one to slip his massive hand under my panties replays fresh in my mind as I move my fingers toward the tingling bundle of nerves between my legs. "Ahh," I gasp, into the darkness of my empty bedroom. Circling my middle finger around the moistened skin and my breath catches in my throat. The feeling of soaring taking over my nerve endings.

I slip my finger down between my lower lips to gather my arousal for lubrication. Nudging the edge of my middle and index finger into my entrance I envision it being Zac's penis. I angle the pads of my finger upward towards the front wall of pussy and arch my back at the tingling heat coursing through my body. The blood running in my veins begins to boil.

Pulling my fingers back and out towards my clit and add just enough pressure to keep the heat rising. Circling harder and faster, my frenzied fingers are blurring below my shorts. One last image of Zac reaching over his hood to finish cleaning his jeep like he would lean over me while inside my silky lower lips. The thought of Zac inside me adds more pressure against my clit and I barrel over the edge of pleasure climaxing into the clouds.

Sweaty and thoroughly sated, I close my eyes and think about what the morning has in store. 'He has a girlfriend, he has a girlfriend.' If I repeat this manta, maybe I'll make it through tomorrow.

Maybe!

"Fuck, I shouldn't have done that," I say, under my breath. The guilt of what I just did with the visions of another woman's man bubble up inside me and threaten to strangle me.

Wearing a pair of cut off shorts and a vintage batman t-shirt, I sit on my couch waiting for Zac to come get me. My parents picked up Wyatt half an hour ago and I have been watching the clock with eager anticipation ever since. Why does Zac have to be so punctual? Why can't he be a little early? Another minute ticks by, slow as molasses and I can't take it any longer. I stand to make the trek over to Zac's when there's a light knock on my front door.

"Thank God." I walk to the door and open it. I find myself slightly regretting being thankful that he's here. Zac stands there with dark jeans hung low on his hips and a pale green v-neck shirt that makes his eyes look more golden than I've ever seen them before. Not to mention the way the shirt stretches across the large plane he calls a chest. His arms straining the sleeves to the point that it looks like the fabric might give out and weaving separate at any moment.

The intense orgasm I had, with this very attractive man as inspiration, causes chills throughout my body. A light shiver overtaking my muscles. Then Zac smiles, and I'm reduced to a puddle of lust. 'He has a girlfriend, he has a girlfriend' I repeat over and over. The guilt over what I did last night making my head spin.

"Mornin'. You ready?" Zac asks, surely noticing the way my body trembled at his presence. Maybe he'll just think it's nerves over getting my first tattoo.

"Yeah, of course." I grab my purse from the hall table and locking the door behind us. "Do you want to take my car? I don't know exactly where we're going, but I know it's an hour away so we might as well use my gas and mileage." God, I need to stop talking. I hear myself rambling and I'm physically missing something and I can't figure out what it is. The way the two of them talk is like they're talking in code and it's not making any sense to me. Not to mention, the two of them in such a small space is intimidating. I thought biting my bottom lip to keep from saying anything more.

"I'll manage the mileage, Ty. Shall we?" Zac gestures for me to walk ahead of him towards his Jeep.

The hour went by without much talking. It was early and I didn't get much sleep so the humming vibrations of the Jeep caused my eyelids to droop and I was asleep before we made it halfway through the trip. Now we sit in his car, waiting for his buddy to open the shop. Zac said he normally doesn't open until three in the afternoon, but he owed Zac a favor and is seeing us before hours. Next to us, I catch the blur of a black shirt and turn to see a large, ponytailed guy walk up to the front door of 'Tatted by Trey.'

"There's our guy," Zac says, reaching for his door handle and I follow suit. "Trey, thanks for opening up for us. This is Tyler. Ty this is Trey." Zac introduces us as I make my way out of his Jeep and towards the front door of the store. For the first time since I left my house the nerves of what I'm about to do hit me full force.

I'm about to mark my body. Like permanently. *Can I do this?* I mean I've wanted one for way longer than I can remember, but girl, this is like permanent, permanent. Like, won't wash off like those henna tattoos I used to get when I was younger. I know that if I say I changed my mind Zac won't try to convince me otherwise, even though, he did drive all the way here at nine in the morning on a weekend. A weekend that he could have spent with his red-nailed girlfriend.

Don't even go there, Tyler! I say hello and shake the artist's hand then let Zac take over the conversation. Watching the two of them catch up feels as if I'm missing something and I can't figure out what it is. The way the two of them talk is like they're talking in code and it's not making any sense to me. Not to mention, the two of them in such a small space is intimidating. I thought Zac was abnormally Hulk-like, but Trey is just as big and muscular. I wonder if they're on the same workout plan. Then, Trey steps behind a desk and looks over at me.

"So, what are we doing for you today?" he asks, taking out a sheet of slightly transparent paper.

"Well, I've wanted something for my daughter for as long as she's been a little bug on a sonogram screen. Now that she's nine, I've used her personality and likes to shape the idea of what I want. I'm no artist, so I'll just explain all the elements I want and leave the rest in your capable hands." I pause, looking at his handiwork on Zac's arm as proof of his capability. "So, I'm thinking I want a mother and child elephant and a pocket watch that looks like this." I say, pulling out my grandfather's antique pocket watch. "If you can have the watch face set to 5:32 that would be great, but if not it won't be the end of the world. Also, I'd like My daughter's name, Wyatt Alexandra, and her birthday, 06.21.09, written somewhere."

"Anything else you specifically want before I play with it?" Trey asks, looking at the list he's written with all the parts to the working puzzle.

I look over at Zac and hesitate before adding, "I'd also like it to say, I am because you are. If at all possible." Looking down, I can't meet Zac's eyes, even though I feel the heat of his stare searing through me.

"And where do you want this?" Trey asks, looking over my body. Not in a sexual way- thankfully. More like an artist looking at his blank canvas. Waiting for the moment inspiration hits for him to let out his artistic genius.

"I was thinking here." Pointing to my right rib cage, I see both Trey and Zac's eyebrows raise.

"The ribs are a tender canvas. It's hardcore for your first tattoo. Are you sure you don't want to think about it for a minute? Once we start there's no going back." Trey says, sincerity for my well-being evident in his voice. For a heavily tattooed man with a ponytail and more piercings than I know what to do with, he's kinda endearing.

"I think I'll manage." I say, not missing the ill hidden smirk from Zac as he tries to hold in his chuckle by bringing his hand to the back of his neck and biting that full lip. God, how I want to bite that bee-stung lip.

Whoa Nelly, slow down there tiger!

"Alright then, let me just take a measurement. If you'll give me about an hour to draw this up we can get started." Trey steps closer holding up the sheet of paper to my side. After a few questions about exact size and location against my tank-top-covered skin, he draws a circle on the paper to represent the area of skin he will be working with and turns back towards the desk. "One last thing, Tyler." He pauses before facing me, "color or black and white?"

I look down at Zac's colorful, vibrant tattoo on his arm and remember the black and white one on his rib cage. "Black and white, please. Thank you, Trey," I say, turning to Zac. "Hungry?"

CHAPTER NINE
ZAC

Thank God Trey owed me a favor or- from the looks of his appointment book back there- Tyler wouldn't have gotten tattooed for a month or so. Trey's good people, we served together for a little while. When I got accepted to the K-9 unit of the Army Rangers, he took his break from the military and used all his money to open his shop. He had been apprenticing before he joined the army. I'd never go to anyone else- the man is a genius with a gun. Tattoo gun or otherwise. Trey is definitely one of the men to have on your side. Dude is deadly with a weapon.

Tyler and I decide to head to one of the small sandwich shops on the strip near the shop. Tyler gets this roast beef with cheddar cheese sandwich. It has a horseradish mayo spread and the smell of the warm sandwich is making me regret my cold club with only warm toast.

"Want a taste?" Well, that caught me off guard. As much as I want to try her sandwich, the idea of tasting something, anything on Tyler's body has my brain running with the possibilities. My dick starts to harden with the dirty images of Tyler spread on my bed. My head between her legs with her on the edge of orgasm. Pulling myself back to the present, I nod and lean forward taking a bite of the food that just touched Ty's lips. Shit, I'd have said yes even if it looked good or not. "You looked to have buyer's remorse over your selection." She winks at me.

She fuckin' winked. Is she flirting? God, I hope so. I lean in to take a bite off of the corner of the sandwich half she's holding out to me. Her thumb nail brushes against my bottom lip as I close my mouth around the food. My eyes never leave hers and I see the shiver overtake her body as our gaze remains locked and I lick my lips as I lean back in my seat.

As I pull away, she looks down and I see the gorgeous blush creep over her cheeks and disappear into the neck of her washed out, black batman shirt. "Hey, I wanted to ask, what's the quote about?" I ask, remembering the words she requested accompany her daughter's name and birthdate on her tattoo. Words that will be forever embedded into her skin. They must mean a lot for a newbie like her to want as her first tattoo.

"I am because you are?" Tyler questions as she repeats the words she spoke to Trey. "You'll laugh at me." she says, trying to get out of the conversation.

"Try me," I say, finishing my food and urging her on.

"Well, I first saw it on Pinterest. I know, of all places. But it struck a chord. After everything Wyatt has been through at such a young age I look at her and the strength she possesses. That girl is filled with so much life and love and fearlessness. She's stronger than anyone I know. She's my reason for everything. I hope the world is kind to her and she never loses her fun-loving, strong, free, wild, fearless attitude. And I hope that one day I'll be all of those things like she is.

"I have only gotten through the things I have because I was doing them for her. I am only as strong as I am because of her. I am, only because she taught me how. Most people think that children learn from their parents, but I'm telling you that girl, I learn from her every day." The conviction of Tyler's words force the memories of another strong, free, wild, fearless girl to escape the vault of my mind and pull me into one of my favorite memories from high school.

"I think I remember meeting a girl that had all those qualities, once upon a time. In fact, you may know her. This girl was hanging out with her friends. Everyone was at 'The Gorge' hanging out and having a good time during spring break my senior year. A lot of people were drinking, but not her. She didn't feel the need to keep up with her friends just because they wanted to forget the night. My buddies and I were cliff jumping off the fifteen-foot ridge. The same one that happened to be nearest this girl's group of friends." I continue getting lost in the memory.

"Do you believe them?" I hear the jerks; I mean jock blockheads hooting and hollering behind us. While we're having a blast jumping into the cool water on this hot ass day, these fools are drinking away their last brain cells.

"You know if you're not man enough to try it, I'd save the judgements for someone who cares," I call back to them. My head swiveling back to the edge of the cliff when my eyes fall on the

clear eyes of Tyler Thomas. I drink in her lean figure resting on a rock next to Kent. Fucking tool. He doesn't even know what he has.

Tyler doesn't look away. Her blue-gray eyes daring me to do something. What I'm not sure, but in her stare, there's no mistaking the challenge. Before I can figure out what she wants from me she's standing. With one step towards me she reaches for the hem of her shirt. Lifting it over her head, her lacy bra comes into view with the slender curve of her ribs and hips. I raise my eyebrow noticing the swell of her breasts begging for release from their cages. Tyler breaks contact to unbutton her Daisy Dukes then looks back at me to shimmy them past her alluring hip bones revealing a matching set of boy shorts panties.

"What in the hell do you think you're doin'?" Kent stands, twisting Tyler to look at him by pulling her arm.

"I'm bein' man enough to try it," Tyler says, looking back at me then over my shoulder at the ledge behind me.

"My ass." Kent picks up her shirt and hands it back to her.

"Will be just fine sittin' on that rock waitin' for me to make my jump." Tyler turns and kisses his cheek before moving past me to the ledge of the cliff.

Fuck if I'm missing this. I think, hopping down to stand beside her. Close enough that she can feel my warmth, but far enough away that I'm not going to get myself punched by Kent.

Tyler is looking over the ledge at the water below with what might be described as joyful apprehension. She's getting a thrill off the fear of the jump. Her blue-gray eyes have taken on a purple hue under her excitement and she looks at me with a dismissive glare. "If you're waitin' for me to ask to hold your hand, I don't think…"

"Oh, I'm just waitin' to see that cocky smirk disappear as your skinny ass hits that cold water," I interrupt and look down over the ledge at the water. Over exaggerating how far I have to look

down to see our destination.

"Funny, but you'll have to take your eyes off my ass long enough to see my face," Tyler says, then turns and places her heels just over the edge of the cliff. I step up beside her and she holds out her arms just before winking at me and letting her weight shift backwards.

I jump alongside her as her body slowly drifts backwards. The smile on Tyler's face is contagious. I fight the urge to laugh just as my feet breach the water. I'm not really sure how Tyler landed, due to all the bubbles and water blurring my vision. However, seconds after my head breaks through the water, Tyler's head bobs, treading water less than five feet from me.

I swim closer to her, her white, blonde hair cascading over her shoulders and into her eyes. Reaching forward, I brush a strand of hair behind her ear. Tyler's smiling and looking up at the cliff, then turns to me and the smile disappears. Alone, at the bottom of the cliff we're just Tyler and Zachariah. We don't have to act a certain way. We don't have to pretend we don't ignite something in the other. We can just be.

Swimming just a bit closer, I let my hand slide south from her hair. Slowly moving down to Tyler's neck, she ever so slightly lulls her head towards my soft touch. It's so slight that if my entire body wasn't buzzing with focus from our nearness, I would have missed it. Sliding my hand down further to her shoulder, I brush my fingertips down her arm and gently find rest against her hip.

Under my palm I can feel Tyler's soft skin. Her wet lacy panties and a slight tremble as I tighten my fingers then move them against her lower back. In this matrix, I can, with the tiniest pressure, bring us even closer together. Her body comes inches from my chest and if I take too deep of a breath my entire front would be against hers.

Tyler's next intake of breath trembles. With the closeness, I can see the blush raising from her chest to cast a pink glow along her cheeks. Still treading water, I navigate us closer to the shore until my feet hit the bottom of the ravine. Tyler's tall for a girl, but I still have five inches on her 5'6 frame. With the height of the water, Tyler raises her arms to cling to my shoulders for stability. Her feet stop moving and we're encased in a bubble. The silent serenity of the stillness around us brings us closer together. Tyler's front is completely against mine and we look into each other's eyes.

I'm not sure how long we have been lingering at the bottom of the ravine, but the stillness around us becomes too much and Tyler looks away. Reminding me all too well that Tyler is not mine to touch. We drift apart and the moment is broken. I reach the shore first and turn to give Tyler my hand to help her up.

"I'm impressed you jumped," I say, as she places her hand in mine.

"Never underestimate the quiet ones. We're tougher than we look," Tyler says, but I've always seen how tough she is. Tyler's ability to stand out among the throngs of followers throughout the halls of our high school never ceases to amaze me. From watching her walk down the halls with one of the special education students, to the visible dismay of her friends and Kent. To the way she doesn't feel the need to drink herself into oblivion every weekend. There has never been a question in my mind that Tyler is tough and resilient.

"Who said I was lookin'?" She left herself wide open, I couldn't resist the thought of teasing her. Tyler's face cascades with pink and I see the error of my ways. For as tough as Tyler is- ever since I met her- my words have always been her weakness. I know this and I tease her anyway. Maybe I like to torture myself, because at that thought I move closer, place one hand on her hip and the other under her chin to encourage her to look at me.

"I'd be a fool not to look, Ty." At that, I turn to walk back up the cliff with the nickname only I use hanging in the air.

Peeking over my shoulder I see her standing in the same spot I left her with her hands wrapped around her core. "Come on, fearless," I say lightly, holding out my hand for her to use for grounding. "Let's get you back to that boyfriend of yours." It's more of a reminder for myself than for her, but it needed to be said. No matter how much Tyler makes me feel, she is not mine to feel for.

Tyler holds my hand the entire way up the cliff until we're within a few yards of her boyfriend. Our intertwined fingers break apart and a cool feeling descends over me as I watch Tyler move towards her waiting boyfriend.

Retelling the story of one of my greatest and worst high school memories, I look across the table to Tyler, who is no longer looking at me. I move my hand to gently tug her chin to face me and meet her eyes. Silently imploring her to explain her shift in mood.

"A lot of things change as we get older."

"Not the things that matter," I say, as drink refills arrive. Once the waitress moves away from our table I continue, "I'm gunna show you that girl is still in there somewhere." Tyler's eyes harden and she tilts her head to the side as if studying me like a math problem she can't figure out. "What?"

"What about your girlfriend? What will she think about you spending time with me?" Tyler asks brazenly, but the blush on her cheeks tells me she never meant to ask that.

"Jane isn't what you think." Tyler quirks an eyebrow at me so I continue. "Jane and I have been doin', it's hard to... It's not serious and the other night was the last time. I told her as much yesterday mornin'. It wasn't what I wanted. "*She* wasn't *who* I want." I correct.

CHAPTER TEN

Tyler

I think I'd rather he have a girlfriend. At least with a girlfriend he could remain in my head as the doting boyfriend. Someone who is respectful and loving. Someone that Kent wasn't I've only ever been with one guy. I'm not sure I'm the casual sex kind of girl. I can't even think about the idea of hooking up with random people. It took Kent five years before he even got into any of my clothing and another two years before he got into me. I can't imagine hooking up with someone and knowing it could never happen again. Or not knowing what he thinks about me. Or knowing he's totally capable of making love to me and then turning his back on me the next minute- next morning in Jane's case.

Then the last thing Zac said reverberates through my brain. She's not the one he wants. What's that supposed to mean? I remember watching his face as Jane came up behind him. He was looking me dead in the eyes. A casual smile on his full lips. Tipping his cup in hello, then fingers appeared on his chest and he blanched with what can only be described as dissatisfaction.

I thought I'd made it up in my head. That the look on his face wasn't the look of a guy who was unhappy. I think it was easier for myself to think he was in a happy, loving relationship. It was easier for my libido if nothing else. But then again, if that's the type of guy Zac is-the kind of guy that has random hook ups all the time- I'm not sure my libido needs to be firing for him. I've been with one guy- Kent- how can I keep up with a guy who's got the cream of the crop in his bed every other night?

Do I even want to keep up with him? Talk about cart before the horse. I don't even know if Zac is interested in me. Do I *want* him interested in me? Watching Zac's muscles firing as he brings each bite of food to his delicious mouth I can't help but remember the ache I used to feel each time we were in the same place in high school- yet always ignored.

"Hey, so I have something drawn up and if you like it we can get started," Trey says, as we walk into his shop after finishing our lunch. Besides the awkward booty-call conversation, the rest of the morning with Zac has been great. The time flew by as did the comfortable conversation. Zac makes me laugh more than anyone I know. He seems to be doing it on purpose, but the ease with which he jokes, I find myself smiling even when no words are spoken. Just being near him is bringing me comfort and support and a ball of something in the pit of my stomach I haven't yet found a name for.

"Great, I can't wait to see it." I can't contain my excitement as I leap up to the counter Trey's standing behind. Looking at the artwork he has laid out in front of him I can't bring words to explain the emotions he's captured. There's a realistic mother elephant with a baby elephant at her front, entangled trunks which look to be placed at my hip above my pant line. Above the bigger elephant's head, partially covered by an ear, is my grandfather's pocket watch complete with little kinks and scuffs from wear and tear over the years. My daughter's time of birth clearly displayed on its face. To finish the picture there are two blooming red roses in the top left and bottom right corners. Then the saying along one side of the pocket watch and Wyatt's full name along the other.

The artwork so masterfully bringing life to my vision. Looking up at Trey with tears in my eyes that I will not to escape, "it's beautiful." It's the God's honest truth and with the emotions running through my mind and heart it's all I can seem to say in this moment. Once again looking down at the mother and child elephant that in my heart so much resembles Wyatt and I.

"So, we're good to go then? I can change or move anything you want if something isn't working for you." Trey, being the professional he is, wants to make sure I'm getting exactly what I want.

"It's perfect," I gasp, unable to take my eyes off the paper containing what will be my tattoo. A hand caressing my shoulder brings me back and I hate that I completely forgot Zac was standing behind me. Looking up at him I see the sincerity in his eyes. The understanding of everything this tattoo means to me. The understanding that one piece of art can represent such an important piece of you as a person. The look of deep connection makes me want to take another look at all of the artwork on his body. Zac shifts his hand to my lower back and breaks our eye contact to nod at Trey and fist bump him for his good work.

"Just give me a minute to set everything up and we'll be ready to roll," Trey says, leaving Zac and I in the front of the shop to ready the table and send his drawing through a copier that makes it a stencil. Zac explains that the copier has a special paper in the tray instead of regular printer paper. The paper transfers ink to wet skin, like a temporary tattoo, to give Trey reference lines.

"Even though Trey drew it, it's still easier and turns out better having reference lines then free handing a tattoo," Zac explains. "Although, Trey's freehanded some pretty damn good tattoos over the years." He begins to roll up his pant leg, "this one he did while we were," he pauses, "traveling and it was all free hand." I'm not sure of his pause, but I look down at the gorgeous tattoo of a German Shepard in the middle of his calf. It's incredible. It's also, not the only German Shepherd marring his skin- but it doesn't seem like the right time to bring that up- they must be his favorite.

"That's incredible." I lean down to get a better look at all the detail that went into the piece. The idea that Trey did this without any reference lines on Zac's skin makes it that much more amazing. I'm lifting my hand to trace the line of the dog's snout when Trey comes back in the room startling me.

"Ready?"

"Absolutely," I say, jumping to my full height. Fingers tingling from the simple touch of Zac's calf.

Walking to the cushioned table my heart is hammering against my chest. I know I want this. It's not the fear of altering my skin. I'm not sure what it is, actually. Maybe the idea that I'm doing something I know Kent would disapprove of is making my nerves raw. Kent would be flipping his shit if he knew where I was, what I was about to do. It's a freedom I haven't felt in so many years that's too embarrassing to count.

Standing there, I lift my shirt and roll it under the bottom band of my bra to keep it in place. Revealing my entire midsection. Trey takes a cold, soapy paper towel and cleans the skin causing chillbumps to spread along my arms. He then brings the stencil a breath away from my hip bone. "You good with it here? I think this is best for the movement of your waist," Trey asks, looking up at me for approval.

"I trust you." With my excited smile, Trey places the stencil against my skin then peels the transition paper away. Holding up a mirror to my hip so I can see the full extent of the image. I nod and bite my lip with enthusiasm. Trey takes that as my acceptance of the placement. Laying on the cushioned table, Trey positions me where he has the best angle to start. On my stomach.

His foot tests the peddle and I hear the electric buzz of the tattoo gun for the first time. My pulse sky rockets for a whole different reason and I'm really nervous. I close my eyes to try and calm myself when I feel a hand firmly grab mine as they rest on the table above my head. Opening my eyes, I fall into the caramel depths of Zac's. The calm that blankets me from his simple touch and concerned eyes brings me the strength I need.

"Ready," Trey asks. Gun in hand, hovering over my hip. Petroleum Jelly looking gooped in the webbing of his glove between his thumb and forefinger and a paper towel looped around his pinky.

"As I'll ever be," I say, glancing away from Zac's hazel eyes to reassuringly nod at Trey. The needle pierces my skin at an alarmingly fast rate. It's an odd feeling of vibrating pain and pleasure. The majority of the tattoo is tolerable, but there are places, like right over bone, that I grit my teeth and close my eyes. Those are the moments I love the most.

No, I'm not some sadist, before you go getting ahead of yourselves. The moments when the pain of the needle becomes almost too great, Zac squeezes my hand and leans in to whisper into my ear.

The spicy mix of his cologne with the mint of his gum causing my head to spin. The sweet words of encouragement he whispers that bring me peace also cause my libido to spike. The tenderness in his eyes as he drags them up and down my revealed midsection and the heat that sparks behind them when he gets lost in my creamy skin there, causes my core to catch fire. Yeah, those moments, where the pain is almost too great to bear is what I enjoy most.

Wrapping my hand around my left side, I fight the urge to scratch at the tape holding the protective sheet over my sensitive skin. I can't believe that took as long as it did. We got there this morning and now we're driving back as the sun sets behind us. I can't wait for Wyatt to see all the work Trey put into making my tattoo personal. All the images are vibrant and the level of his work is astonishing. She's going to love it. I just know it.

"Where are we going?" Zac is veering off the road, and even though there are aren't many cars on the road, this doesn't feel like the safest action. We're still thirty-five minutes from our houses and there's nothing around this stretch of road for miles.

"We're just making a stop." Zac parks the Jeep and walks around the front to open my door. "Join me?" he asks, holding his hand out to help me from my seat. Placing my hand in his I give him a quizzical look, but a soft smile slips from my lips at the spontaneity of his actions.

Zac moves us to the front of his Jeep then turns to me. "I was just thinking, it's been a long day, why not stop and enjoy some nature." He drops his hand from mine. His gaze never leaving me, he lifts both of his hands to my hips- careful not to catch the angry skin of my new tattoo. He leans in, and even though he doesn't ask permission or voice his intentions, I find myself falling under his spell. Whatever he does at this moment, I'm too weak to protest. I close my eyes, reveling in our unbridled connection only to feel my feet leave the ground and my back hit the hood of his jeep.

Before I can open my eyes and enjoy the image of him hovering over me while I'm laying down, his presence is gone. Trying to catch my breath, I feel his shoulder bump against mine on his hood. Zac moves to rest on his elbows, propping up his upper body to look out and I turn my head against the hood to soak in his profile against the setting sun. That's when I realize, we must be here to watch the sunset. The thought that Zac is trying to provide me with a perfect ending to an already great day melts my heart just a little.

He is a good man. Even in high school when he was running around being a jack-a-loon he always had a good heart. Back then it was hard to take him seriously with all the shenanigans he and his friends pulled. Although, he was always there when one of them, or I, needed him. That is the boy I remember and the one that shaped the great man Zac has seemed to have transformed into.

I wish I knew how he had spent all these years between high school and us sitting on the hood of his Jeep together. I wonder if the hard edges he's trying to hide tell a story all on their own. The tattoos tarnishing his skin tell a story. All the pieces of his life, I haven't been privy to, shaping him into the man that's quickly becoming one of my favorite enigmas.

"It's beautiful," I say, looking away from his profile and towards the glowing oranges and pinks taking over the soon to be night sky.

"It most definitely is," Zac says, but the way it falls from his lips- in almost a whisper- has goosebumps breaking out against my skin. The intensity of his whisper, a novel worth of emotion more than the words themselves. Turning my head, I fall into the golden eyes of Zac. "Go on a second date with me?"

My eyes widen with the bluntness of his question. "I wasn't aware we had gone on a first one."

The smile that splits Zac's face, causes my own lips to turn up in the corners. "Well, what do you call this?

We've been together all day. I picked you up, we had lunch, we had an emotional adventure with your tattoo, and now we're watching the sunset. I'd say that's one hell of a good first date." This is the side of Zac I love the best. The playful, engaging side that you can't help but agree with everything he's selling.

"I see your point, Dr. Jacobson. You're very smooth." Zac nudges his shoulder into mine in jest. "I'm just not sure I'm ready to date. After everything that happened with Wyatt's dad, and you don't even know the half of it, it just feels odd. I think I just need more time. You've been nothing but sweet and I really appreciate you calling your friend and convincing him to see me before hours. I saw his schedule for today and the next month and he's completely booked. I'm still not sure how you managed to get him to agree to cancel his appointments. None the less, I just don't think my mind or any other part of me is ready to take on the idea of dating." I pause and try to force myself to look at him, but can't find the courage to lift my eyes. "I'm sorry."

"Hey," Zac lifts my chin with a little pressure from his finger and holds my eyes prisoner. I can't look away, even when I feel the heat rising to my cheeks. "There's no reason to be sorry. I was just teasing. Although, if I'm being honest I'd be honored to take you on a real date. Until then, friends?" Zac lets the question hang between us for a beat then continues, "I enjoy spending time with you and I'd hate for that to stop because I couldn't keep my big mouth shut." The urgency in his eyes of possibly losing me as a friend is so endearing. I nod my acceptance of his friendship before I can change my mind.

We're friends.

I can totally be *friends* with Dr. Zachariah Corey Jacobson.

CHAPTER ELEVEN
ZAC

Last weekend was great. Tyler and I talked and it was unbelievable. Watching her golden hair shine under the pinks and oranges of the setting sun will be ingrained in my mind forever. She was always the girl I compare everyone to. Calling Trey and asking him to open his shop early got me a quick 'fuck you' followed by a deadline. Then I texted him saying it was for Tyler. Trey called me back immediately.

"If Tyler's a dude I'm going to drive down there and kick your ass," Trey groans into the phone.

"No, I mean Tyler, Tyler. A couple days after we went to the range the house next door was bought. Tyler fuckin' bought the house fifty feet away from me."

"No shit." Trey chuckles like the asshole he is. *"Well, I assume you still have the hard on from Hell for her. Didn't you used to have her photo taped to your helmet?"*

"Can we focus on getting her in to see you tomorrow for a tattoo?

I need this, Hicks."

"Yeah, yeah. I got your back. No more blue balls for you. Head to the shop tomorrow morning and I'll draw something up."

"I owe you, dude."

"We're square," Trey says, remembering the mess I saved him from during his divorce.

I didn't mean to talk about her during my deployment. I didn't intend to take her with me when I left Georgia. I was young and we had nothing else to do but get drunk on our nights off. Getting drunk just poured pop rocks on my memories. Dredging up the smallest interaction between Tyler and I. Unfortunately, it also opened up old wounds of Kensie. Crazy bitch sent Trey a 'Dear John' letter during his first long deployment. We shared a lot those months in the sandbox. Which is what got him opening up his shop without question.

Walking past my back window, I'm blinded by the bright sun reflecting off the blonde streaks in Wyatt's hair. The lighter blonde she gets from her mother. Wyatt is dribbling her soccer ball and I have to admit she's pretty damn good. She pops the ball into the air off the tip of her toe and begins bouncing it from knee to knee. After several high knees, Wyatt bucks the ball in the air to hit against her forehead once.

As the ball starts to lose altitude, she lowers her chest while keeping her eyes locked on the ball. When the ball reaches her waistline, Wyatt lifts her chest using the momentum to strike the ball with her shoelaces. The ball skyrockets towards the goal where- for the first time I'm noticing her- Tyler stands no chance of catching the round projectile. Wyatt's incredible, a mini-powerhouse with a ball.

Although it took a while, now that I've noticed

Tyler, I can't bring myself to look away. She lifts a water bottle to her lips. Closing her eyes to cool her overheated body. She's in track shorts and a workout tank top. For someone who bakes sweets for a living, you definitely wouldn't be able to tell from her figure. She's lean and muscular, yet curvy in all the right places. I would assume Wyatt had a little to do with adding those curves to her hips. Leading to toned, tan legs that go on for days. Tyler's hair is pulled back with wisps of fallen stands framing her face from the excursion of keeping up with her daughter.

Both Wyatt and Tyler have rose tinted cheeks. I wonder how long they've been working out there. As my mind envisions all the different ways I can exhaust Tyler, I hear a splash pulling me from my depraved thoughts. Looking towards the sound, I see the black and white ball floating in the deep end of my pool. I smile thinking of the force Tyler put behind a kick that sent the ball sailing past Wyatt and into my backyard. At least she's letting off steam in her own way. Although, my idea of letting off steam would sure be more fun for the both of us.

Before my thoughts can run away with a naked Tyler, the doorbell rings. Wyatt and Tyler stand at my door. Tyler has pulled on a loose t-shirt hiding her curves from me. Such a shame. Trying to fight the disappointment of not being able to see Tyler's body up close, I smile and ask how they are. As if I hadn't been watching them and didn't already know their ball is in my pool.

"Well, we were practicing and mom kicked the ball past me and it landed in your backyard. I was wondering if I could get it back," Wyatt said, twiddling her fingers. Am I that scary that she would be nervous around me?

Tyler lightly swats her shoulder for ratting her out and my smile turns softer at the sight of their bond.

"Of course, must have been a good kick." I send a teasing side glance to Tyler. Turning back to Wyatt, I point to the sliding glass door that heads to the back yard. Wyatt moves towards the back of my house and I gesture for Tyler to come in as well. There's no real reason for her to wait on the stoop. Granted, there's no reason for her to step inside either. Other than the idea of having her in my house sends a thrill down my spine. *God, get yourself together, Jacobson.*

"You have a great space here," Tyler says, trying to make conversation. I know she's nervous about being in my house because there has never been anyone who described my house as great. Plain? Yes. Sterile? Maybe. Great? Never.

I look around my living room with her and try to see what I've done with my space through her eyes. Everything has a function. I have no pictures of family or friends. I have furniture that I use, for a variety of different things. Thoughts of Tyler bent over my couch flood my brain and I have to look away. I shrug it off by saying, "it gets the job done."

Trying to rid myself of the different surfaces that allow for easy access in my living room, I look out of my glass door towards Wyatt. She has already plucked the ball out of the water and is currently running her fingers in small circles to watch the drops fall from the tips back into the water.

"She loves the water," Tyler says, following my eyeline.

"I never use the thing. You're more than welcome to come over whenever to use it."

"Oh, that's sweet. I wouldn't want to overrun your

pool."

"Nah, it's no problem," I say, reaching for my keys. "In fact, here, take this." Handing Tyler the key to the fence, her fingertips brush against mine and a new surge of heat courses through my body.

"What's that for?" Wyatt asks. Her sudden appearance made Tyler jump backwards. Breaking our connection.

"Zac said we can use his pool whenever you want, bug," Tyler says. Watching Wyatt's face fill with joy, I feel like I'm ten feet tall. *Man, that kid is cute.* Just like her momma.

Jumping up and down on the balls of her feet, Wyatt asks if she can swim now. Tyler looks to me for help and I simply nod my affirmation. Wyatt disappears back into her house to change into her suit before running through my house and jumping into the pool.

Two hours of swimming and that peanut is still going strong. "She's like a fish," I say to Tyler. We've been sitting on my patio with a few beers between us since Wyatt started swimming.

"Yeah, she's got gills hidden in that one piece," Tyler jokes. "Are you getting hungry? I thought I'd order food since we've monopolized your entire afternoon."

Monopolized, my ass. This has been one of the best afternoons I've had in a long time. "Dinner sounds great, but you don't have to do that. I'm glad to see the pool is finally bein' put to good use. I feel like it's been a waste on me. It came with the house and I haven't been able to stop long enough to enjoy it."

Wyatt keeps swimming while Tyler and I continue to

regale stories of our lives since high school. There are so many blanks she's leaving out between then and now. Watching Tyler talk about her life since high school, I notice now more than ever, that she's lost the spark that could light the whole school a blaze when we were young. The woman she is now with her snuffed- out inner flame.

However, I'm not being totally forthcoming with my life events either. I'm not sure why I haven't told her about my service. It's not like I'm hiding it. Anyone could find out if they asked the right people; the whole town knows. Bad boy turned good, thanks, in big part, to the military. Maybe I just want her to see me. Not the pain and angst that went into my joining. Or the hurt and suffering that went into my discharge. Just me.

Once again, my deep thoughts are saved by the doorbell. Our Chinese food arrives and as I'm bringing it to the porch table, I see Tyler already has Wyatt out and wrapped in a towel. Wyatt grudgingly sits at the table, when I'm sure she'd rather be swimming. Tyler takes the bag from me and I grab the stack of plates and silverware I set out earlier from the kitchen counter.

Food is shared and a pleasant silence washes over the three of us as we dig in. Wyatt keeps looking out at the pool; I'm sure hoping she'll be able to swim more before the night is through. She could swim all night, for all I care. As long as it meant I'd have all night to peel back the thorny layers of her mother. And I thought I was closed off.

Trying for a distraction I say, "Wyatt, you have such a unique name for a girl. I like it. I think it fits you well." Turning to Tyler I ask, "What made you pick it?"

Tyler opens her mouth to answer, but Wyatt beats her

to it. "Well, Momma always liked it. She said having a boy name makes a girl tough, just like her. That being a girl with a name like ours reminds us that we can be just as strong as anyone. I like it. I like being different. Daddy never liked it though. He didn't think it was right for a girl to have a boy name. That never made much sense to me. I mean, Momma has a boy name, too." Wyatt said her piece and now she's turned back to her food. Unaware that everything she just said was like dropping bombs for me. How could a father let his own child know something like that? What kind of man talks to his own blood like that? It's just a name. Yet, with one comment he condemned both Tyler and Wyatt.

Beside me I can feel the tension rolling off Tyler and I wish there was something I could do to calm her. Before I can find the right words, she turns to Wyatt, "don't you have some homework to finish, bug." She speaks carefree, but I can see the tides are turning inside her mind. She's unhappy at the memory Wyatt has brought up.

"Oh, yeah." Wyatt jumps to her feet and runs towards the door. I look over to Tyler and open my mouth to talk, but before I can get a word out Wyatt is back in front of us. "Thank you for letting me use your pool."

"Anytime, peanut." I wasn't really planning on the nickname coming out, but the look in her eyes when it did hurts my heart. The look of sheer joy that someone other than her mother was showing her affection was clearly a new feeling for her. Wyatt takes one step to leave, then changes directions and comes to give me a hug where I sit stunned. I turn to look at Tyler while Wyatt holds on to thank me, she lifts her hand to hide is back in front of us. "Thank you for letting me use your pool."

"Anytime, peanut." I wasn't really planning on the nickname coming out, but the look in her eyes when it did hurts my heart. The look of sheer joy that someone other than her mother was showing her affection was clearly a new feeling for her. Wyatt takes one step to leave, then changes directions and comes to give me a hug where I sit stunned. I turn to look at Tyler while Wyatt holds on to thank me, she lifts her hand to hide the smile this interaction has produced. I'm sure the look of shock on my face is priceless. This is why I deal with dogs; I don't understand children.

Watching Wyatt once again head for the front door, I'm oddly happy that she felt comfortable enough to hug me. Considering when she and Tyler showed up on my doorstep this afternoon, she looked as nervous about me as a timid bunny. "Well, that was unexpected," I say, looking over at Tyler, who has begun to clean-up from dinner. "Leave it. Talk with me for a minute."

"We've been talking all afternoon," she teases, continuing to stack plates and trash.

I grab her hands to still them. "True, but now I'd like to ask you a question." Tyler stops moving and looks frightened about what I'm going to bring up. Talking to Ty is like walking through a field of landmines. She has deep emotional scars that I'm sure no one even knows are there, hiding just under that tough skin of hers. Manifestations of the ugliness she must have endured. "You don't have to answer, but I'd like it if you did. And know that I don't judge you."

I raise my eyebrows and Tyler nods in understanding. "Why does Wyatt know that her father doesn't like her name? Did he say it to her or is she just really perceptive?" It's the one thing I can't get over. Treating a spouse poorly is one thing- as bad as it is- but treating your children badly is a whole different level of scum. How could Tyler have associated with someone of that level, let alone married them and procreated.

"Unfortunately, that was the least of our problems with Kent."

And there it was. The last piece to the puzzle that has become Tyler's adult life since she left for college. Everything is starting to make sense and all the loose ends getting tied into place in my mind.

"Ah, I was wonderin' if he was Wyatt's father," I said more to myself, but by the time the words left my mouth, I knew I'd fucked up. The look of sheer pain and- worst of all- hurt that flashed across Tyler's face was deafening without her saying a word. While my words were innocent enough in my head, I shouldn't have said them out loud. I can only imagine the thoughts running through Tyler's head revealed by the emotions running like a marathon across her face.

CHAPTER TWELVE

Tyler

"Excuse me?" I ask, although, don't really care for an explanation.

How dare he? What did he think, I left for college and started sleeping around? No wonder he wanted to go on a date with me. He probably thought I was a sure thing and he'd have me in the bag before the meal was over. *The pig!*

I pull my hands away from his and throw down the napkin balled up in my fist. I can't stand to even look at him. I'm fuming. After everything Kent did, I didn't think anything would make me feel that defeated. Yet, hearing Zac talk as if I might have become the school slut after graduation cuts deep.

Turning to walk away, Zac reaches for my wrist. It's not hard like Kent used to grab me, but enough to get me to stop. "I'm sorry. That came out wrong." Zac pauses. I don't turn, but I don't try to get away either, so he continues, "I just mean that I lost track of everyone after high school. I didn't even know if the two of you went on to college together. Let alone stayed together romantically." I turned then to look back at him and he took that as his sign to keep going with his apology.

"I swear I didn't mean it the way it sounded. You were never the type to sleep around in high school, and I didn't think your morals changed. Only that I hadn't heard anything or kept tabs on you two to know if you made it or not as a couple."

I can't look at him. There was no judgement in his voice, but I couldn't shake the tone of accusation from his original statement. My body turning against my brain's objections, I can only look into the golden, remorseful eyes of Zachariah. He truly looks as sorry as he sounds.

Getting lost in his caramel depths, my body calms and I'm having a hard time keeping my temper fuming. The softness in his eyes licking the wounds of my ego. As the thought enters my head, I can't help the naughty images that accompany it.

My back is against the kitchen counter, Zac moving closer until he's directly in front of me. Breathing each other's air without so much as a whisper between my chest and his. Zac's hands graze my sides, lightly tracing an imaginary line from each of my shoulders to my hips. There his fingertips will slip beneath my shirt and play with the hem of my bottoms. Before my next breath, his mouth is on mine. Stealing the air from my lungs. The force of his need mixed with the softness of his lips causes me to gasp; opening my mouth to allow his tongue access.

A heady feeling overtakes my body and I hold onto

Zac's shoulders. If it wasn't for my back against the counter, I'm not sure I'd be able to keep myself upright. Zac's fingers start inching further into my shorts and his mouth moves to my neck. Due to my choice of clothing my loose shorts are around my knees with minimal effort on Zac's part. Then, I'm sitting on the counter and my shorts fall to the floor between us.

"Tell me you want this?" It's a question I don't expect. Zac asks the question while his hand moves up my inner thigh. I know he can feel how wet I am the closer he gets to my core, because I'm dripping. My slick cream sliding down my legs like sweet syrup down an ice cream sunday. "I need you to say it, Ty." The use of my nickname is my undoing.

"Yes, I want this," I whimper. "I want you." I repeat with more confidence. My head falls back as Zac's kiss swollen lips break into a beautiful smile. A smile that would melt my panties if they weren't already forgotten on the floor.

Then he's there. I can feel Zac's breath against my right thigh before his lips touch me. I gasp, more from the anticipation of what's going to happen then the actual feel of his lips. Although, his lips feel damn good against my skin. The heat rolling through my core is on the verge of catching fire. Zac can sense my urgency and luckily doesn't keep me waiting. He lightly swipes his tongue from my opening to my clit and my mouth falls open. Another whimper escapes my lips with the trembling of my core. Before my heart can catch up with the current events Zac's mouth closes around my clit and I cry out in pleasure.

Zac clears his throat pulling me from my mental-fantasy. My cheeks blush a deep red as I look at Zac with his sincere eyes still trained on me. "I'm sorry. I know you didn't mean it the way it sounded. I'm sorry I freaked. There's just so much that happened between Kent and I. I tend to react poorly without thinking."

Zac registers my blush, but only breaks eye contact briefly. "Will you tell me what's happened since graduation?"

"It's not glamorous," I admit, trying to back away from the subject gently.

"Even so. I want to know you." Zac's hand rests on mine atop the table and I tilt my head at the contact-his tanned skin against mine. Somewhere in my subconscious I recognize how nice our complexions compliment the other, but choose to ignore it. I've been through too much to even entertain the thought of being with someone romantically again.

I take a deep breath then start at the beginning. "We went to college together. I thought once we were away from our families and the usual circle of friends we'd have the whirlwind romance away at college. That Kent would have time for me and we'd continue to grow closer and closer.

In high school our relationship was good, but that was the problem. It was just ok. He was always so busy with his friends and the team I was an afterthought many times. But we had been together for so long I figured we owed it to ourselves to see it through. And, everything was great, at first. I thought things were going well. Things were headed the direction I thought-we thought-they would. Kent wasn't playing his first season. He told me he thought he was going to be redshirted. Although, he never got any official word on that from any of the coaches.

"Then, in the last game of the regular season, the coaches put Kent in when the quarterback went down and the second string QB was looking at an injured rotator cuff from practice drills. I was so happy Kent was finally put in, but apparently that wasn't a good thing. I didn't get it." I look up at Zac and he's shaking his head in understanding.

Essentially, Kent had missed out on an entire season. He would only be able to play three more years; so, this year was a waste-since he only played one game all season. "As you can imagine he was pissed. We didn't make it to the post season playoffs that season which added to his aggravation. Adding salt to the wound he was stuck at third string quarterback the last three years of school. I'm getting ahead of myself, though." I collect the plates and move to place them in the sink. Looking through the window and at my daughter doing her homework on the kitchen table.

"Back to freshman year after the playoffs, though. I was stressed out trying to pull Kent out of his funk. After a few weeks, I started throwing up anything I tried to eat. I thought the stress of trying to be perfect for Kent was the cause, but after three weeks of not being able to keep anything down, I had no choice but to go to the student health center. Needless to say, I was told I was pregnant and my stomach dropped to the floor. I was so nervous to tell Kent, but I knew I had to sooner rather than later. I was nine weeks pregnant according to student health and eventually I'd start showing.

"I made myself sick with nerves and worrying about how Kent would react. I went back to student health and the doctor urged me to find a way to calm down. The stress I was putting my body through was not good for me or my baby. Eventually, I just bit the bullet and told Kent.

"To my great surprise, Kent was ecstatic. I was shocked, but he became so attentive. He became so loving, caring, and intuitive of my needs. I needed him- really needed him- for the first time in our relationship and he was there for me. I thought I was floating on cloud nine. When I was past my first trimester and we knew the baby was in the clear, Kent proposed. We were married with just our close family and friends over the summer between freshman and sophomore year.

"Everything had been going so well. I should have been waiting for the other shoe to drop. And oh, the size of that shoe as it trampled on my life. As soon as Wyatt was born, everything went south- and quick. She kept getting sick. I swear that girl had croup about seven times before she was two years old. Each time resulted in a midnight trip to the emergency room for a breathing treatment and steroids. All of which were left to me. Kent argued he had to focus on football and his grades to stay on the team. My classes be damned. It was 'me who wanted the baby anyway.'

"As I mentioned before, Kent kept getting overlooked for better players. He spent his college football career playing third string quarterback and blamed Wyatt and I more and more as time passed.

"By the time we graduated, the NFL wasn't even a pipe dream; and it was our fault. Kent had the credits to graduate- but since he had put all his eggs in the NFL basket- it was only in general studies. Unable to get a specialized job with that, he decided to follow a buddy of his to the academy. Before we knew it, Kent was a cop." I pause here to catch my breath- or my emotions, not sure which- and turn to look at Zac. "Are you sure you want to hear about this? It's kind of a mood killer." My cheeks redden. I didn't mean mood, that had all been in my head, shit.

"I want to hear anythin' and everythin' you're willing to tell me." Zac's voice calms the storm of emotions within me.

"Well," I pause, turning back to the window. "What came next was worse than everything leading up to this point combined. All the guilt was laid on me of his stinted football career. The guilt pushed to me of feeling like I pressured Kent into marriage and children. All of that was child's play compared to what came after Kent became a cop. Kent started spending all of his nights off drinking with the other cops from his precinct. They knew he was drinking more and more and did nothing. As time went on the anger got worse every time he drank. They would get him good and plastered, then send him home to Wyatt and me. Wyatt was six when the threats started.

"At first it was little things. Calling me names- any and every name imaginable-to belittle me when I did something he didn't like or approve of. Then there were bigger threats of hitting or smacking me if I didn't have something done or ready for him when he wanted it-or done the 'right' way." At this, I look down at the sink at my waist-ashamed. I should have gotten us out then. I will hate myself every day for not leaving sooner than I did. "The threats started becoming more frequent and I started second guessing myself. All of my choices were finalized through Kent. All of my decisions were run by Kent. All of my plans and appointments were organized through Kent in coordination with his calendar. If I wasn't doing something for Kent or Wyatt, I was home doing laundry, cleaning, cooking, or hiding in Wyatt's room with her as long as I could after I put her to bed."

I pause and I can feel Zac's body heat move closer behind me. "Kent was always so angry. His threats became too close for comfort. I lived every day afraid that, maybe, that would be the day Kent crossed the line from emotional to physical abuse. I couldn't take it anymore. Watching Wyatt walk on eggshells with her own father was my breaking point." I pause again and look up at Wyatt, studiously working at the table.

"Kent wasn't granted any visitation. He has to attend anger and alcohol management classes for six months consistently before he'll be allowed to see Wyatt, but only with supervision. After a year of classes, he'll be able to try for joint custody. I'm so scared for that day. Thankfully, the last I heard from my lawyer, he's not making any effort to attend any of his meetings. So, it's a long way off, but it still terrifies me to leave her with him for any extended period of time." With that final concern, my story is finished. The soap opera that has been my adult life to lead me here is over.

Zac reaches forward and I feel his hands on my shoulders. The warmth of his body causes anything tense remaining from my memories to relax at his touch. I feel myself drift back against Zac's chest. My back to his front, and I know I shouldn't, but I can't bring myself to move away from him. His heat is drawing me in and at this moment I'm too vulnerable to ignore the pull between us. I want to forget the hurt that is my life.

Zac's breath grazes past the side of my neck. The gentle physical contact making me shudder. It's been so long since someone has touched me this way. So caring. So- dare I say- loving. The simple connection is healing my outlook on the opposite sex and he doesn't even know it.

"I'm sorry you've had to go through that. I'm sorry Wyatt had that as a male role model. I hope she knows that's not how a man treats a woman. But mostly, I'm sorry you didn't get the 'happily ever after' you wanted. I've only ever wanted to see you happy." Zac's husky voice softly speaking against my ear- his lips moving, brushing my earlobe and neck- sends goosebumps down my arms.

I don't need to see his face to know Zac means every word he just spoke. He has always seemed to put my happiness above his own. Even if it was letting me have the lunch we both wanted when it was the last one. I'm not sure where to go from here, though. I'm still not ready for anything to move forward with Zac-with anyone. No matter how he's healing my male outlook. If I turn and see the sincerity in Zac's eyes, I know I'll break. Hell, I'm already on the verge of agreeing to give it a try and he hasn't even asked me on a date, yet- again?

"Thank you." It's all I can think to say, as I extract myself from Zac's innocent caress. "I should go check on Wyatt." Another awkward pause. Still unable to look at his caramel eyes, I focus on his chest and continue, "this was nice. Thanks for letting Wyatt swim. And for listening. I'll see you later, Zac." With my farewell said, I beat feet for my house and away from that distractingly gorgeous, sweet man. I need to stay away from him. He's too dangerous for my already shattered emotional state. My heart can't take another break, yet. Not before it's fully healed from Kent.

Yes, I need to stay away. If only someone would relay that message from my brain to the rest of my body and my overactive libido.

CHAPTER THIRTEEN

ZAC

Two damn weeks and *nothing*.

Fucking radio silence from Tyler ever since she opened up about Kent. I thought we were finally getting somewhere. Apparently not, since Tyler has gone out of her way to avoid me for fifteen fucking days. Fifteen days where I can still smell her vanilla scent and feel her soft skin against my fingers.

"I can't," I say, pushing myself off of my kitchen island counter to look out the sink window at Ty's closed window shades.

I can't keep watching her house for a sign of life. I know she and Wyatt are out. I'm looking for breadcrumbs when there are none. I can't keep this up.

I haven't met up with the guys for drinks. I haven't replied to any of Jane's texts or calls. Even when they're getting more and more detailed. Her last voicemail nearly did me in. With her husky voice she explained-in no uncertain terms- what she wanted me to do to her. Unfortunately, all I could think about was doing all of those things with Tyler's lithe body instead of Jane's. And Jane's a good girl-she doesn't deserve that. She's a friend and I shouldn't use her the way I do.

Walking to the fridge, I figure I'll drown my self-imposed loneliness in a beer. Yeah, beer is good. Although, as my body absorbs the frigid air seeping from the open fridge door, I see the evidence of my total lack of shits given to stop at the grocery store over the past week.

"Fuck," I mutter under my breath at my very empty cold shelves. As if it's the appliance fault for not restocking itself. "Welp," I shut the door and grab my keys, phone and wallet off the counter and head for the door.

I'll grab food and restock a little at the store near the clinic. I need to grab some paperwork I left on my desk anyway. My mind has clearly been elsewhere this week and has made my memory it's bitch. Because while I can't remember groceries or paperwork, I could tell you exactly what Tyler wore out of the house the past six days.

Pulling into the marketplace that houses my clinic, I take stock of my options for lunch. I can't decide between fake Mexican and fake Chinese. Parking near my clinic I walk towards my top two options.

Beep

Looking down, I see yet another text from Jane trying to get me to stop by later. I swipe to the left to delete the temptation and run right into a bench. Wait, that bench has little hands grabbing my arm.

"Uff," Wyatt says, holding my arm to steady herself.

"I'm sorry. I wasn't watching…" She looks at who she's ran into and breaks off mid-sentence and smile. "Zac."

"Hello, Wyatt." Looking around I expect to find Ty lurking nearby trying not to get too close to me, but still be with Wyatt. Or is Wyatt old enough to roam alone? I right Wyatt onto her feet and make an apology of my own. "You have no reason to apologize. My eyes were on my phone and I clearly ran in to you. I'm sorry. Where were you headed?" I ask, hoping it was inside to her mother.

"To Chipotle," she points to the store window in front of us.

"What a coincidence, I was headed there myself." Well, it's half true. It was the fake Mexican I was debating. "Is your mother inside?"

"No, she's back at the bakery. We're painting, but we got hungry. Mom sent me for fuel. Plus, my arms were about to fall off from the rolling brush and the high walls of mom's new shop. It sucks being short," Wyatt finishes and looks down dejectedly.

"Look at your parents, peanut. You're goin' nowhere but up." I say and nudge her into the restaurant. "Now, let's get you ladies some sustenance." We make our way through the line and I insist on paying. This actually causes more of a huff in Ty's mini-me than I would have thought. I think she wanted to feel grown up paying for her own meal.

"Chin up, Peanut. There's plenty of time for that. Don't grow up too fast." I pause with an idea. "Want help back?" I ask.

"Yeah, just wait till you see what mom and I did to the shop." Oh, peanut, I can't wait. Although, it has nothing to do with the shop and everything to do with the woman inside it.

Jingle. Jingle. Jingle.

The small bells looped around the inside door handle alert everyone the doors have opened.

"Bug, is that you?" Ty's disembodied voice calls from the back of the shop someplace.

Looking around the shop, it looks amazing already. The majority of the front room is painted and decorative touches lay on the edges of the floors as a blueprint for where I assume they will be placed on the walls. There are framed pictures of cakes and pies, wooden utensils, and antique looking pans as the primary décor. The open storefront windows have stacked trays for displaying the goodness from within. There's a soft layer of fabric as the base and various levels of tiered trays and cupcake towers. I can almost see the truffles and cakes Tyler's going to produce and display here. Just inside, there are a few quaint two and four top tables arranged in the lobby area.

The kitchen is behind a partially cleaned display case and a doorway with a rod that holds a curtain as a door. Presumably to hide the interior of the kitchen. The painting is mostly done, but there are still many things to be done.

"Mom, look who I found," Wyatt says and I turn to lock eyes with Tyler just as she comes around the corner from behind the partially drawn curtain.

Tyler misses a step and grabs hold of the wall, but recovers quickly. "Zachariah, we weren't expecting you."

No, I don't guess you would with you doing everything in your power to avoid me. "Ah, but I was in the mood for fake Mexican and it looks like great minds think alike." Nudging Wyatt next to me, I say, "What do you say, peanut? Eat then we help your momma finish makin' this place shine?"

"Yeah, I'm ready to finish this up and go for another swim. Maybe?" Wyatt looks hopefully to her mother.

"We'll see. First, we eat. Then, we work. After that, if there's still time, maybe a swim." We step up to one of the four top tables and distribute the food. I opted for a bowl so I didn't make a fool of myself in front of the ladies. As we eat in comfortable silence, I can't help feeling how nice this is. So domestic. So unlike anything I thought would ever make me feel anything other than my chest tightening in paralyzing fear. Not just because of the domesticity of everything, but the clutter of opening the store would normally make me break in a cold sweat claustrophobia if not for my PTSD therapy.

The idea that I'm not breaking out in a cold sweat being in this domestic situation aside, I need to come up with a reason to be around her. Then I remember the dog treats.

"I've been looking into those," Tyler says, around her last bite of chicken and rice. "From what I've found I can use many of the same ingredients I use for any of my vegan cakes. Applesauce for eggs and what not."

"Sounds good to me. When do you think I could get some samples?" I ask, putting the lid back on my empty bowl.

"Depending on how much we get done today, I can probably get you some by the end of the week."

"Perfect, should we get to it, then?" I ask, standing. "Where should I start, Boss?"

Tyler looks around and motions towards the display cases. "Maybe get those in order? I need to focus on the kitchen."

"You got it," I say, moving towards the cleaning supplies and starting on the trivial task. When that's done my back is killing me. I'm going to need a pain pill later, but hell if I'm going to stop helping now. Looking around, the paint is dry in the lobby for the most part. I start walking around the base of the room and hammering the décor according to the blueprint Tyler organized.

Before I know it, the sun is setting and I've- we've- been working all day. I've been working alongside Tyler and she seems to always find a room to keep between us. This won't do. I need to find a way to get close to her again. My back won't let me keep doing grunt work to weasel my way into her presence.

Looking over, I see Wyatt has clocked out and is softly snoring at one of the tables in the lobby. "Looks like we should call it a night." I nod towards the sleeping girl.

"It does appear that way. Let me close down the back, then I'll grab her and follow you out." Tyler looks positively exhausted. She doesn't need to be dragging a sleeping ten-year-old from her limp state. Granted, I don't either, but hell if I'll let her know how much pain I'm in. She's been at this longer than I have today. I'm not ready to open that can of worms if I talk about where I got my back injury.

As Tyler returns to walk towards Wyatt, I raise my hand to stop her. "I got her." I lift the girl into my arms and I'm surprised at how solid she is considering how tiny she seems. Walking Wyatt to the back of Ty's car. I catch Ty watching from the doorway as she locks up the shop.

"Thank you for helping today. We got way more done than I anticipated," Tyler says.

"Just doin' my neighborly duty," I say, softly closing the car door. "I'm always around to help," I add, stepping closer to Tyler. I don't want to press my luck, but I have to be close to this woman. My body yearns for her nearness just as it did in high school.

I need to calm down. I can't do this tug of war thing. Tyler has let me back in slightly. I will not scare her away again.

I can't-she helps keep the nightmares at bay.

CHAPTER

Tyler

Watching Zac's thick, muscular form lifting my slumbering child into his arms was the single most caring thing anyone who wasn't family has done for me in a long time. Never would Kent have been considerate enough to be concerned for Wyatt or my well being to help. He probably would have nudged Wyatt until she woke and grumbled to her to get her ass in the car.

While Zac looks like this hulking, moody giant sometimes, it's times like these that I'm hit with just how gentle and caring he can be. Is he like this with everyone or just children? My mind wanders to what Zac must be like in other contexts of his life. Is he a gentle lover? Kent was always so rough and would only get worse the more I showed the pain I felt. I can't imagine that is how it's supposed to be between two people who love each other. Although, Kent's all I've ever known and while Zac may make my panties damp, my heart race and my mind wonder where it shouldn't I'm not sure I could ever cross that line with him. No matter how sweet he is to me or my daughter.

"I think she's all set," Zac says, closing the door with Wyatt safely tucked and buckled inside.

"Dinner?" I blurt out without my brain entirely caught up with my mouth. "I mean as a thank you. I'm cooking, you're more than welcome after helping all afternoon." Smooth Tyler, real smooth. God, I'm giving myself a mental facepalm right now. Could I get anymore awkward?

To his credit, Zac just smiles while I make a fool of myself. "Dinner sounds great." His reassuring smirk doing everything, but calm my nerves.

"Then, I guess you can follow us home. I-I mean to our home. Er, my home. Unless you want to change first. Not that you have to, just," I pause, looking over Zac's body until my eyes hit the floor. "I'm just going to stop talking now."

"Hey." When Zac doesn't pull my attention from the hole I'm trying to burn into the ground to swallow me, he places two fingers under my chin and with gentle pressure he brings my gaze to meet his. "There you are. How about I stop and grab somethin' from my office and meet you at your house in about fifteen minutes?" I nod and let out a sigh of relief that the awkwardness is over.

How does he do that? Zac is the only person who can calm me while at the same time making my heart race. He makes the butterflies in my stomach flutter to no end while clearing my mind of any nerves and embarrassment. God, how am I going to get through this dinner? How do you ignore the pull in your gut towards something you've lost faith in? I loved love. I loved the feeling of being loved and loving someone with your whole heart. But, love hurt me and it's not the type of injury that heals overnight.

With the exception of the love between a mother and their child I don't have any faith in love anymore. Kent saw to that. Kent made sure that I never believe in love again. Love only ever turns to hate, the fine line between the two blurring until it is gone and all that remains is contempt for the person you swore to love and cherish. I can't do that to myself, but how do I ignore how Zachariah makes me feel? How he's always made me feel?

Can I?

"Baby, go get a shower, then start your homework while I work on dinner." Wyatt isn't happy about waking up to do homework. She slept the whole way home, which for me was great. Helped me work through my Zac issue in my head. Hopefully, so I don't make a fool of myself.

Walking into the kitchen I'm thanking the forethought I threw chicken and dumplings into the crock pot before we left for the shop this morning. I knew we'd have a long day there and either; A. I wouldn't have time to cook a decent meal or B. I wouldn't feel like cooking after working the majority of the day. And oh, does it smell good. I look at my watch and figure dinner is pretty much ready, I have time to grab a quick shower before Zac is supposed to me here.

As I close the bathroom door behind me and begin

to strip my clothes off the heat of the day, and being around Zac doesn't wane. Maybe I'll need to take a *cold* shower. Anything to cool off from the way my body warms due to all things that is Zac.

Watching his muscles pull and tighten beneath his shirt as he hammered in nails to hang my decorations. Then the way he scooped Wyatt into his arms holding her against his firm chest like I'd like to be. Shit, this is bad. A cold shower is definitely what the doctor ordered. Cool down these damn hormones.

Just as I finish dressing and start towel drying my hair there's a soft knock on my front door. "God, grant me strength," I whisper to my reflection in the mirror before heading down the stairs toward Zac waiting on the other side of my door. Blowing out all my breath to psych myself up, I open the door. "Hey." I'm all smiles. He'll never know the internal battle I fought to not touch myself in the shower with thoughts of him in my head.

"Hey." Zac has changed into a pair of cargo shorts and a v-neck showcasing bulging biceps and long lean calf muscles. Since when do I find calves attractive? What is this man doing to me? Zac stands there with his hands in his pockets watching me struggle not to look over his body with a smug smile spreading across his face. He knows this is hard for me. Then I realize he's still standing on my porch and I'm holding onto the door like it's the only thing holding me up. "Sorry, come in." I open the door farther and step back to allow him in. "I hope you like chicken and dumplings."

"I love 'em," Zac drawls, walking past me, his clean soapy smell wafting after him as he goes. Oh God help me, I pray as I close and lock the door, then turn back to Zac to lead him into the kitchen where Wyatt is already working on her schoolwork.

The smell of the crock pot consuming the entire space and my stomach rumbles quietly at the idea of eating it. Walking to the fridge I take out broccoli and start to steam it. "Dinner shouldn't be too much longer. Bug, you gunna be ready?" I ask, looking over at Wyatt working at the table.

"Yeah, I just gotta finish this math, but I don't get it. Can you help me, Momma?" She asks, looking over her shoulder at me.

"Baby, math is not my area of expertise. I don't think I'd be much help at all. History or English and I'm yours, math and science are dark and scary places for me," I say, apologetically to my daughter.

"What math is it?" Zac moves towards the table to look over the paper laying in front of Wyatt.

"Decimals and fractions," Wyatt says, in the most self-deprecating way a 9-year-old can.

"Ah, let's see here. My older buddy taught me this trick when I was in school," Zac says, sitting next to Wyatt to show her an easy trick to figuring out the math problems. I rest my hip against the kitchen counter and watch as Zac leans towards my daughter to praise her on picking up the trick so quickly. The light shining in my daughter's eyes from the male praise breaks my heart. She's needed a male influence, other than my father, for so long. The scars may not be visible for her, but the pain from Kent is definitely there. Just like mine will always be there, just underneath the surface.

Watching the two of them work while the broccoli softens reminds me of my childhood. My parents were fantastic. My mother always had a home cooked meal for us while my dad sat and worked through our homework with me. The love in my home growing up was what I had wanted for my family. God, did I mess that up.

Yet, watching Zac and Wyatt working together, a smile on both their faces sends a joyful spasm into my ovaries that most definitely needs to be ignored. Those two organs have no say in my life anymore.

Just as I'm straining the last of the water off the broccoli and adding butter to the bowl Wyatt jumps up, "finished!"

"Perfect timing. Baby, go put it in your bag and set the table for dinner."

"I got it," Zac says, walking behind me toward the plates and silverware I took out earlier. The gentle graze of his hand on my lower back as he passes behind me causes my body to shudder at his nearness, his caress. Thankfully, if Zac noticed he's not mentioning it.

CHAPTER FIFTEEN

Tyler

"You ready for your game in a couple weeks?" I ask Wyatt, trying to occupy my mind so I can stop filling it with the way Zac looks sitting at my dinner table. The moan from taking his first bite ringing in my ears. My brain playing the sensually low groan on a repeated loop just to cause my core to ache in the most delicious way. I can feel myself getting wet and I need to switch gears as quickly as possible.

"Yeah, Coach said he's going to start me as forward. So I'm super stoked," Wyatt says, then looks to Zac who's nodding towards her with a vaunt look in his eyes. "Will you come watch me play, Zac?" Wyatt shy's away from her question like she's anticipating the let down. Kent couldn't be bothered to show interest in Wyatt's soccer talent, and all she wanted was to make him proud of her.

Zac looks to me and I can't read his expression.

Maybe he's looking to me for help. He doesn't want to go, but he also doesn't want to hurt Wyatt's feelings. He's a good guy, "Bug, Zac probably…"

"I'd love to come watch you play," Zac interrupts me while still holding my gaze. Then, he looks over to Wyatt with a wide grin that would make me weak at the knees if I wasn't already sitting. Wyatt is positively glowing which causes my heart to break and my head to cloud with my feelings for this man.

Easy conversation continues over Wyatt's soccer prowess until dinner finishes with excitement. "Wyatt, go on upstairs and get ready for bed," I say, clearing the dishes from the table. Just as I'm turning toward the sink Zac reaches out for my elbow. I turn to find him standing much closer to me than I expected causing my breath to catch in my throat. He takes the plates from my hand. "I got this, you go help Wyatt for bed."

There's no use in arguing with him. By the time I can think properly, Zac's already at the sink rinsing the plates and reaching for the pot I steamed the broccoli in. Can you say swoon worthy. This whole day has been one long swoon-fest for the bad boy next door. Although, this man in front of me is so different from the boy I once knew, while still holding all the endearing qualities I remember.

I don't say anything as I walk up the stairs to help Wyatt with her nighttime ritual. When I get there she's just getting into bed with her hair brushed and pj's on. "Did you brush your teeth, bug?" I ask, walking into her room to tuck her in.

"Yeah, I'm good to go." She lays her head on her oversized furry pillow and I walk over to bring the covers to just under her chin. Sitting on the side of her bed by her hip, I lean over to kiss her forehead. "I love you, baby girl. Always know that. You are the best thing I have ever done, never doubt that." I recite the same three sentences, just as I have since she was a baby cooing in my arms.

"I love you, too, Momma," she says as I get up and check her night light before turning off her overhead light. Just before I close the door behind me I hear her soft voice, "Momma?"

"Yeah, baby girl?"

"I like Zac."

"I like him, too, baby. He's a good friend," I say, then turn to walk back downstairs.

As I make my way toward the kitchen, the view of Zac's back muscles has me walk slower than normal. His bulging muscles performing a cacophony of movement as he finishes the dishes. Like a choreographed dance used to set me in a trance of lust. Then he wipes his large hands on the towel hanging from my oven and I know my private show is over. As he turns around, I rest my hip against the doorframe and slip my hands into my shorts pockets. "Hey."

"Hey," Zac says, mimicking my posture against the granite countertop. Crossing his arms over his chest, causing his shirt to stretch to its limits over his hulking pecs. I tear my gaze away from his body to see the mirth behind Zac's eyes. The heat rising from my chest to my cheeks almost unbearably embarrassing.

"Thank you for doing the dishes. You're the guest, you didn't have to do that," I say, rambling yet again from the nerves he causes coursing through my body fogging my brain.

"It's no problem. You cooked, it's only fair," Zac

replies, taking a step toward me and dropping his hands to his sides.

"Well, thank you. I normally leave everything until Wyatt goes to sleep then conquer the kitchen. So it's nice to come down to it clean already." Zac simply nods and takes another step toward me. My heart is in my ears and I'm afraid if he comes any closer he'll hear it, too. "It was sweet of you to offer to come to the soccer game, but if you're busy Wyatt will understand." I'm giving him an out that I'm sure he'll pounce on. No one who's not family would willingly sit and watch a bunch of nine and ten year olds play soccer.

Zac shrugs and takes yet another step closer. "And what if I want to go?"

"Why would you?" Another step from him and my ribs might break under the pressure of my heartbeat.

"Because you'll be there," Zac pauses and takes one last step until he's right in front of me. He raises his hand to brush his fingers over my cheekbone. Rough fingertips catch my fallen bangs and brush them behind my ear, then he drops his hand to my neck. The calloused hand a contradiction to his gentle touch. "You look like you need someone to help you live a little."

The harsh words stop me from leaning too far into his caress. "I do live," I snap. Looking into the sincere thoughts behind his eyes. I realize I may have misjudged the intention of his words.

"No, you survive," he says, reaching up with his other hand to tangle his fingers in the loose hair by my ear. "I want to remind you how to live, if you'll let me." Then his lips are on mine.

Zac's kiss is soft yet insistent. Gentle yet needing. I

can't help but lean into his hard body. The pressure of his lips freeing me from all other thoughts. The graze of his tongue against my lower lip pulling slightly. Without thinking I open to his exploring tongue and lift my hands to his biceps to keep my knees from buckling under the pleasure coursing through my body.

His adventurous tongue tasting every inch of my mouth. Swiping past mine, silently begging for me to join. My chest heaving for a normal breath. Lungs screaming for oxygen. My tongue begins to move against Zac's. Then it hits me all at once what I'm doing. My hands move towards his firm chest pressed against mine and I push slightly. I don't need to put in more effort. Zac understands and breaks our connection, but only slightly. We're still sharing the same oxygen, eyes searching the others. Then, his lips are against my forehead. "It's too soon. I'm sorry" I say, unable to meet Zac's eyes as he pulls away.

"You're stronger than the storm I see brewing behind those pretty eyes of yours." With his final words, Zac moves towards the door and I'm left frozen against the doorframe with my fingertips against my lips.

My head is spinning from the lust and confusion running through my head. If that's what a kiss is supposed to feel like than what have I been doing all my life? The pure oneness that came over me while Zac and I were connected was something I've never experienced before. It was light years ahead of what I felt when I connected in anyway with Kent. How can I keep comparing the two?

There's no competition.

CHAPTER SIXTEEN

ZAC

The water pelts down on my head as I rinse the cold sweat from my body. My nightmares. My memories, which is worse. They're coming back more frequently now with no way to block them out. It always starts the same. Mac and I are walking down the dirt path with my men behind us. There's no raid planned. We're simply supposed to make our presence known and investigate anything suspicious. Sounds easy enough. Grady and I shit talking the newest member to the team. A scrawny kid that never would have made Ranger had we still been working the school. We'd have to whip him into shape, especially since he took the place of Trey. Fuckin' Trey. I should have left with him. Although, he would have stayed in if not for his ex leaving him high and dry on our last deployment.

Grady's still razzing the damn newb, but my thoughts go to *Trey and how he's doing now that he's out. Man, I can't even imagine what my life would be like if I left. He's a damn good sniper, but he's also a damn good artist. The tattoo currently healing on my skin proves just how good I think his work is. But, he needed out-damn Kenzie. She nearly got us killed with her lame 'Dear John' letter. I don't even want to think about getting married let alone married and then divorced because of my job protecting civilians.*

Struggling from my thoughts, Mac pulls on his lead. I trained him myself and I know what this could mean. The hairs on my neck stand tall. Mac isn't a fickle one like some of the trained ones out here. If he's catching wind of something then we should all take caution.

I hold up my hand in a fist and everyone falls quiet. I give my command to Mac and he takes off with us following. The men bring their weapons to the ready in case they're needed. With my own weapon raised, I take note of my surroundings and look for possible evac routes. Noting the people around us shying away. Shying away from the building Mac is leading us towards. Mac gives me his signal as we approach the door. I motion for him and Grady to go in with me. Motioning the other four members of the team going the opposite direction.

We clear rooms one by one until we're down to the last two in that back corner of the compound. I motion for Grady to sweep the room on the left while Mac and I head for the room on the right. I hear Grady yell clear, just as I notice the timer in the middle of the room I'm clearing with two tubes of PVC pipe underneath. "Fuck," I yell.

"Grady out. Everyone clear the compound. Bomb!" I move closer to the device in the center of the room to see the countdown is at less than a minute. Even if I could get someone to walk me through disabling this bomb, there's no time.

"There's no time. Get the people back. I saw kids in the courtyard, take care of it!" My last command before all I see is

white.

Every time the dream is the same. I begin to feel the heat from the flames around me. The absence of something or someone I know is important. The searing pain in my back and immobility of my body. Then it hits me like a bullet. Mac isn't with me. He's taken the brunt of the bomb to save me. He's gone. My partner is gone.

Waking from my memories drenched in sweat is the worst way to wake up. The strangled scream falling from my lips is something I can't escape. Something I'd never force upon another person. The sheer pain and loss in my own voice scares me. There's no way I could allow another person to endure my pain and loss. What was I thinking trying to get close to Tyler?

Here I stand, head down and hands holding my body up against the cold glass of my shower wall. Water threading through my short hair and down my cheeks to hit the tile under my feet. Deep breaths. Inhale. Exhale. I'm alive. The scars on my body prove I'm alive. I lived when others didn't. When Mac didn't. I can't think about it anymore. It's been four years and still the pain in my chest from the loss of Mac crushes me.

I can't remember the last good night's sleep I had, but it was too long ago. Fuck, it's been close to three weeks since I last slept the whole night without reliving my losses. The ramifications that clouds my mind when I think of the last good sleep I had causes my eyes to close. Three weeks ago I was knocked on my ass with the softest lips and sweetest taste I've ever known. The memory of Tyler's lips on mine has been on a constant loop in my mind since it happened almost a month ago. Since our kiss Tyler has been friendly, but never overly so. It's killing me and the nightmares are back with a vengeance as a result.

Mainly I only see her when she's bringing Wyatt to swim in my backyard. She never swims with her daughter, but that doesn't stop my brain from conjuring how great her body would look in a bikini. The images circulate through my mind and I can feel myself getting hard with the thought of a half naked Tyler in my backyard. Moving to rest my back against the glass with the water hitting my chest, I lower my hand to my throbbing cock.

Wandering back to the memory of the kiss we shared three weeks ago, I can feel the throb start in my lower belly. Tyler's soft tongue, curious, but cautious as she started to explore my mouth. The way her hands clung to me as if I was the only thing holding her to this earth. If only she'd let go of what's holding her back. If only she'd let me help her move on-move through it.

If she were here I would have picked her up onto the counter. Moved between her legs and freed her perky breasts. Tasted the silky skin of her neck until I pulled her tight buds into my mouth. The taste of her tongue still on my lips as my hand blurs around my cock. The pre-cum dripping from the tip only adding lubrication.

My brain switches gears back to Tyler here with me. I'd lay Tyler back and remove her tiny shorts until nothing was hidden from my eyes. Dropping to my knees, I can see myself getting lost in her tight pussy. I can imagine how sweet her wet folds would taste against my tongue after how sweet her pretty mouth was. God, that mouth. Before I plunged into her, I'd pull her off the counter and onto her knees to get her pretty mouth wrapped around my weeping cock. Then, when I couldn't take it anymore I'd pick her up and push her back against the wall. Wrapping her arms and legs around me as I lose myself in her warm pussy with one hard thrust.

I can barely make out my fingers as my hand slides faster against my cock. I want to know how Tyler feels everywhere. I want to know how Tyler tastes everywhere. God, I could smell her during our kiss. She was wet for me and I could smell her. The taste of her lips on my tongue and the smell of her pussy swirling around my brain, I cum in bursts with light and heat behind my eyelids.

I'm so tired of jerking off in my damn shower to a woman not 200 feet from where I stand. Three weeks is far too long. I need to see Tyler again. I need to feel Tyler again.

Walking out of my office all I see is Tyler's shop, 'Ty's Pies.' It's fuckin' taunting me. Shannon says I don't have anymore clients and I know she'll call if that changes. "Shannon, I'm takin' a long lunch. Not sure I'll make it back in if there aren't anymore appointments."

Shannon, my sixty-something assistant, looks up from her desk with a warm smile. "Alrighty then, Zachariah. I'll holler if you need to come back to put out any fires, hon." Shannon is a kind and gentle soul. How she puts up with me and my moodiness I'll never know.

"Thank you," I say, before kissing her on the cheek and heading towards Tyler's shop.

Tyler opens in three weeks and there are fliers hung all around town about the big opening she's planning.

Hopefully she's not ready for it and could use my helps. Cause I'll use any excuse at this point to spend some time with her without Wyatt around. Not that the little thing isn't growing on me.

"Knock, Knock." I say, opening the door and sticking my head in. Tyler peeks her head around the corner. Hair falling from her ponytail, flour on her right cheek, and dough in her fingers.

"Hey, what's up?" Tyler asks, heading back behind the curtain separating the kitchen from the display case and lobby.

I follower her back until I can rest against the silver table she's rolling out dough on. "Just thought I'd check into see how it was goin'. See if you had any dog treats for me. Or maybe a sample or two for me to try. I also don't have anymore patients today so I thought I'd help you get ready for the opening, if there's anything I can help with." Ok, that wasn't smooth in the least. I sound like a pussy. Whatever, at this point she knows I want her.

"Actually, I just finished some of the dog treats. They're so good." She points to a cooling rack with one inch bone shaped treats on a pan.

I walk over to try one for myself. I'm surprised at how good they are-considering they're glorified dog food-but these cookies taste as good as the real thing. I'd buy a box of these just to eat while not sleeping at night. "And these are usin' only the ingredients you and I spoke about?" I ask, surprised she could make dog friendly ingredients taste so damn good.

"Yeah, why? Do you not like them?" I can see the concern etched all over Tyler's beautiful, flour-caked face and it's cute how concerned she is with her dog treats.

"No, they're great. That's what was so surprisin'," I say, reaching for another small cookie before walking over to her.

I step up slightly behind her right shoulder, a little closer than necessary and take a bite of the cookie for her to see then ask, "so, could you use me anywhere?" I enjoy the labored intake of her breath. She's flustered by my nearness, but she hasn't stepped away. This is a good sign.

"Sure, can you start packaging up the cupcakes over there? The ones already iced and decorated," she asks, pointing to three pans of cupcakes that look better than good. They look magazine-worthy good.

Five hours later and I've finished packaging while Ty finished decorating the last of the online order as well as the dog treats for my office. We've also packaged up some of the extras for me to take home. The time has flown by, and thankfully, Tyler eased up and we were able to talk through the whole thing. We talked about all things irrelevant. Nothing too deep or emotional. Just shooting the shit, but that was enough.

That was everything.

"So what's the damage, Thomas?" I ask, then freeze, "Williams?" Damn, I don't like to think of her having Kent's last name.

"It's Thomas, again. Just got the paperwork back last week. It's odd to be a Thomas again. Kinda like coming home," Tyler says, a gentle smile on her lips. "And you don't owe me a thing. You helped all afternoon. Just enjoy the treats and tell everyone how amazing I am." Tyler leans her back against the silver table we just finished wiping down and grabs the edges firmly beside her hips.

I step close and lean towards her to put my hands on the table beside hers. "I already do." She tilts her head confused by my meaning. She is amazing and anyone that will listen knows what I think of her, but before she can answer I continue, "but you have to let me pay you back some way." Leaning even closer to her until I can smell her vanilla perfume, or maybe it's extract from the baking, coming off her skin. "How about I take you out?"

"I-I," Tyler stutters.

"If only to pay you back for the food," I add. There's a long pause while Tyler stares at the ground, chewing on her bottom lip. I'm about to give her an out when she speaks.

"Okay." It's almost a whisper, but I'll take it. I'll take whatever I can get at this point. I've been jerking off to this girl since high school. Foreplay is long over.

"Great, I'll pick you up tomorrow at six." I don't give her time to change her mind. Pressing a lingering kiss to Tyler's cheek, I push myself off the table and head for the door. "See you later, Ty." Then I'm gone with my hands full of sweets, my head in the clouds, and Tyler taste on my lips.

CHAPTER SEVENTEEN

Tyler

I hear the bells above the front do sound and Zac softly closing the door behind him, but all I can do is lean against the cold metal of the table behind me. What the hell did I just agree to? I'm going on a date with Zac? Three weeks ago I told him it was too soon, now all of a sudden I'm ready. *Am I ready?* He was leaning so close. His clean soapy smell mixed with a spice that only he possesses and I was lost. The nearness of his lips to my skin without touching me caused my breath to shallow and my chest to heave. My heart was going a mile a minute and I was afraid he could feel my body buzzing.

I had to get him to back up. Agreeing with him felt like the easiest way to accomplish that. I couldn't take the heat coursing through my body anymore. Zac is the only one who makes me ignite this way and so I said yes. I said yes to a date with a man that could quite possible be the death of me. Granted, it's right now that I wonder what might have been if I hadn't put the town and my parents' wishes above my own and followed these feelings in high school.

The conversation with my dad comes to mind when he caught me coming out from behind the bleachers with Zac. It was an innocent thing then, but he knew there was something there and he squashed it. Now, look at Zac. Would the heat between us have burned out? Would my life have been totally different? Would I be totally different? But, it's no good wondering because then I wouldn't have Wyatt. And Wyatt is my reason for everything.

Wyatt. Once the warm and fuzzy clouds clear my head, all I can think of is Wyatt. What if she's not ok with me dating. I know she likes Zac, but that's as a friend of the family not as my boyfriend. Whoa, Whoa, Whoa, there brain. Cart meet horse, we haven't even gone on a first date yet. This could just be a friendly dinner to repay me for giving him the sweets today.

"Who am I kidding," I say under my breath. The way he caged me in. The way he kissed me three weeks ago. There's no way this is just to repay me for being kind. I need to talk to Wyatt. Now.

Finishing the cleaning and closing up the shop took virtually no time at all. Zac helped with the clean up since he said the 'artistic expressions' were left to me as I decorated the last batch of cookies for an online order to ship out. Which was extremely nice of him, since cleaning is my least favorite activity.

Driving to Wyatt's school, I'm just this short of a full on anxiety attack. I could tell myself until I'm blue in the face that I want Wyatt to tell me she doesn't want me to date. I know if that were the reason Zac would back off without an argument. Yet, there's this part deep inside saying that it wants to feel special- the way Zac makes me feel- but I'm not sure I should listen.

As this mental war is waging inside my head, the carpool line outside my daughter's school chooses today to run smoothly. Crap, I had anticipated another fifteen minutes of waiting in line before I had to face the inquisitive eyes of my daughter. Within seconds Wyatt is pulling at the back door of my car and climbing in. My bundle of energy.

"Hey, bug, how was school?" I ask, driving away from the curb and heading towards the house.

"It was great. Mrs. Godek gave me a nickname," Wyatt says, buzzing with excited energy that needs an outlet. We'll be doing something about that later. I meet her eyes in the rearview mirror while at a stop light, waiting for her to continue with her story. "Yeah, she called me Tic Tac today. When I asked her why, she said it's cause I'm cute and pocket-sized." I laugh at the nickname, because it's perfectly fitting for my pint-sized powerhouse.

"That's awesome. I think that's a suits you perfectly. As long as you like it." At the stop light by our neighborhood I look back at her again, expectantly.

"Oh, I *do*. I think it's cool to be different than everyone else in my class." Of course, my daughter the performer.

Pulling into the driveway, Wyatt asks, "Mom, can we go to Zac's to swim tonight if I finish all my homework with enough time?"

I know she needs to let out her energy, but does it *have* to involve *him*? "Actually, tonight's probably not a great night." I need a break from him to wrap my head around tomorrow night. "But I did want to talk to you about Zac. He asked me to go to dinner tomorrow night."

"Sweet. Where is he taking us?" Oh, sweet, sweet Wyatt.

"Baby, I'm going to see if Nana and Pop Pop can watch you. Zac wants to take me out just the two of us? Like a date, bug." And there it is-a date. It's out in the open and Wyatt has all the power here.

"Oh," Wyatt says, looking down at her backpack and visibly working through this information in her head before looking back at me. "That's cool. Do you think Pop Pop will take me over there to swim while you guys are gone?" I let out a breath that I didn't realize I was holding. "I think that can be arranged." There goes my hail mary for a cancelation. It looks like the date is happening.

"Mom, you look so pretty," Wyatt says sitting on my bed and looking over my curled hair and subtle makeup as I walk out of my bathroom still in my robe. I don't normally spend as much time on my appearance, but something about knowing Zac will appreciate it makes it worth the effort. Kent never seemed to notice the effort I put into my appearance for him. Yet, he sure mentioned when I put my hair up and went without makeup because I just got home from work or was doing laundry and cleaning the house. That was not acceptable in his world. Just another thing that I put up with because I thought we were in love. "Come on, help me pick out what I'm going to wear," I say, pulling Wyatt into my closet with me.

After ten minutes of searching, Wyatt pulls out a white spaghetti strap dress with a delicate lace overlay. It's loose and flowy and the hem pushes just this side of a conservative length above my knees. It's cute and comfortable, but nice enough for a first date. First-as if it's a done deal that there'll be more.

I haven't worn this dress since before Wyatt was born. Kent always said it looked too country. Although, wearing it now, the neckline is a little more revealing than it was before I got me new boobs. One good think pregnancy gave me-or two I guess. Looking at myself in the mirror I'm afraid it might be too revealing. Heading back into my closet for a different outfit I see my cropped jean jacket, *perfect!* Rolling the sleeves up to my elbows and clasping the 'Momma Bear' necklace around my neck, my phone rings from my bed. That terrifying ringtone I set just for Kent blares through the suddenly frigid room.

God, what does he want? "Hello, Kent. How can I help you?"

"Always the charmer, Tyler. I want to talk to my daughter." Kent's voice a demanding boom over the phone.

"Kent, my parents are here and Wyatt needs to start getting ready for bed." At least the first part is true.

"Then let me say goodnight to her. Man, have you always been such a bitch?" Hearing Kent call me names used to be a common occurrence, but after not hearing his degrading tone for so long it's like a slap in the face. Just like the first time he called me a choice word. At first, I thought it was just a bad day. Or he saw something horrific during a call. Then, it started happening more often than not.

"Always a pleasure, Kent." I say, pulling the phone to my chest and calling down the hall for Wyatt. "Bug, Daddy's on the phone. He wants to say goodnight." I try to sound as little phased by the phone call as possible. I don't want to sway Wyatt's opinion of her father at all. That is not my place. No matter how rotten he is to me, he's still her father and she deserves the right to make her own judgement about him.

Wyatt looks around and hesitantly reaches for the phone. I busy myself with getting my cowboy boots from the closet so I can't obsess about what is being said. This is much harder than anyone ever tells you. How can I hate the man while still wanting him to be there for our daughter? I may not need, or want, him, but Wyatt is just a child. She needs her daddy and he's not here- physically. Or emotionally. Unfortunately, I don't want her to grow up to hate or resent me. Hate me for separating her from her father. Or resent me for not choosing a better man to be her father.

Stepping out of the closet, all I see is the worried look on my poor daughter's face. If I'm confused on how I feel about this situation, it has to be 100 times worse for her. Her innocent nine year old mind not able to comprehend all that goes on in the adult world. She's having to grow up well before her time.

Then the doorbell rings and Wyatt's face shift to one of felicity and emprise- and it warms my heart. "Daddy, I have to go. Mommy's date is here and I can't wait to see him." Wyatt says, handing me the phone and running to the door. Well, shit- not good.

This is not a conversation I wanted to have tonight.

So, I hang up. What's the harm? Hopefully, he'll think it was Wyatt hanging up. I'm sure I'll deal with the drama her farewell caused later. Apparently, Kent isn't happy with my decision and calls back the second my phone hits the bottom of my purse. He'll have to deal with it. I'm not letting him ruin my first date in fifteen years by being an ungrateful ass like he ruined much of my young adult life.

Walking into the foyer, I meet Zac's golden eyes first. The caramel hue that only brings thoughts of safety and security-like a man's gaze should. I could get lost in those eyes. Then, I notice the button up flannel shirt stretched across his expansive chest. The green in his eyes stand out more than normal. It must be the subtle amount of purple coming through the linework of his shirt. Man, those eyes. That chest. Don't even get me started on how those perfectly worn out jeans wrap around his muscular thighs like he was sown into them.

Deep breaths, Tyler. Just take deep breaths. Although, moving closer to Zac, that may not be so wise. His woodsy, clean musk engulfs me as I reach up to give him a hug in greeting. Okay, this is going to be one difficult date.

Wyatt is looking up at us still at the door. Looking much like my parents did when Kent used to pick me up for dates in high school. The memory makes me laugh and love her even more than I did earlier today, if that's possible. "Alright, peanut. I'll have her home in a timely manner." Zac says, looking down at Wyatt and roughing up her hair. Then looks at my parent., "It was nice catchin' up with you again." He shakes my dad's hand and we're off.

Boy, is tonight going to be interesting.

CHAPTER EIGHTEEN
ZAC

Holy Fuck!

This is going to be a long night. I've been excited for this date since she agreed to it, but nothing would have prepared me for seeing Tyler walk down the hall in a short, lace dress with her tits almost hanging out in an 'I'm still respectable' way. Everything about her outfit from the jean jacket to the short hemline was sexy as fuck- in the classiest sense of the word. And all of her long, tanned, toned legs on display. As my eyes take in Tyler's outfit, I think my breathing stops when I see cowboy boots finishing off her look. Yeah, tonight's going to be difficult-if only just distracting her from seeing the hard-on she's causing in my jeans all night.

Closing the door and walking to my car, I open the door to my Jeep and help Tyler step inside. As she bends to crawl in, the bottom hem of her skirt slowly lifts higher against the backs of her thighs and I have to close my eyes to keep from seeing the tiniest glimpse of the lacy panties flirting with the edge of lifted material. I shut the door and adjust my dick in my pants before walking around the back of the jeep- the long way- just to give myself a little extra time to get myself under control. What does this woman do to me? Man, it's just a dress and cowboy boots. Not something all that uncommon to see here in southern Georgia. Get a grip, Sergeant.

"So, where to, Doctor Jacobson?" Tyler asks tentatively. Glancing over, she's playing with the hem of her dress. I assume it's something to exhaust the restless energy coursing through her body. *I know the feeling, Tyler*, I think to myself. Although I wish I could put her at easy somehow. Right then, I silently pledge that before the night is over she will be at ease.

"I was thinkin' dinner at this Mexican restaurant not too far from here. They have live music there on the weekend. So if you're up to it, maybe I can teach you somethin' on the dance floor," I joke, trying to make her more comfortable.

"Yeah right. The day you teach me anything on the dance floor will be the day Kent stops drinking. I remember your two left feet at prom. In fact, I was surprised you even showed up," Tyler jokes, and I can see her body sag with relief. As if she's letting out the breath she didn't mean to be holding. That's right sweet Tyler, relax- tonight's going to be one to remember.

"Things have changed a lot since twelfth grade, Thomas. And if I recall there was a particular gray eyed blonde with an allurin' peach strapless dress."

"It wasn't peach, it was coral and the jewelry was teal. Come on Mr. Army Ranger, what do they teach you in school?" Tyler jokes.

"I don't think I can eat another bite," Tyler says, gently rubbing circles on her lower stomach. Luckily, as we talked and ate she seemed to let go and started becoming the easy going Tyler she's was since high school. The more free she let herself get the more she seemed to glow from across the table. Man, I sound like a fucking pussy- this girl doesn't even understand how tied up in knots she has me. She had two blackberry margaritas and after every sip she licks the residual moisture off her lips. If she sticks out that tongue one more time to wet her lips, I might lose all self control I thought had left.

"I'm glad you enjoyed it." I look over at the couples dancing on the makeshift dance floor across the room from us. "How about we go work off some of those calories?" Tyler cocks an eyebrow at me, questioning my meaning.

Standing, I reach around to grab her hand off her stomach and pull her to standing in front of me. I must have surprised her because she stumbled into me. Her other hand coming up to rest on my chest to catch herself. "As nice as this is bein' close to you- I meant dancin'." I say into Tyler's ear. Her eyes drop to the floor and her hand falls off my chest, but not before I feel her body shudder against me.

Groaning inwardly, I lead Tyler to the dance floor. Thanking my Bolivian college roomate, I spin her in front of me until we're facing each other, chest to chest. Stepping back I grab each of her hands to keep distance until she's comfortable, then I begin to move. The easy flow of my foot work causes Tyler to lose her footing a few times while I step closer to her. The rock of her hips closing in on mine. Thank you Salsa Gods, for creating a dance that is easier the closer you get.

Letting go of one of Tyler's hands, I spin her around twice before pulling her into me and closing my hand around her hip. "Who do I have to thank for teaching you how to dance?" Tyler asks, resting her hands on my biceps.

"My roommate in school had a sister. She wanted to take classes, but never had anyone to go with. Her brother offered my services. Plus, I thought if I knew how to move, it would help with the ladies." I tightened my hold on Tylers hip, causing her to look up at me. "Is it working?"

"Well, it definitely doesn't hurt." She smirks before losing herself in the music once again.

Time passes as we work our bodies against each other. Tyler's curls are loose from the heat and her running her fingers through her hair lost in the movement. One turn and she's got her back against my front. Continuing to grind our bodies together, I reluctantly glance down at my watch to see it's much later than I thought. "Should we get you back, before you turn into a pumpkin?" I whisper into Tyler's ear, just loud enough that I know she hears me.

Tyler's eyes close and leans her head back against my chest before she nods. As much as I don't want to walk away from her slick body fit so closely against me, I know this evening has to end at some point. I already paid the check before we began dancing, so, we walk toward the exit and to my Jeep. All the while, I can feel the warmth seeping away from my body the further we get from the dance floor.

Driving in comfortable silence, Tyler keeps adjusting the air vents, while looking frustrated. "You doin' okay over there?" I ask, without taking my eyes off the road in front of me. We're already almost to our houses. The night is just about over and I can't believe I'm just going to have to say goodnight and leave her- probably for another three months of "friendly" encounters.

So, help me God, if we just go back to be neighborly- I'm going to kill someone.

"I'm just really hot. All that dancing is still overheating my system," Tyler says, fanning herself.

Think, Zac, think. How can I make this evening stretch farther? "We're almost back- do you wanna hop in the pool for a bit?" Please, please say yes, Tyler. I'm mentally begging her to agree to swim with me, as we pull into my driveway.

"I don't have a suit. If I go into my house I'm not coming back out. My bed is already calling my name," she says, reaching for the door handle.

"Well, I could make it even and wear my boxers too." I swear I catch Tyler's eyes glance down at my pants at my suggestion. "Come on, where did that free spirit from high school go?" I razz her, until that spark ignites. I know Tyler won't back away from a challenge-at least she never had before.

"Alright, Romeo. We'll swim- but only until I cool down. Then, I'm going home," Tyler clarifies. I smile knowing I've won, but also because there is no way I'm letting Tyler get away after that dress comes off.

Instead of walking through the house, we go through the back gate to the pool deck. I don't need the temptation of fuckable surfaces. When we get to the back, I start to unbutton my shirt and turn to see Tyler staring at me. Her eyes glazed. Mouth hung slightly open. Oh yeah, she's not leaving. As I slip the shirt from my shoulders, I clear my throat and Tyler's eyes meet mine. I look at her expectantly and she blushes knowing I caught her staring. Then, she slinks out of her jean jacket. Toeing off her cowboy boots as I slip out of my Vans.

Tyler reaches down to take off her black ankle socks and as she straightens she catches the hem of her dress. Slowly lifting the lacy material. Her eyes meet mine as the bottom of her dress rests just below the tiny V between her legs.

Now, I'm the one staring, with my hands frozen against my belt buckle. Tyler's cheeks redden further than I've ever seen them and she looks down at the floor. Shaking my head out of it's lustful trance, I unbuckle my belt and make fast work of the button and zipper until my jeans are pooled at my feet. I step out, then, ship off my socks, standing before Tyler in nothing but my tight boxer briefs, I love the look of shock that comes over her. She knew I was built, but I'm sure she was in no way ready for me with so little clothing on. Then again, maybe it's the scars she's staring at.

Taking a deep breath, Tyler lifts the fabric of her dress up until lacy gray and light pink panties come into view. Shortly followed by a toned stomach. Then a matching bra with soft mounds of flesh barely contained. And finally, the material is over Tyler's head and flowing to the deck floor. I have to physically remind myself to keep fucking breathing.

Tyler's body is incredible. She's toned and tan, yet,

she still holds the subtle signs that she's a mother. Widened hips, accentuating her curves and small silver lines along her hips. Nothing overtly standing out, just small signs that she's a strong sexy woman. Before I can tell her just how beautiful she is, her back is to me and she's walking to the stairs of the pool.

What's that country song, "hate to see her go, but love to watch her leave." The lyrics have nothing on watching Tyler's firm, bubble ass bounce with each step she takes closer to the pool. The way her ass is mostly covered by her cheeky panties, but the small swell at the bottom lures my eyes and body closer. I want to sink my teeth into that swell of muscle until she's begging for me.

Shaking my head, I smile at this evening's events and walk toward the edge of the pool and jump in. As my body disappears into the water, I hope it will wash away the images of Tyler running through my brain enough to loosen my quickly tightening underwear. I don't want to make her uncomfortable, but fuck, she's driving me to my God damned limits.

While I'm thinking of guns and grandmas, Tyler makes her way toward me in the deep end. Treading water as she floats in front of me. Standing at just over 6'3, I needed a pool that would allow for my height. Although, watching Tyler struggle to hold a conversation while trying to stay afloat, I take pity on her. *Who am I kidding*-I just want my hands on her. I reach out and take her hip, pulling her closer. Tyler puts her hand on my forearm to hold herself up without getting too close to my nearly naked body.

Quiet engulfs us, with the new nearness. I don't want to say anything. I don't want to breathe. I'm afraid anything I say will alter our bubble. Tyler pulls her bottom lip between her teeth. Just as I lift my hand to pull her lip from her teeth, she sucks in a breath and disappears under the water.

I chuckle and lower myself to match hers. We're looking at each other through the chlorinated water. Her hair floating around her like some Greek water Goddess that hasn't been established yet. I can't help it, I lift my hand to caress her cheek with my palm. Tyler's eyes close and she leans into my touch.

Slowly, her hand moves to cover mine, twining our fingers against her cheek. Before our lungs give out from lack of breath, I turn my palm and gasp her hand to pull her towards the edge of the pool with me. The vulnerability streaming off Tyler, as she leans into my hand, was too much for my self control.

Before Tyler can complain, I have her back against the edge of the pool and she's caged in by my tattooed arms. "What's goin' through that head of yours?" I ask, brushing stands of too wet hair behind her ear. Tyler looks down, until I lift her chin to look back at me. "Not this time. You're not shyin' away from the hard questions anymore." I will her to let me in. To let me help her. To let me heal her. "What are you thinkin'? What's brewin' in there?" I ask tapping her temple.

"It's everything. I feel like I'm drowning. Everything is pulling me under and it's so dark. I've been so oppressed for so long. After everything with Kent, I feel like everything I touch is dark. It's all going to go wrong and I'll fail. He called today. While I was getting ready. I haven't spoken to him since the court ruled against him. It was as if he knew I was going out tonight. As if he knew I was beginning to live my life without him. He knew and he called to remind me just how broken I really am." Tyler's out of breath by the end of her confession. She's struggling to keep the tears pooling in her eyes from cascading down her cheeks. If I could kill one more man it would be Kent Williams. One last bullet from my gun chamber with his name on it.

"Hey," I say, gently lulling her into safety with my voice. "You're gunna make it through this. Kent was horrible to you and Wyatt, but that's not all men. That's not even most men. The darkness will recede. The scars Kent left behind will fade. What is that sayin', it's always darkest before the light, or some shit. You'll find that light, Tyler. You've been my light for years." With that confession, I freeze. I hadn't meant to say it, but it's out now. I'm glad she knows how she's always made me feel. If she knew it was her graduation photo in my helmet that kept me safe and sane overseas. We'll leave that confession for another night.

Tyler lifts her hand to my cheek, pulling me closer to her. "Zac," she pauses, "be my light. Make me feel better." Her vulnerability slays me. I'd give this girl anything. Then her lips are on mine. It takes several seconds of her soft lips pulling at my bottom lip before I'm contributing to the kiss.

We start slow. Exploring each others lips before she opens for me. I take advantage and dive into her mouth. Caressing her tongue with mine, teasing her into moving with me. I can taste the blackberry margarita she had with dinner, but the undertones of sweet honey is all Tyler. The same flavor that's haunted me since I stole a kiss senior year. I'm lost in her taste, then, a soft moan escapes her throat and I'm a goner.

My left hand moves to her hip and pulls her lower half against me. I know I'm pushing it, and she could pump the breaks at anytime- like she did the last time we kissed- but something about the vulnerability in her words has the protector in me reeling. Tyler's hair tangles around my right hand at the nape of her neck. With the pressure of my hands, she arches into me. The heat from her core unmasked by the water or the thin material against my boxer briefs.

She wants this-at least her body does. Testing the waters, I grind my hips against her. Showing her exactly how she makes my body react. This time she pulls away from my lips and my breath catches in my throat. I pushed too far. I'm already thinking of the blue balls I'll have crawling into bed tonight.

"Zac," the desperation in Tyler's voice not helping with the calm I'm trying to force my body into. The desire dripping in the word exposed in her eyes and mirrored in mine.

"Tell me what you need, Ty," I say, lips against her neck, before placing the softest of kisses to her pulse point.

"Make me forget him, Zac. Make me *yours*," she says, leaning her head back against the deck with my hand as her pillow. Rolling her neck to give me more access and wrapping her legs around my body. Rubbing her heat against my hard-on.

Leaving my hand behind her head, I move the other to her ass. Cupping her and moving her against me until she's short of breath. My kisses moving lower to the hollow of her neck. The dip between her collarbones where dried sweat pooled from our dancing after dinner.

She's sweet even when she's salty from sweat.

Tyler arches against me further so the swell of her breasts brush against my lips. Nipping at the soft, supple skin around her bra, I lift her to sit on the edge of the deck.

"I'll make you forget, Ty," I say, against her stomach, gently pushing her shoulder to lay her back on the deck. "Lift up," I tap her hip. As Tyler lifts her hips off the ledge, I drag her panties down her legs. With the lacy fabric sinking to the bottom of my pool, I spread Tyler's legs and kiss the inside of her left knee. Turning my head and moving closer to her core I kiss her right thigh. A small quake runs over Tyler's body. She arches her back and closes her eyes.

Then, I'm there. Lightly blowing warm heat into the apex of her legs. Her lips glistening from the pool water and her own desire. I can smell the sweet nectar coming from within. With one final look at her face, I pause until her eyes open and she cups my cheek with her hand. With her encouragement, I flick at her little nub.

The gasp that escapes Tyler's lips is music to my ears and I suck her sweet clit into my mouth. Earning me a full blown moan, before she covers her mouth with her forearm. I'm not sure if it was the fear of us being heard or the reality that I am making her feel so good, but the shy reaction caused me to smile against her. I continue exploring her lower lips as she's grabbing at my hair trying to guide me with little tugs. It's cute, but unnecessary.

I raise my right hand to her entrance and look at her face as I slip two fingers into her pussy. She's so wet they slide in without a problem. Her eyes fly open and she's up on her elbows instantly. "Oh, God," she breaths and she watches me move my fingers in and out of her hole while feasting on her clit. I look up at her and wink just before I hook my fingers and rub at the spongy tissue against the front of her pussy walls.

Tyler's head falls back and her eyes roll into the back of her head, before my name on a moan escapes her lips. I continue moving my hand until I know she's making her way back down to me then slide out and kiss the crease between her hip and her left leg. "Oh my God, Zac," she says, still stunned by her orgasm.

Hopping out of the pool, I sit beside her on the pool deck. Almost stunned myself that I finally fulfilled one of my high school fantasies of Tyler Thomas. I can't help the satisfied smile on my face when I look over at Tyler still feeling the aftershocks of the orgasm I gave her. That's right-I gave her that. I helped her try to forget. I helped her heal.

I reach over and brush a strand of hair behind Tyler's ear and she turns into the caress. Leaning in, I press a kiss to her forehead and then her lips, but I try not to linger. "You're beautiful. Everythin' about you is light and free. And if this is all we do tonight, I'll go to sleep a happy man. You've always been the one to make me happy," I say, pressing my forehead against hers and close my eyes.

"So you're saying if I get up and leave now you'll have no quarrel?" Ty asks, gesturing down at my clearly still rock hard cock.

"I'm sayin' that if you got some peace because of what we just did, I'm happy I could give it to you. And I'm saying that, while my body may have other plans, if you are done for tonight, I understand and I won't push you for anything you're not ready for." Still unable to open my eyes, I feel Tyler lean forward a press a kiss to my cheek. Then my lips. Then my jaw where it meets my neck.

"It's a good thing I'm not done," Tyler says, reaching for my shoulders and straddling my lap with her legs. Pressing her naked heat against my pulsing dick.

I groan and my hands hook around her hips- my fingertips on her ass. "Then, should we move this party inside?" I ask, moving to stand while still holding Tyler to me. She wraps her legs around my waist and arms around my neck.

"I thought you'd never ask," she says, leaning in to kiss me again.

Once we reach my room, I kick the door closed behind me with my heel, then move to the bed. We haven't stopped kissing the walk here and now my lips wonder to her neck as I drop her on the bed and remove the last remaining article of clothing separating her body from my lips.

As the straps fall away from her arms, my mouth forms a strong suction around her nipple. The hard peak like a small gumdrop against my tongue. Before I release her I lightly close my teeth around the nub and scrap outward until her nipple pops free from my mouth. Then I repeat my efforts on her other nipple. My large hand palming the first.

Tyler is writhing on the bed. Trying to grind against my hips that I have pulled just far enough away that she can't quite reach. Gentle grazing of the fabric tenting my boxer briefs is all the relief she gets. "Please," Tyler says, trying in vain once more to gain friction against my hips.

"Is that what you want, baby?" I ask, leaning forward

just slightly. Enough that she can feel the ridge of my bell head without enough pressure to get her off. Tyler opens her eyes and nods- looking directly into my eyes, but she looks a million miles away. Even after everything we've done so far. Is she still nervous? Is she thinking of Kent? At this moment I'm reminded of her saying she's only ever been with Kent. This is all new to her.

"Where'd you go?" I ask, rubbing my bell head against her. Giving her the friction she wants, but not enough that she'll come without me.

She shakes her head and arches into my hips.

"I don't believe you. Where are you?"

"I'm with you," Tyler finds her voice.

"Say my name," I urge.

"Zachariah."

"That's right. It's just you and me here. Don't let Kent come between us," I say. Tyler's eyes welling with unshed tears. I lean forward and kiss each of her eyelids before removing my boxer briefs. "I've got you, now. I'll be your light. Just let me," I say, as I slowly enter her for the first time.

Tyler's head falls back and I kiss her jaw. Holding still inside her, waiting for her to adjust to my girth. The girl may have had a child, but her pussy clamps tight against my cock and I have to fight the urge to pound into her at full speed. Tyler is better than that. Tyler deserves more than that. When her back flattens against my mattress she lifts her hips. Silently telling me she's ready for more.

That's when I start to move. Slowly at first, making sure she's stretched to fit all of me. With each thrust into her silk she meets me with her own. We get lost in each other. Her fingers leaving nail prints down my back. My hand grabbing at her hip just this side of too tight.

Reaching up, I pull her hand above her head and twine our fingers. The pendulum motion of my hips hitting her right at her G-spot. Her eyes roll into her head. Her back arches and I know she's close. So am I.

"Let go with me," I say, and on the next thrust she breaks free. Her pussy muscles clamping down on me sending me into the most euphoric orgasm I've ever felt.

My thrusts slow to a stop and I hover over Tyler. My name falling from her lips as small aftershocks run through her body and against my cock still inside her. "Baby, you're amazing," I say, rolling off and pulling her into my arms. Tyler rests her head against my chest until our breathing slows and our hearts normalize. That was the single most gratifying feeling I think I've ever lived through. And I've lived through a *hell* of a lot.

Without even realizing, my fingers have been combing through Tyler's tangled hair. Her breathing normalizes and her eyelashes fan out against her cheekbones. God, she is gorgeous. And she's *mine*. Whether she knows it or not, I'm going to make her mine. After all, I've been hers since I was seventeen. I look over to my dresser where her frayed senior picture sits in a box hidden within.

"I have to go," she says, looking up from her position against my body.

"Not exactly the words one wants to hear after great sex," I say, trying to make light of the situation. I know she has Wyatt and her parents waiting next door. And I know it's way later than we had anticipated her getting

Whether she knows it or not, I'm going to make her mine. After all, I've been hers since I was seventeen. I look over to my dresser where her frayed senior picture sits in a box hidden within.

"I have to go," she says, looking up from her position against my body.

"Not exactly the words one wants to hear after great sex," I say, trying to make light of the situation. I know she has Wyatt and her parents waiting next door. And I know it's way later than we had anticipated her getting home, but I don't want her to leave. It's the first time I have felt at peace in my own bed in years. The first time the nightmares aren't threatening a headache as my head rests on the pillow now.

That's when it hits me. I haven't had sex with anyone in my bed-ever. Not since I've been out of the army. Yet, with Tyler in my arms, I didn't even think twice about bringing her into this place that holds so many of my secrets. The place that holds my fears. That sees how deep my scars go. I'm not sure what this means, but I know I'm not going to figure it out with Tyler leaving and heading back to her house never to come back.

"I know, but I have to be there when Wyatt wakes up and my parents need to get home. As it is, I already know I'm in for the second inquisition when I walk through my door," she says, sitting up. I follow her lead and swing my legs around the side of the bed, resting my elbows on my knees. Tyler leans against my back and places a kiss to the top of my shoulder. "Where did you get these?" she asks, gently running her fingers over the silver patchwork of lines across my back.

I don't know how to answer her. The truth is much too long. If she's worried about getting home late now, there's no telling how late it will be once I retell my living nightmare. My past is much darker than she knows and I'm not sure I can let her into that darkness yet. She thinks her world is dark. She wants me to be her light, but what will she think of me when she knows the truth? What will she think when I tell her about Mac? That my physical scars have nothing on the mental ones that never seem to heal.

I turn my head and I'm sure Tyler can see the indecision in my eyes and kisses my cheek. "How about you can tell me over dinner tomorrow?" she says, then kisses my lips. Standing she looks around just now realizing all her clothes are either on the deck or in the pool. "Can I borrow something to wear next door?"

"Anythin' you want it's yours," I say. Tyler blissfully unaware of how true that statement is. Tyler would want for nothing if she were mine. Anything I had the ability to get her I'd move heaven and Earth to make it happen. Such a fuckin' pussy I've turned into.

CHAPTER NINETEEN

Tyler

Rolling over in bed, a smile spreads across my face as my slightly sore body objects to my movements. Muscles I didn't know I had are groaning with the exertion from the previous night. Although, if it weren't for my sore body, I might have thought last night was a really, really good dream. God, a really good dream- I think, sliding my hand down my stomach to my most sore spot under the sheets.

Memories from my night with Zac as inspiration, my fingers start moving against the sensitive bundle of nerves swollen with need. Arching my back- my fingers become a blur in my panties. Thinking of the way Zac's hands held my body. The way he filled me to the brim- like nothing I've ever felt before. Closing my eyes, I relive the pleasure as my body undulates.

I'm so close, now. I can taste Zac on my tongue. I can feel him against my skin. Hear his groan- sexy and gruff- as he released. The sound fresh in my ears sending me over the edge into a world of pleasure only Zac has been able to bring about.

Coming back to myself, chest heaving, sweat dampening my skin, I know I'm in trouble. I want more of him. I want more of this. The thing is though, it wasn't just the sex. As amazing as that was, it was the whole night. From the moment Zac picked me up there wasn't a moment that I didn't think his every focus was on me.

It was a sensation I'm not used to. Even in our earliest days as a couple, there was never a time that I thought Kent's total focus was on me. There was football, and when football season was over it was training for the next football season. Or catching up with friends that he couldn't do during football season. I was always just expected to be there *for* him. Be there with him wherever he went. Enjoy just being able to be around Kent while he lived his life. It never changed in all the years we were together.

Being with Zac is like nothing I've ever felt before. From sitting across the table from him, he'd asked many questions, as if an urgent need drove him to get to know me better. To walking into the bar where women turned to appraise him with appreciative eyes-looks that he didn't even seem to notice let alone acknowledge. Then, dancing with me like we were the only two people in the room. There is one thing I know for sure-I haven't gotten enough of the sensation Zac gives me.

"Mom, should I get cereal or are you making breakfast?" Wyatt yells up from downstairs. Crap, it's still a school day. "I'll be right down, bug," I holler.

Quickly, I change my too wet panties and putting on sweatpants.

"What would you like for breakfast, baby?" I ask, washing my hands in the kitchen sink. Wyatt shrugs, "How about eggs and bacon. It's quick," I suggest, looking at the clock and the lack of time before Wyatt needs to leave for school. Standing at the stove as the bacon crackles in front of me, I turn to look at Wyatt. "Are you ready for tomorrow?"

"Mom, I can't wait for my first game. It's going to be so much fun." Wyatt is positively buzzing. "Do you think Zac will really come?" she asks, looking out the kitchen window towards our neighbors house. "Were you nice to him last night? You didn't run him off, right? I like him." Oh my sweet child.

"Bug, I don't think I ran him off. Actually, I think he's going to come over tonight," I pause remembering the scars on Zac's back- I really want the story behind those, but I'm also terrified to know what happened to cause those types of gashes. "You can ask him at dinner."

"Sweet!" Wyatt is almost bouncing on her chair.

Wyatt eats and collects her bags to head to the bus stop and the rest of the morning flies. I'm trying to work on new recipes for healthy desserts, but it's fruitless- no pun intended. All I can think about is the deep scars marring Zac's back. The disfigured skin at various stages of roughness. What would cause scars like those? He's a veterinarian, for God's sake. Was he attacked? The scars are only on his back. Unless, some of those tattoos are covering more. I make a mental note to feel around the next time I have the opportunity. Geez, listen to me- it's like I'm already assuming it's a sure thing. He may not even want to see me again that way. He probably doesn't. We just got carried away last night. I'm getting way too ahead of myself. Who'd want a single mom, divorcee with so many issues-courtesy of my ex-to last a lifetime.

Just then I'm alerted to a text. **Are we still on for tonight?** It's Zac. My stomach flutters and my breathing quickens.

Tyler: I was just thinking about you. How'd you know?

Zac: Cause I haven't been able to get you out of my head all God damn day.

Cue the swooning. Luckily another text comes in before I can reply with something stupid. **So tonight?**

Tyler: Yes, dinner?

Zac: Should I bring anything?

Tyler: Just yourself. Wyatt is excited to see you.

Zac: Glad to hear one of you two is. I'll see you at 6?

Tyler: Sounds great!

And with that the date is set. Screw the recipes, I shove the papers I've been pretending to work on to the corner of my desk and move to the bathroom to shower.

"Wyatt, can you get that?" I ask, as the doorbell rings. I'm finishing the mashed potatoes for dinner and I can hear Zac and Wyatt talking in the foyer.

"Mom, we're going to go out back and practice until dinners ready." I hear just before the side door opens and closes.

Dinner's ready, but I can't deny Wyatt the chance to interact with an adult male figure-in a *positive* way, for once. Looking through the glass I see the smile on my daughters face as she laughs at something Zac said. A rampant tear slides down my cheek that I refuse to wipe away. After all the years we've been trapped in a loveless family to now see Wyatt without a worry in the world is unbelievable. She can clearly let new people in, why can't I?

Burying my emotions, I open the door and call out to the two, "Dinner, guys." The motley two sit at the table sweaty and breathing deeply. Throughout dinner, Wyatt dominates the conversation allowing me to sit back and relax. Not to mention, it gives me the opportunity to look over Zac's visible skin for additional scarring. As we finish up, I look over at Wyatt asking Zac if he's really going to come tomorrow to her game.

"Of course." My daughter looks back at me to make sure I'm still ok with him going. He and I haven't really had a chance to talk about what happened last night. And ever since he's been here, he's been nothing but friendly. Granted, that could be because of Wyatt. Why shouldn't I let him be out family friend?

I smile, at Zac then to Wyatt, "there you go, bug. Now, hope upstairs and shower before bed. You have a big day tomorrow and an extra person to impress," I say, collecting the dishes from the table and heading to the sink as Wyatt bounds to her bathroom.

I can hear Zac's chair scrap quietly across the floor even with the water running. My pulse spikes. Heat radiates behind me just as hands grab the countertop on either side of my body. My audible gasp giving away my surprise. "Dinner was fantastic," Zac says, much closer to my ear than I expected. His lips grazing down my throat, my head lulling back to give him access, where he places a soft kiss on my pulse point.

Zac moves his hands to my hips and turns me to face him. I don't have the courage to look up at him pretty sure my cheeks are the color of a tomato. Zac clears his throat and I know he's waiting expectantly for me to meet his gaze. Looking up, his face lowers and his soft lips touch mine. Our mouths glide against one another. Neither one trying to push for more or to deepen the kiss. Content with the innocent connection.

Pulling back he says, "I've been waitin' all day to taste you again." Blowing out a deep breath, I have no clue what he wants as a reply. Zac notices my speechlessness and leans in to kiss me again. I pull his bottom lip into my mouth and suck. Earning a groan from Zac's chest that I feel to my core.

As I hear Wyatt bouncing down the stairs, I nudge Zac away and bring my hand to my lips. "Mom, I'm going to bed. I can't wait for tomorrow." She turns to Zac, "I'm so happy you're coming. I'll see you at the field." She hugs Zac, then turns to me and hugs me as well. I'll follow her up the stairs and tell Zac I'll be just a minute. As I close the door after our nightly routine, I stop in my room to look over myself.

I feel so flustered, but with one more deep breath, I head back to Zac. Once again I come down to Zac finishing the dishes. What did I do to deserve him? If someone had told me my life would have had a severe one eighty change in a matter of months I would have laughed in their faces. If someone had told me the boy my parents warned me about is now the one they're pushing me toward I'd have punched them. What would have happened if I followed my feelings toward him then? I keep coming back to that question, but I can't dwell on the past. I have Wyatt and therefore the past was worth it. Well, now what?

"You gunna keep starin' at my nice ass or are you comin' over and help?" Zac says, without taking his eyes off the dishes. How did he know I was here? It's like he sensed it or has eyes in the back of his head.

Walking up behind Zac, I reach around and turn off the faucet. "Actually, why don't we leave it for later," I say, pulling his elbow to turn him to face me. His smirk tells me he's more than ready to continue where we left off. "Before we continue, I want to talk." Zac follows behind me as I walk to the couch, where we sit facing each other. Worry rolls across Zac's face.

"What's wrong, Ty?"Zac's use of his nickname for me, leaves me in a blanket of safety. Leaning forward, I rest my forehead against Zac's chest. Without hesitation his fingers thread through my hair.

"I don't know how to do this. I've only been in one relationship- with one guy." I pause, because now that is no longer the case and the weight of that fully hits me. "Until you, I thought my life was going to revolve around Kent. I thought I would die loving one man."

"Tyler, you left Kent. You did that before me. Your

world doesn't revolve around him. And it won't revolve around me. I don't want to be the center of your world, I just want to be a part of it," Zac says stroking my hair gently, a small piece of the hurt left after Kent begins to heal with his words.

Looking up, I gaze into his eyes. "That's the thing though, Zachariah. I can't just be casual. I don't know how. I don't want to, but I'm also not sure I'm ready to jump into the deep end."

"What are you talkin' about? I don't want to have a casual relationship with you either, Ty. I've wanted to be with you since I was seventeen years old. Now that I have a chance with you, I'm not lettin' you go." Zac leans forward to kiss my forehead. "I can be patient while we date and get to know each other again. I just want you to know, I'm not the type of man that needs to be your everythin'. I just want to be somethin'. I would never try to be your world. Wyatt, she's your world. That is undeniable and unconditional. I would never interfere with that. I just want to be with you-and Wyatt. That little girl already has me wrapped around her finger. I'd do anythin' she asked."

Tears sting my eyes as I take in the words Zac has said. He's the total opposite of Kent and everything I need-everything I deserve. Leaning my chest against his, our lips crash together. We literally just said we'd go slow, but his words were too perfect and I can see the sincerity in his eyes. I can't hold back.

My hands quickly find the buttons of his shirt. Fingers grazing against the tanned, toned skin of his chest as his shirt falls open. Zac deepens the kiss as I move my hands to his shoulder, slipping his shirt to the floor.

I pull away to catch my breath as my fingertips brush

against a raised scar behind the base of Zac's neck. "Zac," I whisper, breathless.

"Mmhmm?" Zac asks, nuzzling my neck.

"Where did you get this?" I ask, bringing both hands to caress his back-his scars. "Where'd you get these?"

Zac brings both his hands to cup my cheeks, a pained look washes the lust from his eyes. "It's my nightmare, Tyler." I can see every second of agony on his face and it pains me to my core.

"I can take it if you can." I caress his cheek, the day old stubble rubbing against my palm.

CHAPTER TWENTY

Tyler

"Come here." Zac pulls me into his lap. I move to straddle him so we can still look at each other. "After graduation-when you left-there wasn't much to keep me here. My pop had no use for me. He wasn't around much anyway. If I went missin' it would have taken a good few weeks before he'd notice, if not longer. It was a depressin' thought, but it was my reality. Then, my buddy came over sayin' he'd just signed up for the army. I laughed in his face and told him how much of a fool he was, then lit a joint."

Zac laughs at the memory and the warm rumble brings a smile to my face as I picture the scene he paints. "When he left, I got to thinkin' about how much we really had nothin' to do in this town. I wanted to get out, but had no clue where to go. Not to mention, I had no damn money. A few months later my buddy came back from basic trainin' and he was still the same dude, but cleaner. It wasn't what I thought would happen-I thought he's be a total douche when he got back. That really got my wheels turnin'.

"Well, long story short, I ended up enlistin'. Turns out I was really good at listenin' to people who yelled at me." Another small chuckle comes from Zac. I play with the hair at the nap of his neck, engrossed in his story. Fearing the end- the nightmare part. "I moved up the ranks quickly. Re-enlisted until they sent me to Ranger school. It was insane, Ty. I was finally good at somethin'. People looked up to me. People asked me for help and entrusted me with important tasks. I was a teacher at the same Ranger school I graduated from for a while and it was like I finally found my stride. My place in the world.

"Then, a spot on a special team opened up. I was going to be an Army dog handler. I got paired with a German Shepard named Mac. They have specially trained dogs for a lot of reasons, but mainly to make our jobs easier. They're called Multi-Purpose Canines and they get assigned as puppies. They train and work with one soldier their entire lives. Mac was the best friend and partner I'd ever served with. We were a team-him and I-and we trained hard. Next thing I knew, we were headin' an op at one of the cities in, well in a bad area of a bad country. I can't really tell you all of the details," he says, brushing my bangs out of my face and tucking them behind my ear.

"We went in to clear a compound. My men and I went to sweep the area and Mac and I must have drawn the short end of the stick. We ended up in the room with a bomb. I called the code through my radio and the men rushed out. There was no time for Mac and I. I made sure my men got the kids out of the courtyard instead of comin' in to help us. I don't remember much of the explosion. My memory shoots from callin' the code to wakin' up with my name bein' called while I'm flat on my back. My brain was fuzzy and eyes needed time to adjust. But, by the time I'd adjusted to my surroundin's again, I was unable to move. I couldn't lift my arms or legs. I was paralyzed from the neck down. I'm so concerned with myself that it took me probably a good ten minutes of strugglin' to move and recall what happened before my brain circled back to Mac."

A lone tear falls from Zac's eye as he clutches his side- the one with the tattoo of boots and dog tags. "All the kids were safe and unharmed and I was alive because Mac did what he was trained to do. Mac sniffed out the bomb and posted on top of it. We'd done the drill countless times, but I never thought we'd need it. My best friend was saving my life while he lost his.

"It took five surgeries on my spine, back, and sides to remove as much of the shrapnel as possible before I was cleared to leave. Only to get papers for my medical retirement nine days later. I gave my best friend and my back to the Army and they were dropping me with no second thoughts. I was no longer useful at my post so I was no longer needed." Zac shakes his head in disgust. "My rehab got me walkin' again and eventually I used my GI Bill to get my degree in veterinary medicine- for Mac. I still have limitations and I still get bouts of pain so bad I can barely stand. But, aside from that, for the most part, I'm healed. Well, if you don't count the nightmares I still get of that night. I still smell the sulfur and see the flames. I hear the aftermath every time I close my eyes."

Turning to face Zac, I place my palms on his jaw. "You're a hero. You saved those children. And I know if you could have saved Mac you would have. He was doing what he was trained to do. You can't feel bad about that." Zac closes his eyes and I kiss both lids before placing my forehead against his. "That's how you know Trey. You served with him." It's not a question, just an observation, but Zac nods his confirmation. "And the tattoo on your side it's for Mac." Again Zac nods. "You are a strong, brave man, Zachariah. Why couldn't it have been you?" The question comes out without thought. It's not fair to either of us to play what if.

"Could have been me what?" Zac opens his eyes looking deep into mine.

"Why couldn't it have been you I chose to spend my life with? We would have lived much differently. I'll never regret Wyatt, but she would be a much brighter child with a father that loved her." It makes me a bitch to say it, but it's truly how I feel. I had feelings or at least the beginning of feelings for Zac in high school, but because of his bad boy tendencies my parents didn't approve. And Kent seemed like the safe route at the time.

Zac, moves my hair out of my face and wraps his fingers behind my head holding my curls back. "It had to happen this way, Ty. But it can be our time now, if you let it. We can heal each other-together." Zac doesn't give me time to respond before his mouth crashes into mine. His lips are rough and desperate. I drape my arms around his neck and move my hips against his growing crotch.

"Zac?" I can't wait anymore. The rawness of his

emotions during his story. The vulnerability he shows when he talks about us together. It all adds to the anticipation.

"I've got you, baby." Zac pushes forward, forcing me to fall backward. He sprawls over me, his biceps rippling as he covers his chest a whisper from mine. His mouth moving to my neck and chest as his hands discard my clothing at a record pace. His clothes following, my shaky hands working the fabric from his beautiful form exposing the tattoos that give him equal parts joy and despair. My body undulating under his weight. As he hovers, I can feel his cock against my entrance. The anticipation is too much, I arch my hips to grant him access. "Ty, hold on. I know last time we got swept up in the moment, but do we need somethin'. Are you on the pill? I'm clean, but I want you to be comfortable" God, I didn't even think of that. I never had to. Kent always took care of it when in high school. Then, after we were pregnant then married it was a moot point. He's right, though. We didn't use a condom last time. I'm not on the pill- it's way too early for any of those repercussions. I nod and Zac reaches for his pants off the floor to produce a small foil square from his wallet.

"Planning on getting lucky, huh, Soldier?" I joke.

"I like to think of it as bein' prepared, Darlin'."

"It's a good thing one of us is." I caress Zac's cheek "Thank you." There are no other words. I'm thanking him for letting me into his nightmare. I'm thanking him for making sure to keep me safe with his 'preparations.' I'm thanking him for trying to heal the broken woman Kent left me.

Zac now fully wrapped, hovers back over me. Our eyes lock, my name a whisper on his lips as he slowly enters me for the second time. The stretched feeling radiates through my body. The stretch only he brings out in me and my eyes roll back into my head as my moan fills the space between us. He stills inside me, fully seated, but doesn't move. "Look at me, baby." My eyes open to rough hands softly caressing my face and honest eyes taking in every flinch of my pleasure.

Bringing my hands to his neck, I lift my upper body to connect with Zac the only way I know how. Our lips meet in the most genuine kiss I've ever experienced. My breasts press against his firm, uncompromising chest. In this moment I'm not worried about Kent. I don't even register that Zac is still inside me. The only thing my brain can compute is how good Zac's lips feel against mine. How sweet he tastes against my tongue. How whole I feel when it is just us. Zac pulls back and exhales a breath. "I've never-" he pauses, eyes locked with mine. "You're incredible."

Our lips connect again, while Zac gently lowers me to the couch. My hands release their grip on his hair dropping to Zac's shoulder and back as he hovers above me resting on his elbows by my ears. His lips brushing against mine, though never fully connecting for a kiss. The soft caress causing my eyes to close in anticipation of his body moving in mine.

Zac traces his tongue across my bottom lip. My lips part and instinctively invite him inside. He doesn't taste me. He doesn't dip his tongue past my lips, instead nips at my plump, kiss swollen bottom lip from the scruff on his chin. My sharp intake of breath cutting through the silence of my living room.

Then Zac's lips are gone and I hear myself whimper in his absence. A soft chuckle vibrates against my chest as he presses a kiss to the tip of my nose, followed by a kiss to first my left then my right eyelid. "Eyes on me, baby. I wanna see those pretty blue eyes watchin' me move inside you. I want to see that creamy skin blush as you come around me. Only me. Kent can't take anythin' from you anymore. I'm the one that's gonna give it all back. So, eyes on me, Ty."

My eyes flutter open at Zac's insistence and I'm locked with his unyielding gaze. The emotions bleeding into his hazel irises as he looks at me is breathtaking. The touch of his arm traveling down my side to my upper thigh does nothing to break the connection. Without looking away, Zac hikes up my knee to his shoulder and slides deeper inside my channel.

Deeper inside me than anyone has ever been. My back arches and I cry out. Through sheer willpower alone, I'm able to keep my eyes on his. A soft moan escapes my parted lips as Zac stills, allowing my small sex to accommodate the wide girth of him. My breath comes rapidly, raising my chest until my hard buds brush against the hard planes of his chest.

I don't know how long we stay like this, but as my body loosens to accept Zac time seems to halt. Then, without warning, he's moving. Zac starts slow with a gentle pendulum swing of his hips. As he moves, my body begins to undulate and meet him thrust for thrust.

Zac's grip on my hip tightens and his shoulder slips into the groove behind my knee giving him more access. My body is climbing, but I'm not quite there. I need more. I need everything. "Zac, please." I'm not sure what I'm asking for but I need it.

"I've got you, baby." Zac says, as his thrusts take a punishing rhythm. The slapping of his skin against mine the only sound in the house. The grunts escaping the back of Zac's throat pushes me closer to my orgasm. "That's it, Ty, relax. Let me catch you. Let me heal you. Let go, now."

At Zac's words, I hurtle over the cliff. I'm thrown from this world of unimaginable pleasure. My body has never felt this weightless, this satisfied. I'm no stranger to self-fulfilled orgasms, but even my own ministrations haven't brought about an orgasm this strong.

As I fall back to Earth, Zac has slowed his pace to revel in my pleasure. His lips come to mine and I whimper as he pulls out. Did he come and I missed it? "Don't worry, I'm not done with you yet." Zac assures me, as he collects me in his arms.

My legs straddle him as he moves to stand. Zac's hands under my ass holding me close as if I weigh nothing in his strong grip. Leaving our clothes where they lie, we take the steps two at a time until Zac has me pressed against the upper landing wall. His lips and teeth nip at my neck as he enters me again, thrusting so deep the drywall threatens to give out behind me.

"Bedroom?" Zac growls against my earlobe, before taking the fleshy skin between his teeth. Unable to form words, I point to the room at the end of the hall. Without pulling out, Zac moves us towards the door and sets me down among my unmade bed sheets. Zac's eyes travel from my toes up my body. At my knees he brushes his fingertips against my overheated skin. "You're so damn beautiful," Zac whispers, as he moves between my legs.

This time when he enters me he doesn't take his time. In one thrust he's stretching me then pulling back to thrust again. The rough onslaught pushing my body to its limit. Without much warning, I'm crushed by another unworldly orgasm. Zac thrusts through, prolonging the flying sensation coursing through my body, until I feel him swell and spill his seed inside me.

Left to catch my breath, Zac pulls out and ties off the condom before disposing of it. When he walks back into the room from the en suite bathroom my eyes watch the sinew muscles move with his stealthy gait. "See somethin' you like, sweetheart?" Zac teases, as he joins me on the bed and pulls me in close.

"More than you know," I say, snuggling into Zac's warmth, my back to his naked front. Zac's calming breath evening out behind me. Resting my head on his bicep I struggle to stop my brain from running. Willing myself to let this play out, but I'm not used to this gentleness. I'm not used to being this happy. I'm afraid to give in- waiting for the other shoe to drop. Like it did with Kent. Maybe Zac's right and I do need to heal after everything my ex did to me. If he is right, I know exactly who will be able to give me the healing touch.

CHAPTER TWENTY-ONE

Tyler

My eyes flutter open and I can feel the slight stretch between my legs from last night. Zac is by far the best and biggest I've ever had, bar none. Granted, I don't have much to compare him to. Slowly rolling to my back, my legs feel like Jell-O. How am I supposed to function at a soccer game today? I don't feel like adulting, I'd rather bask in the afterglow that is having sex with Zac. Groaning I roll toward Zac, only the bed beside me is empty. The sheets are cold and my mood plummets along with it.

Where did he go and when? I think about the night and his sweet words the whole way through my shower. Washing the smell of sex down the drain and hopefully the thoughts of Zac along with it. He seemed so sincere when he was talking about his feelings. Who would lie like that just to get into someone's pants? I guarantee I'm not that good in bed.

Maybe that's the problem. Maybe I suck in bed. After all, comparatively, he's the freakin' sex Greek god of sex. Is there a Greek sex god? Anyway, compared to that, who am I-inexperienced Tyler- only been with one man. Well, two now. God, I feel like a slut. Not again. Here and now I vow, no matter how good he is-I will not fall for his words and fall into bed with him.

Dressing in the most comfortable running shorts I own and an appropriate motherly V-neck shirt, I head down to get Wyatt her breakfast. As I walk down the stairs the smell of maple syrup and burned chocolate chips fill my nose. Alarm has me running the last few steps only to see Wyatt covered in pancake mix by the stove.

"Bug, what are you doing?" I hip bump her out of the way and dispose of the burned cakes in the trash.

"I wanted to make us breakfast. It's an important game today, both teams are undefeated and I couldn't sit still." I can understand that. Cooking has always been my peaceful place when anxiety was dominating my life. In fact, that's the whole reason I started my online site. I just needed something peaceful that was my own that would make me forget the stress of life with Kent.

"I get it, bug, but why don't I help you?" Wyatt nods, jumping on her toes. "Go, get the stool- you'll be able to see better." By the time Wyatt is back, I've replaced the pan with the electric griddle. It makes a more even pancake and it is so much more kid user-friendly than the stove. "Alright, why don't you get the measuring cup and get me a cup and a half of flour." As I riddle off ingredients and measurements, Wyatt is diligent to follow, while I get my coffee percolating in the single use coffee pot.

Single use-talk about reminding me how lonely I am. Especially after waking up alone in my bed this morning.

"Alright, Momma, everything is in and mixed," Wyatt calls, just as I'm stirring the creamer into my coffee.

Looking at the mixture in front of her, it doesn't seem quite right. "Did you decide my measurements weren't acceptable?" I ask, noticing the amount of chocolate chips to batter.

"It's more like improving," Wyatt says with so much confidence and sass. The mini-me I was always worried she would be.

I can't help but laugh. "I'm only going to allow this because you're so nervous about today and you're right, it is a big game." Reaching for the mixture, I start leveling out dollops of batter.

The cakes come out perfectly. Very chocolatey, but perfect nonetheless. As I finish my coffee, my mind wanders to the man next door. Wyatt has disappeared to finish getting ready for the day and I can't help but look through the kitchen window. The window that faces Zac's kitchen. Will he be sitting at his table drinking coffee? Did he leave my place and hook up with someone else? What if I see him shirtless with arms wrapped around him like I did with Jane?

Placing the empty coffee cup in the sink way more forcefully than strictly necessary, I steel myself to not worry about my night with Zac- or my morning without him. He's not worth it. All the lies he fed me last night. He's not worth my time and I'm not going to waste anymore of it on someone more focused on getting laid than human decency. And to think, I thought he was different than Kent. I thought he could heal what Kent broke. I guess I do have a type, assholes. Zachariah Jacobson is not the man to heal my scars. Hell, he's just the type to make more.

"Ready, Momma." Wyatt calls from the doorway and we're off. A day in the sun watching my daughter play the game she loves. Now that is exactly what I need right now.

We arrived early to the field. Wyatt and her coach are the only two working on drills to warm up. The dedication she has at her age is remarkable. I hope she never loses it. I wish I had even an ounce of it when I was her age, but I know she's special that way. When she loves something, she puts her whole self in it.

I'm so entranced in Wyatt working, I didn't even notice people had started to mill around the base of the stands. As I turn to look for some of the other moms of Wyatt's teammates, I see the one face I didn't except. Well, maybe not the one face I didn't expect, but I'm sure as hell shocked he's here.

Zac walks to the bottom of the stairs leading to my section of the bleachers and starts to make his ascent. Why is he here? He was so quick to leave this morning just to show up at my daughter's game where he knows I can't yell at him. What did I do in a past life to deserve the men I've chosen to share a bed with. "Uhh," I groan inwardly as Zac works his way to me, moving past the family sitting to my right.

"Mornin', this is for you," Zac says, sitting so his outer thigh brushes against mine. As good as the coffee smells and as good as Zac feels, I can't cave. I can't let myself fall for another Kent. Turning so I'm not longer flush with Zac even as my body longs for his warmth. Traitor body.

Holding the coffee cup to me, "no coffee?" Zac looks over at me, confusion stretched across his handsome face. "Tyler, look at me." Pulling at my chin, Zac leans to meet me halfway. I continue to look at the floor while Zac tries coaxing me to look at him.

"Ty," at my nickname the tears form behind my eyes, "what's wrong? What did I do?" The sincere tone to his voice is so endearing, so believable.

How can someone so rotten sound so innocent?

"You didn't do anything. It was obvious this morning what you wanted." Scuffing, I turn more towards the field.

"I'm sorry, what? This mornin'?" Realization dawns on him. He finally knows I have his M.O. down. "If by this mornin' you mean prying myself away from your beautiful, naked body so I wasn't sneakin' around when your daughter woke up?

"I know the relationship you have with Wyatt. I may not have kids of my own, but I know if I had one, havin' my child walk in on my new relationship while we were indisposed in bed, I'd be mortified." I turn to look towards Zac, dumbfounded- he's totally right. Zac reaches for his coffee from the floor of the bleachers between his feet. "So, if that was the wrong decision, I'm sorry. Next time I'll meet everyone downstairs for breakfast in my boxers."

Turning towards Zac, I feel like a fool for the second time today. "Next time?" I ask, trying to plow through my blunder. "You really think you're that good in bed?"

"Oh, Darlin', you know I'm that good." Zac says,

handing me the coffee once again.

"Maybe," taking the cup, I hook my arm through his and lean my temple against his shoulder. "I'm sorry I overreacted. I'm not good at this. I'm damaged goods. I understand if you don't want to stick around." I need to give him an out. I need to let him go gracefully before it gets too messy. I am too damaged- Kent made sure of that.

"Hey," Zac cups my cheek and brings our foreheads together. Breathing his air into my lungs it's like he's giving me life- a new life. "Ty, I'm not goin' anywhere. Everythin' I said last night I meant. I've been waitin' on you in some capacity since I was sixteen years old. Now that I have you, you're not gettin' rid of me that easily." Zac moves to kiss the tip of my nose then a light pec to my lips before we turn back towards the field.

Trying to give my daughter my full attention, the heat radiating from my right side is causing my concentration to deviate. Yet with every advance or assist Wyatt makes, Zac is on his feet cheering louder than me. Cheering like Kent could never be bothered to cheer. The ugly images of Wyatt's crestfallen expression every time she would look in the stands to see Kent looking down at his phone flies through my mind's eye. These new images of her pride and kidlike wonder shine through as she looks up, seeing Zac and I cheering with the best of them.

When the game comes to a close, Wyatt has four assists and one goal. I'm so proud of her and the dedication she has to the game she loves. As snack and water bottles are handed out, Zac and I make our way to the home bench.

"Ugh, bug," I groan as Wyatt gives me a sweaty hug.

Pulling her in closer, I whisper, "you did great. How about a celebratory lunch?" Wyatt turns to look at Zac, asking him the unspoken question of his company to lunch. With his small nod, Wyatt looks to me with a bright smile repeating the gesture.

Off to lunch we go. One big happy… *something.*

CHAPTER TWENTY-TWO
ZAC

Waking up, the first thing I notice is it's morning. I can't believe I slept through the entire night. Since Tyler and I made things official after Wyatt's game last week, my nightmares have drifted further and further into my subconscious. It started simple. Like the night I first made love to Tyler my nightmare was a passing dream. There was no earth shattering fear or pain associated with it. I woke up, took a leak, then I went right back to bed.

Normally, a nightmare would leave me debilitated for at least an hour. Since then, I've had a few nights where my back would bother me as my mind played back the night I lost my best friend, but I'm able to manage my nightly outbursts. And I know what the change was- Tyler.

I'm happy, truly happy for the first time in years. When we came home from Wyatt's game we played around in the pool. The memory of throwing Wyatt around the pool and sneaking a kiss from Tyler when her mini-me wasn't looking is quickly filling my soul and dissipating the bad dreams. We were giant prunes by the time we stepped out of the pool for dinner, but it was totally worth it. Just to see the looks Tyler shot me from across the pool, I'd have done anything. The mix of admiration and-dare I say it-love shining through her purple eyes was life altering.

We moved to Tyler's house after dinner so she could put Wyatt to bed. I waited on the couch for a much needed talk. Tyler had hinted toward this talk all afternoon. I get it, it's not just her and she needed ground rules for our relationship to not confuse Wyatt. I respected the hell out of her for it.

The deal was, at the beginning, three nights a week I'd come over for dinner. I pushed for five, but Tyler wasn't having it. We established the schedule and what she was comfortable doing in front of Wyatt and what she didn't think was acceptable. Kisses on the cheek and hugs, assuming they weren't lingering, were fine. Hand holding was a given, but those were my lines and as much as I wanted to cross every one of them, I've done my part to stay in my lane.

It's worked, we've been dating, seeing, fucking-whatever you want to call it- for a little over a week and I couldn't be happier. We've been out in public and I bet the whole town knows the ex-bad boy finally got his girl. I remember the conversation I had with Mrs. Betty at the market the other day.

"Dr. Jacobson, I'm so happy to see little Tyler has finally come home." The nearing ninety year old pushed.

"Yes, it's great seein' Tyler again."

"The way I hear it, you got yourself a little romance abrewin'." She leans in conspiratorially.

"You hear right. Tyler and I are datin'." The broad smile can't be stopped as I think of Tyler being mine-finally.

"It's about damn time, darlin'."

"Excuse me?" I'm taken about by the statement.

"With all the games the two of you played in school, you weren't foolin' anyone. We all knew you had it bad for each other. Rotten thing that Kent did to her and sweet baby Wyatt. You're a good man, you be good to them."

I'm surprised, the whole damn town must have known my feelings for Tyler-everyone but her clearly. "I plan on it, Mrs. Betty," I say, helping the old busy body to her car.

I guess I shouldn't be too shocked that people knew my feelings for Tyler. I didn't really keep them a secret. While I never told anyone how I felt about her in high school, I was definitely different around her. Only her. She made me want to be a better person. She saved my life before I knew it needed saving.

Tonight, I'm taking her on a date. We haven't been out just the two of us since our first date and Wyatt's soccer games-which don't count. Reaching into my bedside drawer I pull out the tattered box from under the books I stashed for nights when sleep evades me. Taking a deep breath I open the box that hasn't seen the light of day in too many years to count.

Laying right on top is the senior picture of a young blonde with blue-purple eyes. I plan to remind Tyler of the day I got this photo and what the photo meant to me overseas. I've made sure to tell her exactly what she means to me, but this is one conversation I need to have with her. She needs to know what she does to me. What she's always done to me.

"Darlin', you had enough to eat?" I wrap my arm around her shoulder and pull her in close, my stubble brushing against her cheek as I kiss her temple.

"Yeah, we can walk over to the shop and I could make dessert," Tyler suggests linking her fingers with mine as they hang by her shoulder.

"Or, I could take you home and have you for dessert." Nibbling on her earlobe, I know I've got her where I want her. I need her loose and relaxed if I'm going to have this conversation with her.

"Mmm, I like the sound of that. Lead the way, soldier." We walk back to my Jeep and I help her in.

As we drive back to our houses, Tyler explains everything she wants to do for the opening. I mentioned the idea of having a huge opening day party. I offered my practice as a sponsor. I'm totally whipped; I'm finding any excuse to see this woman and I'm hoping that after I tell her she's the one that kept me pushing on in Afghanistan she won't go running for the hills.

We pull into my drive and my hands remain on the wheel. I'm trying to psych myself up for this conversation. What if she thinks I'm creepy. Or worse, what if she doesn't want to continue seeing me after I everything.

"Zac, are you ok?" Tyler's hand brushes her hand along my cheek and I close my eyes relishing in the way she makes my body tingle.

"We need to talk, Ty." Her sharp inhale only adds to my raw nerves and she pulls her bottom lip between her teeth in fear. "I'm sorry, Darlin', not about that.

You're mine and that ain't changin' unless you decide otherwise." I pull Tyler into my arms to cut the tension.

"But let's go on in. I got somethin' I want to show you." We make our way into my house and I lead her up to my room. Depositing her on the edge of my bed I move to the tattered box sitting on my end table.

"What's going on, Zachariah?" Tyler seems apprehensive and I know it's my fault. I've been so nervous that I haven't done a very good job at talking her through things here.

"Do you remember graduation day?" I ask, as I find the beginning of my confession.

"I remember the bright white gowns. The lame jokes Mr. Buckwalter tried to make in his "look to the future" speech. Although, now looking back, they were kind of funny." Tyler chuckles quietly and I wait. "What is it I'm supposed to remember exactly?"

"Our first kiss," I say, lifting her senior portrait out from inside the box.

"Zac, Zac wait." Turning I see Tyler jogging down the hall toward me. "I wanted you to have this." She holds up small wallet sized professional photo of her in one of the fields around town. She looks beautiful. The sun is shining behind her making her blonde hair look golden. Her smile is wide like someone just told her a joke and her eyes are dancing with warmth.

It's the most captivating image I've ever seen and I can't believe I'm letting her just walk away without even trying. Ok, so she's not walking away-she's going to college, but the outcome is still the same. She'll still be leaving town without knowing how I truly feel about her.

Without thinking about the consequences, I take her hand and pull her into the nearest classroom. As the door shuts quietly behind us we're entombed in silence. The beating of my heart in my ears makes it hard to think.

"We shouldn't be here. My parents will be lookin' for me."
Tyler's right, her family is probably looking for her as we stand
here, but I'm not holding her here and she's not moving her feet.

"I know." I step toward her and she steps back into the desk
behind her. "If your folks found you in here with me they'd be
pissed, but I couldn't let you leave this town not knowin'." I take
one last step forward until I'm chest to chest with my dream girl.

"Knowin' what?" Tyler asks breathily.

"Knowin' that there isn't a day that I don't think about you.
Knowin' you're the sole reason I made it to graduation. And
knowin' this." I lean forward and touch my lips to Tyler's for
the first time.

My hands go to her shoulders and I put everything I have into
the kiss. Her lips are slack, but I give it my all. She's not into
it. I read her all wrong. Everyone was right, she's just a good girl
who's nice to everyone. I'm a prick for thinking I was anything
different. I move to pull away, but before I break contact, Tyler's
arms snake their way to my neck.

She grabs hold of my flannel collar and meshes her lips to mine.
She's kissing me back. We're making out. I adjust closer and tilt
my head, she mirrors my movements perfectly. We're in the erotic
dance and I can't get enough. I slide my tongue along her bottom
lip and she opens to tangle her tongue with mine.

As we get lost in the moment, I allow my hands to roam her
back, her sides, her hips. I can't get close enough. Gripping her
hips tight, I lift her onto the desk and nudge her knees apart so
I can step between. I'm so close now there's no denying what she
does to me and she gasps. Moving her hands to my chest, she
applies light pressure and I retreat a few steps back. We're both
looking at each other, catching our breath.

"I'm sorry, Zac. I can't." Tyler looks down at the floor and I'm
kicking myself for putting her in this position-feeling guilty. "I'm

with Kent. I don't know why I did that?"

"Hey, you didn't do anything, darlin'. This was all me. I've been dreamin' bout doin' that since sophomore year. Call it a graduation present."

Tyler looks up at me with a sad smile. "Alright, Zac. It was your secret graduation present. I'm gunna miss you."

"I'm gunna miss you, too, Ty. You be good in school, ya hear?" I say, defeat written all over my face. "Now, run along. I'm sure your daddy's ready to tan someone's hide if you don't show up soon." She hops down from the desk and moves toward the door.

"Zac," Tyler turns with the door slightly ajar. I lift a brow in question, "if things were different."

"It would still be you," I cut her off. I don't need to hear her say she'd be with me. I don't want to think about "what if's." In the end I still don't have the girl.

"I can't believe I forgot," Tyler says, as recognition hits her. "I gave you my graduation photo and you dragged me into a classroom and molested me." She pulls me close, laughing at her not funny joke.

"I remember it quite differently, darlin'." I hand over the photo in my hand. "That day was ingrained in my brain. The way you felt against me. Your smell. Your taste. Everythin' about you I had committed to memory. So, when I left for the Army, I couldn't get away fast enough. I left with the clothes on my back-and this." I look down at the photo in Tyler's hands.

"Why?" Tyler looks up at me, moisture accumulating in her eyes.

Lifting a finger to catch a tear I continue, "I needed to take the photo of the girl that stole my heart and never gave it back. I put this picture in my helmet durin' every deployment. You were my guardian angel. I wanted to make it back so that, maybe, one day I'd see

Lifting a finger to catch a tear I continue, "I needed to take the photo of the girl that stole my heart and never gave it back. I put this picture in my helmet durin' every deployment. You were my guardian angel. I wanted to make it back so that, maybe, one day I'd see you and we could try again."

Tyler looks down at the ratty photo and turns it over. Her teenage handwriting is faded, but still legible. The words that I always thought to mean more than they were. She places the picture on the bedside table and stands in front of me. "Zac, I can't give you back the years that I gave to Kent, but I can give you everything I have left. You made me see that not all men are the same. I'm falling in love with you."

"Tyler, I think I've been fallin' in love with you since I was sixteen years old. It's about damn time you caught up." The time for talking is over. We have no more secrets and now I just want to make love to the woman of my dreams-the woman of my past, present, and future.

As Tyler lies on my chest, I look over to the photo sitting on my nightstand. The photo that kept my hope alive that one day we'd find a way to make this work. Lifting the dingy paper, I read the back one last time.

SOMETIMES THE PATH NOT TAKEN IS THE MOST FUN. WHAT IF THE FIRE IS MEANT TO BE TOUCHED. ISN'T IT BETTER TO LIVE WITH THE BURN OR TO NEVER KNOW. I HOPE YOU RUN THROUGH THE FIRE, I SOMETIMES WISH I

I EXPECT GREAT THINGS ~~COULD~~ FROM YOU, ZACHARIAH.

♡ TY

CHAPTER TWENTY-THREE

Tyler

"Zac, are you ok?" I ask, resting my shoulder on the doorframe to the bathroom.

"Yeah, just needed some water. I didn't want to go downstairs and wake Wyatt up." He sets the cup down on the counter and walks toward me.

"It wasn't a nightmare, was it?" Zac hasn't had a nightmare in a month and a half. In fact, in the time we've been together I've only seen him have a PTSD nightmare once. It was during our first week officially together and it scared the living shit out of me. He swung his arms and thrashed around on his side of the bed. He whimpered softly and called out Mac's name. He jolted awake in a cold sweat. It broke my heart. The memories this poor man lived through over and over again would strangle a lesser man.

"No, Darlin'. I'm good. I haven't had one since we've been together." He wraps his arms around my waist and he presses a kiss to my temple. "Come back to bed." Zac pulls me with him and positions me against his side with his massive pec under my head. As hard as his muscles look, I've never had a more comfortable pillow.

Zac's rhythmic breathing lulls me to sleep and I don't think I moved a muscle until I felt Zac nudging me, "Darlin', I'm gunna leave now before Wyatt gets up. I'll be over in twenty to have breakfast with you ladies."

"Mhmm." I sink into the bed a little further. Zac chuckles and kisses me on my cheek before leaving my room to pretend he spent the night anywhere other than my bed.

I must have fallen asleep because the next thing I know Wyatt is yelling down the hallway that we have a visitor and I need to get up. Rolling toward my phone beside the bed I see I slept about forty-five minutes past the twenty minutes Zac gave me. Throwing the covers off my I run to the bathroom to brush my teeth then put on a pair of sweatpants and head toward my daughter.

"Sorry, I must have needed more sleep that I thought." I apologize to Wyatt.

"It's ok." Wyatt is the easiest child, I swear.

"Yeah, no worries. Somethin' must have kept you up late last night," Zac teases.

"Something was definitely up," I flirt back. God, sex with Zac is like nothing I've ever experienced. I'm surprised he doesn't have me waking the whole neighborhood with how good he makes my body sing. "What's that?" I ask, looking at the envelope in Zac's hand.

"Don't know. It was addressed to you and on your

front steps. Thought I'd bring it in with me. There's no return address." He hands me the letter.

Opening it slowly, I pull out the letter. Blood stills in my veins and a wave of nausea rolls through my stomach. Zac must see my reaction and tells Wyatt she can go work on her drills outside and he'd call her in when breakfast was ready.

"Ty, what's wrong? Is there something wrong with the custody arrangement with Kent?" Zac steps toward me and reaches for the letter. My body goes limp as he takes it out of my hands. It's no matter. I may not be holding the letter anymore, but the words are forever ingrained in my head.

You think he can fuck you better than I can? You're mine and I'll remind you of that soon enough. Just wait for me. You don't want to see what I'm capable of. No one else will have you, but me.

"What the fuck," Zac curses. "This has to be Kent, right? I'm going to have some people look into this." He pulls out his phone and takes a picture of the letter, but I'm shocked and scared into immobility. "Ty, darlin', look at me. I will not let anything or anyone get to you or Wyatt. I'll keep you safe."

I know his words are true, but that doesn't make me any less scared. I've been with Zac for almost two months and I know he'd do anything to keep me safe, but I also know that is not Kent's handwriting. If it's not Kent who wrote it, who did? The anonymity of a possible stalker is terrifying.

"Let's make breakfast. I know you won't forget about this, but let's not worry until I hear back from my guys.

They'll look into its credibility. Alright?"

I nod and move toward the kitchen. Zac makes a call then brings Wyatt in and I plaster a fake smile on my face. The last thing I need is to frighten my daughter.

"It's been a month and we haven't gotten anymore letters. My guys have put up cameras and nothin' has been out of the ordinary. I think we're officially in the clear," Zac says as he walks in the front door after work.

"That's fantastic. I'm sorry I've been on edge, that letter just freaked me out," I admit.

"I know, but I'm thinkin' it was a nasty prank some high schooler was playin'. We are all good." Zac reassures me and I'm on cloud nine. My would be stalker is nonexistent and I've been blessed with the best boyfriend.

It feels weird calling Zac my boyfriend, but that's what he is. We've been seeing each other exclusively for two and a half months. He's the most loving, caring, and genuine person I've ever met.

"You know I love you, right?" I link my hands behind his neck.

"Is that right? I think you better show me." Zac bends and places a searing kiss against my lips.

"Ugh, come on you two. PDA much?" Wyatt walks in the room and interrupts our make out session. The girl loves that I'm with Zac, but she's plenty happy with us waiting until she goes to bed to show any 'PDA.'

"Oh, you're just jealous you can't kiss that Harrison boy in your class," Zac teases Wyatt about the boy from her class she blushes around.

"Do not- I don't- Momma," she whines, but she's also laughing and blushing.

"Alright you two. Don't make me separate you."

"Peanut, you know he'd be an idiot not to like you, but I also think you're a little young to be wantin' his attention." Zac walks over and kisses Wyatt on her crown as she wraps her arms around his hips.

And just like that, my broken family has become whole. Zac has filled the void that has been missing since before I ever thought of divorcing Kent. Zachariah Jacobson has become the glue to our mess. *The balm for my wounds.*

"Darlin', if you don't stop you're going to walk a hole in the carpet." Zac reaches for my arm as I pace by the bed for the millionth time- or what feels like it. I've been restless for upwards of an hour. The bakery opens tomorrow and we've planned a huge array of events to mark the occasion. Tomorrow starts the rest of my life.

"I can't." I try to wiggle out of Zac's grip to keep myself moving. "I'm so nervous. What if people don't like my stuff. What if I can't pay my rent every month?" I'm spiraling and I can feel it, I just can't stop it. I can't make my brain stop asking these asinine questions. I can't make my chest stop seizing with worry.

"Ty, come here. Come lay down and try gettin' some rest. Burnin' the midnight oil is only gunna make tomorrow more difficult. You need to sleep to function your best tomorrow," Zac says, pulling me into his arm on the bed.

"I can't stop thinking." Looking over into Zac's creamy caramel eyes, I melt just the slightest bit. "I can't just lay here."

"Then let's not lay here," Zac says, standing and gesturing for me to stand as well.

"What do you mean?" I stand and stare at Zac with confusion.

"Do you want me to make you forget about tomorrow, darlin'?" Zac cups my cheek and I lean into his warm touch. I close my eyes and nod. "Then, take off your shirt." Zac's voice has dropped an octave with a hint of dominance. I'm wearing his shirt and a tiny pair of lace panties. I reach for the hem of the white shirt and hesitate. "I'm not gunna ask again, Ty." Zac has moved behind me and his breath tickles the back of my neck.

Gripping the hem tighter, I lift the light fabric over my head and turn slightly so his lips are against my ear, though. Zac doesn't touch me. He doesn't seem to even register my shirt has hit the floor except for the vibrating energy between us.

"And your panties." There's no hesitation this time. The insistence in his deepened voice not allowing for argument.

My thumbs curl around my panties at my hips and slowly drag the delicate material downward. As my pussy meets the cold air, a shiver runs through my body. My nipples pebble and my pleasure gathers between my thighs. The lace falls to my feet and I step out of them. Standing still waiting for Zac's next order.

After years or Kent demanding things from me, I never thought I'd feel comfortable around this kind of behavior in bed. I never thought I'd be turned on by giving up my will. But the way Zac's voice drops.

The way his silent stare promises pleasure, I find myself getting wetter as each second passes. My desire beginning to dampen my thighs as the anticipation stretches on.

My arms resting at my sides begin to tingle waiting for Zac's touch. "Zac," I moan as I turn to face him. I can't be this close to him without touching him anymore.

"On the bed, back down," Zac orders before I can reach him. Without thinking I drop my hands and knees and move toward the bed. Crawling toward the pillows, I move slowly, trying to draw out the view. Hopefully, give Zac a taste of anticipation. Rolling to my back, I lie with my knees bent. Gazing at him through my open legs, waiting for a command. "Do you want me, Ty?" Zac asks, not moving closer.

"Yes," it's a breathy admission. Arousal pooling on the comforter below me.

Zac moves closer, the bed dipping against his weight. He's taking me in, caressing me without moving a finger. My body overheating with pleasure and he hasn't even touched me. "Hands above your head." Moving without thinking my hands twine with the metal of my headboard. Finally, Zac reaches out and brushes his fingers against my legs.

Starting at my ankle and moving towards my knee. The gentle pads of his fingers drawing invisible lines of pleasure upwards until he stops just shy of where I need him most. He turns and retraces his trek on the other leg.

Stopping at my knee, Zac opens me up to him. I'm on full display as a blush rises to my cheeks. The pure intensity of my arousal surprising even to me. "Zac," I reach for him, to pull him against me. "Please," I whine, the anticipation is too great. I need him to touch me.

Zac takes my wrists in one large hand and brings them back to their place along my headboard. "Keep your hands here or I'll have to tie them there." Oh, God. I'm torn between leaving my hands where they are to please him and moving them to get tied up- knowing he'll please me either way. "What do you want, Ty?" The question all too familiar now. After three weeks of building a relationship, Zac is always concerned with giving me what I want. What I need from him.

"Touch me," I plead with a strained voice.

"I will, sweet girl, but not yet." Zac leaves one hand around my wrists to keep them in place while the other moves up my rib cage. As his rough palm grazes across my sensitized skin, it's as if I can feel ever ridge of his palm print- every imperfection. Then, one finger is tracing the underside of my breast. My back arches and hips undulate, trying to create the friction my body needs. "Such a greedy girl," Zac whispers, planting the gentlest of kisses against the soft spot on my neck behind my ear. Not giving into my body's needs, Zac moves his traveling finger to circle my areola. Never getting close enough to the peaked tips to garnish enough pleasure, but enough sensation to keep me on the cusp wanting more.

"Please, Zac. Please."

"Please, what, angel?" Zac moves his head toward my chest and grants me a subtly flick of his touch against one of my pebbled nipples. "Please, taste you?" Zac places a light kiss against the side of my breast. "Please, touch you?" Another peck between my breasts. "Please, fuck you?" A flick of his tongue against my other nipple. It's torture at its finest.

"Yes!" I want all of them- any of them. I need them. I need him.

Zac removes his hand from my wrists and cups my left breast and squeezes slightly to suck on the tip. While his other hand traces a line from my sternum to my throbbing sex. Sitting to my left, Zac flattens his hand against me so the heel of his palm is moving in small circles just barely against my clit as the tip of his middle finger toys with my entrance. The touch sends my nerve endings pulsing and arousal to drip down my thighs, coating Zac's hand.

My hands drift to Zac's silky hair, pulling his mouth closer to my breast. "Ah, ah, ah." All in an instant Zac's mouth is gone and his hands have left my body to peel my hands away. "Naughty girl, hands up." My hands once again grip the metal bar of my headboard. Zac disappears into my closet and comes back holding one of my winter scarves.

With the skill of the Army Ranger he is, he ties my arms to the headboard at the wrists. As he steps back to look at his handy work, I give my hands a experimental tug. They're securely bound without cutting into the skin, thankfully. Looking back at Zac as his eyes trace ever curve of my body I can't help squirming. I'm building with more pleasure and he's feet away from me.

Catching my eyes, Zac reaches for the hem of his shirt. Uncovering inch after inch of his rippling six pack knowingly taunting me. I groan and dig my teeth into my bottom lip. At last the torture is over and he drops the material to the floor. Then, it's his basketball shorts dropping to the floor. I'm squirming with need and he's taking his damn time. "Zac, please," I beg, pressing my legs together, trying to get a little relief.

"Open your legs. Let me see you." That demanding voice leaves no room for argument. My knees drop open and my heart rate escalates further. "Good girl." Zac leaves his boxer briefs on, denying me the view of his naked body. *Asshole.*

His hands go to my knees and his lips to the inside of my thighs as he lowers his body between my legs. My hips grind against the air trying to get closer to his mouth, but Zac refuses to move faster.

After what feels like an eternity, his mouth finally reaches the apex of my thighs and his warm breath cascades over my sensitive skin. My clit is throbbing for attention and my entrance dripping with desire. I can see the bulge under Zac's underwear, but my attempts to reach for it are futile. The more I try to pull away from my restraints the tighter they become. Damn military knots.

Zac's tongue finally makes contact with my clit and I throw my head back in pleasure. Any thoughts of removing the restraint a distant memory if it garnishes pleasure like this. First, his tongue moves slow. Drawing small, tight circles around my nub. Then as my desire builds, he pulls the little button into his mouth and sucks. I can feel a knot at the base of my spine rolling, waiting for just the right pressure to explode.

My eyes roll back into my head and my hips begin to grind against Zac's face. All at once, Zac drapes one arm over me to silence my hips and with the other he presses two fingers into my entrance. Curling his fingers, massaging the front wall of my sex the ball detonates. White hot bliss tumbles through my body as the orgasm that has been building for too long opens my nerve endings. A kaleidoscope of pleasure tumbles through my body to my fingertips.

I'm falling into another world of pleasure and Zac doesn't let up. The slow circles he was lavishing on my clit have turned into a frenzied torrent of sensation. I'm still flying high and Zac is brushing against my clit and g-spot with each thrust. I'm not able to catch my breath before I'm thrown right into another all consuming orgasm.

As I wind down from the my second orgasm, I open my eyes to see Zac's satisfied smile glistening with my arousal. He wipes his mouth and crashes his lips to mine as he drops his boxer briefs to the floor.

"God, darlin', you taste so fuckin' good," he says against my lips before moving in for another soul crushing kiss. "I need to be inside you."

"Yes, Zac," I plead while Zac moves my ankles to his shoulders and positions his cock at my entrance. I lift my eyes to meet his and he trusts in all at once. He sets a punishing pace and we're building together. Sweat is prickling on my skin and my bound wrists escalating the intensity of his movements. I can't grab onto anything to ground myself so I float higher and higher at Zac's will.

"Come for me, baby," he growls through gritted teeth. Zac's hands wrapping around my thighs and the slapping of our skin pushes me over the edge. I climax seconds before I feel his cock spasming inside me.

Zac and I stay locked together as our breathing steadies. My legs slide off his shoulders and wrap around his hips. He unties my wrists and our limbs tangle while still connected in the most intimate way. Our lips lock and a wave of exhausted flows through me. I rest my forehead against his chest, catching my breath.

"Thank you for getting me out of my head," I say, as I notice my thoughts are nowhere near the shop or it's opening tomorrow.

"The pleasure was all mine." He chuckles, his chest rumbling against my body.

I drift off to sleep in Zac's arms, relaxed and sated. It's hard to believe that forty minutes ago I was stressing out about tomorrow and now I'm struggling to keep my eyes open. I may not have planned him. I may not have even wanted him. But I needed him. Zac has shown me how a woman should be treated in two and a half months than Kent had in all the years we were together.

These three weeks have opened me up to things I never thought would be available to me. I've found myself drifting to thoughts of Zac when he's not around and craving his nearness when he's only a room away. With the misery Kent left behind in my life, I didn't think I'd move on at all. Yet, things have moved quickly for us, much quicker than I thought my heart would allow. And as my brain shuts off to bring sleep one thought remains. I'm falling for the town bad boy. I'm falling in love with Zachariah Corey Jacobson.

CHAPTER TWENTY-FOUR

ZAC

Sneaking out of Tyler's house has become more and more of a nuisance. Leaving the warmth of her bed and the softness of her body wrapped around mine has become one of the hardest things to do. I don't know how to navigate this though. I understand Ty's apprehension to coming out with our sleeping arrangement to Wyatt, but man this sucks.

"Ty, I'm goin'. You should get up soon," I say into Tyler's ear as I pull her back further against my front. "I'll be at the door in forty minutes to get Wyatt and take her to the opening." Groaning, Tyler turns towards me and twines her hands behind my neck. Tyler asked me to take Wyatt to the opening and meet her parents since she needed to be there early and after all I am closer than her parents.

I move to get up, but Tyler won't let go. Her fingers lock around me, keeping me in her bed. "Ty, if I'm gunna get out of here without Wyatt seein' me, I'm gunna need to go now." Reaching for her wrists behind my neck, I can already hear stirring from Wyatt's room down the hall.

"What if you didn't have to leave every morning?" Tyler doesn't open her eyes, or move her head from against my chest. Is she serious? I pull back to catch her eyes and raise my eyebrow in question. "Unless that would be moving too fast." Tyler unlocks her fingers and starts to back pedal. Clearly misreading my expression.

I grip her hand just as she's starting to turn away. "Hey, that's not it. I was just thinkin' how I didn't want to sneak out anymore. I love hangin' out with the peanut and I love wakin' up in your bed. I was just thinkin' how much it sucked to have to sneak out every mornin'. The look was that of surprise that we weren't gunna have to hide this part of our relationship anymore. Not that I didn't want it."

Slowly, Tyler turns back toward me. "You sure? We can just keep doing what we've been doing." The shy coloring in her cheeks I've been missing the past couple months returns with a vengeance.

"No, I want to stay in this bed with you as long as humanly possible." The drop in my voice- that Tyler loves- returns and seems to bring enough confidence to my voice to make Tyler believe my honesty. "Now, get that cute ass downstairs and make me and your daughter some breakfast before you have to leave, woman," I joke.

"Yes, sir." Tyler disappears in her closet and returns minutes later looking like a professional bakery owner- or at least what I assume one would look like. I lounge on the bed, resting my back against the headboard to enjoy the view. Tyler catches my appreciative gaze and winks before leaving the room to start whatever she has planned for breakfast.

I hop in the shower quickly and change into the outfit from last night. I just put it on after the gym and a shower, so I'm as clean as I care to be. God, if people knew the days I'd spent in the same clothes in the desert. This was nothing compared to that stink. These cargo shorts and striped v-neck will work fine for the occasion. Now if I could just find where I kicked off my Vans I'd be set.

Finally, fully dressed and ready for the day, I make my way downstairs. Tyler is behind the counter putting the finishing touches on whatever sweet smelling pastry she's just pulled out of the oven. Wyatt is at the table looking through the newest kid's sports magazine that just arrived in the mail.

For a man that never saw himself with a family, I find myself enjoying the opportunity to be a part of a unit again. I always thought the men I served with would be my family- my brothers. But the two girls turning to look at me as I take the last step down the stairs, are quickly becoming that instead. Their smiles growing as they see me. Tyler nods to the table to get me to sit, and while she isn't looking this way, I know she's listening for Wyatt's reaction to my morning appearance from upstairs instead of next door.

"Mornin', peanut," I say, gently rubbing my palm against the crown of her head.

"Ugh," Wyatt groans pushing my hand away. "You're gunna make me bald before I hit double digits."

"Oh, but you'd still be the cutest bald girl I know."

Sitting at the table, I hear Tyler snickering at our banter. The kid and I have a good rapport, I have to admit. She's witty and quick- much like her mother. She's a pistol and going to be quite the handful in a few years. Might have to start cleaning my gun more often when boys start coming around.

Fuck, is that really where my point of reference is for my gun now? A few months ago, I was meeting Trey at the range and blowing off steam with shells flying from the magazine. Now I'm talking about long term relationship goals, scaring boys coming after a teenage Wyatt, and teen magazine blogs. *My, how the mighty have fallen.*

"Wyatt, are you still ok with Zac taking you to the opening to meet Grandma and Pop Pop?" Tyler sets the sticky buns on the table and moves to collect her purse and phone.

"Yeah, might as well get some free labor out of him since he's here practically every night anyway." And there it is- the little runt has known the whole time. I've gotten rusty with my stealth in my old age it seems.

Tyler stops halfway to the table at Wyatt's back and if it weren't such an important moment for the three of us I'd burst out laughing at the stunned mortification written all over her face. "Well, since the cats out of the bag, peanut, what do you say? We straight?"

Wyatt look between her mother and myself before she nods and agrees, "yeah, we're straight." With that Wyatt reaches for a sweet pastry and looks back to her article.

Bullet dodged.

Tyler steps up and gives Wyatt a kiss on the head and reassurance of seeing her later. Then she comes to me. Her eyes lingering on Wyatt, fearful of how our interactions might affect her daughter. Tyler's an awesome Mom and an incredible person.

With Wyatt uninterested, Tyler looks to me and places a delicate palm on my cheek and a light peck on my lips. She doesn't say anything as she makes her way to the door, but as she's about to walk out I feel her eyes on Wyatt and me. She may not have said anything, but in that second as I turned and caught her stare- her eyes told a storybook of happiness.

"So, peanut, let's have it." Wyatt and I have a bond already and it's something I've grown used to. She's not just Tyler's kid, she's an interesting character and I find myself just as excited to see her as I am Tyler.

Well, maybe not quite the same.

"It's about time you stopped pretending. And you should probably go back for some training in sneaking around. The Army sure isn't making them quite like they used to, it seems." Wyatt barely lifts a brow let alone look away from her article as she reads me the riot act.

"Damn, girl, you sure know how to wound a man," I joke, messing up her hair again. Switching gears before I'm totally emasculated I ask for help. "Alright, I'll work on my stealth if you help with a gift for your momma on her bakery openin'."

That gets Wyatt's full attention. "Shopping? Let's go."

I have to drop my pastry on my plate to catch hold of her wrist fast enough to stop her, but as I pull her back I say, "whoa, where's the fire? We have two hours before your momma's expectin' us. Eat your breakfast then we'll head to the mall." Wyatt sits and reaches for a sticky bun. "So, what do you have in mind?" I ask, leaning in conspiratorially.

"I know just the thing," she says, taking a bite.

As Wyatt and I make our way to the strip mall that houses my office and the bakery, I look down at the small gift I purchased for Tyler. It is as much from Wyatt as it is from me and the importance that we picked it out together is not lost on me. Tyler would like a brown paper bag if it came from the two of us. She is such a good person and I can't believe I get to call her mine. Yeah, yeah, I know it's sappy, but at this point my man card is non-existent.

Pulling into a spot, I'm in awe at all Tyler has been able to accomplish. When I left yesterday, I saw the bare bones of what is an amazing festival of sweets in front of me. The tent I helped assemble had been divided into four stations. First, you pick a flavor of cupcake. Second, select your icing. Third, you pick you decorations, everything from sprinkles to little pieces that look like blown glass. And the final station you sit and enjoy your masterpiece. Tyler should be proud. Shit, I'm more than proud. This is a huge success and everyone around me is singing her praises.

Wyatt grabs my hand as we cross the parking lot to where Ty stands with her parents. "Well, hello there, Bug," she greets her daughter, hugging her and pressing a kiss her temple. "And hello, Sergeant." She grins and kisses my cheek.

As I shake Ty's dad's hand and side hug her mom, the hairs on the back of my neck stand tall. An eerie tingle shoots through my body and I'm set on full alert. I check my six and subtly evaluate my surroundings.

Nothing seems out of place, but I can't shake the feeling of being watched. It's the same feeling I used to get when I knew one of my men had me in their sniper scope. Even from a friendly you can never shake the feeling of being watched. The full body tingling you get with eyes on you, never goes away.

A brush of Tyler's hand against my forearm brings me back into the conversation. Ty furrows her brows and mouths "you ok?" I nod and try to ignore the feeling as nothing seems amiss.

"Alright, Lovebug, you go make yourself a cupcake then Grandma and Pop Pop are taking you for the night." Wyatt leaves the group and her parents follow, helping to make sure Wyatt doesn't try to use every icing and ingredient available.

"Can you do me a favor?" I turn to her with brows raised in question. "Can you run inside and get me more of the cupcakes I made last night? We're running low." She holds out her shop key.

"Of course." I head toward the door and check all my surroundings again and still nothing seems out of place. I refuse to acknowledge the feeling anymore. I'm going to enjoy this time with Tyler.

Walking towards Station one with arms full of cupcakes, I unload before heading for Tyler. Wyatt is sitting and eating her cupcake with her grandparents and Ty is off in the corner between client conversations. Now's my moment.

I brush against her back and wrap my arms around her ribs, pulling her body flush with mine and rest my chin on her shoulder. "I have a surprise for you," I whisper against her ear.

I brush against her back and wrap my arms around her ribs, pulling her body flush with mine and rest my chin on her shoulder. "I have a surprise for you," I whisper against her ear.

She leans into me, groaning. "Mmm, is that right. Should we sneak away?" Tyler asks, subtly rubbing her ass against my hardening dick. That's all it takes from her. A subtle touch and I'm rock hard.

The vibration against her body as I chuckle grants me a soft gasp through Tyler's parted lips. "Naughty girl, I'm more than happy to take you inside and bend you over the counter, but I mean I have somethin' for you in the gift variety, not my cock. Although, bein' that I'm such a generous man, I'm sure there's a way you can arrange for both." I grin and nip at her earlobe.

Tyler groans again and rubs against me. If she's not careful I'm going to make good on my word and drag her inside draped over my shoulder. I'm already so hard my cock is threatening the integrity of my shorts. Reaching into my pocket before they become too restricted to fit my hand inside, I pull out the little box Wyatt and I purchased.

"You didn't have to get me anything." Tyler takes the box from me.

"I know." Brushing my lips against her neck I continue, "now open it."

Tyler's eyes go wide as she sees the silver necklace with a whisk charm and a pair of cupcake earrings. One hand flies to her lips as she gasps. Then she's laughing as she sees the small saying at the base of the box. 'Beat it, just beat it.'

When Wyatt brought me to a jewelry store in the

mall I have to admit I was slightly apprehensive. In the time that I've spent getting to "re" know Tyler, I haven't once noticed her wearing any jewelry. But when she pointed out the charm and the saying on the corresponding box, I know this was made for Tyler.

"It's perfect," she says, turning in my arms to wrap hers around my neck. Looking up to meet my eyes she thanks me then burrows into my chest.

"You're more than welcome. I'm so proud of you! Your dream is finally a reality," I say, bending to kiss the top of her head. Leaning down further towards her ear I whisper, "now about that other surprise." I drop my voice a few octaves, "go inside and get naked. I'll be there in two minutes. Be ready."

Tyler doesn't hesitate. My demanding tone leaving her without argument. We're no Christian Grey and Ana Steele, but I've noticed Ty likes my demanding tone. As she turns to leave I lightly slap her ass and send her on her way. Taking one last sweep of my surroundings, I adjust my aching cock and follow in her wake. God, this girl is going to be the death of me.

CHAPTER TWENTY-FIVE
ZAC

I could smell the chicken as soon as I opened the door. Tyler's house was becoming like a second home to me. Two months and we're still having dinner just about every night. I come home after a long day of animals, shower, change, then head next door. It's a routine and it works for everyone. I like having Tyler's warm body to hold and Tyler likes having a full house to cook for. And Wyatt, well she gets free homework help.

"Honey, I'm home," I say, as I make my way into the kitchen. Tyler looks over her shoulder and smiles at me, but keeps working on chopping the vegetables for steaming. She's wearing blue running shorts and a tank top, her hair in a high ponytail. She looks good enough to eat.

Moving towards her, I rest one hand on either side of her hips against the counter. Caging Ty in, I press my chest against her back and fit her toned ass against my jeans zipper. Running my nose against her right shoulder blade from her lat to the spot where her shoulder meets her neck. Inhaling the sweet smell of sweat from my girl's skin. "Did you go for a run?" I ask, placing a kiss to her neck below her ear causing her to shudder against me.

Tyler leans into my touch and tilts her head to grant me more access to her soft skin. "Mhm, Wyatt and I went for a jog before she started her homework." Tyler turns in my arms and I crush my mouth against hers. Her lips pliable and salty with sweat. Tracing the seam of her mouth with my tongue, she opens to tangle with me. Our tongues dance and taste each other.

Then, at the sound of footsteps in the stairs, I reluctantly pull away from Tyler and spin to place my back against the counter next to her swaying body. Lately, it has been harder and harder to back away from Tyler. Even though we talked with Wyatt months ago about me staying the night, Tyler didn't want to introduce Wyatt to PDA since it would be a new concept for her. Seeing that Kent never showed any.

"Hey, bug," Tyler says, trying to disguise the quake in her voice. The effect not lost on me. "How did your homework go?"

Groaning deep in her chest, Wyatt flails her body into her chair at the table. "Uhh, it's so dumb. I don't get it. Math is way too hard and when will I ever need geometry and planes for soccer." Tyler chuckles at her daughter's dramatics and I try to cover my smile with a cough.

"Actually, peanut, those geometry problems might help with kicking goals," I offer to Wyatt's skeptical face. "Go get your work and bring it here. We'll work on it together."

"Thanks, Daddy," a shocked hush descends on the room. "I'm mean Zac, I'll be right back." The little girl takes the stairs two at a time to get away from her blunder.

Tyler is rooted to her spot in front of the vegetables she was cutting. I'm in a shocked daze myself. I never saw myself as the fathering type, but then with Wyatt it's not like I'm fathering at all. I'm simply over all the time and helping when needed and hanging out when allowed. Wyatt doesn't need punishment because she's never getting in trouble, so, it makes this easy. We have fun together and enjoy each other's company. But a father- or step father?

The longer Wyatt takes upstairs, the more awkward Tyler seemed to feel. "Hey," I reach for her wrists folded against her chest and pull her towards me. This time as our bodies mold together the hormonal charge is less intense. "Hey, it's ok. I get it, I'm always here. It happens."

"Zac, I saw your face when Wyatt called you 'Daddy.' You freaked. You want nothing to do with that. And if that's the case why are you here. You know we're a packaged deal. You can't have me without her. It doesn't work that way." Tyler burrows her face into my chest, hiding her eyes from mine.

"I'm not sure what face you saw, darlin', but I wasn't freaked." Tyler looks up and pleads with me to be honest. "Ok, I was, but not for the reasons you think." Leaning down I place a kiss to her forehead, stalling the inevitable. "The face you think you saw was me freakin' out that I wasn't freakin' out. I never saw myself as a

Dad. You know the point of reference I had for that title growin' up. I never wanted to turn into that. So, bein' called Daddy should have been a rude awakenin' for me, but it wasn't. Hearin' Wyatt call me by a name of reverence- a name that should mean somethin' to a young girl- made me proud. I am proud that Wyatt thinks of me as someone that will always be there for her, because I will. I'll always be there for you too. No matter how this thing between us turns out."

Taking Tyler's cheeks in my palms, I wipe her tears with my thumbs, than bring her lips to mine. A soft kiss to reassure her that I'm not going to disappear now that things have gotten real. I love this woman and I love her daughter. And while we haven't said the words yet, I know she feels the same.

Wyatt comes down the stairs breaking our embrace, than we start working at the table. Tyler moves back to finishing dinner. All thoughts of Wyatt's mishap forgiven, without saying the words. Instead, Wyatt and I joke to make sure our relationship is as sturdy as it was before her accidently calling me daddy.

At dinner, Tyler brings up the idea to Wyatt that I might stay over more often. Which is hard to imagine since I'm here more often that not anyway. But Wyatt takes it with stride and says she can't wait to have a live in tutor. However, I think we're still a little ways away from moving in together, but we're definitely headed in that direction. It may be quick, but Ty and I aren't kids anymore- we have history. We aren't going into this blind. Not to mention when I've stayed the night here over the past few months the nightmares have stayed at bay.

When dinner ends, Tyler takes Wyatt upstairs to go

to sleep and I start on the dishes. The same routine since our first dinner together. The phone rings as I'm putting the last of the cutlery into the dishwasher. I can hear Wyatt's small voice enthusiastically talking to whoever's one the phone.

Wyatt's door closes, and I expect to hear Tyler head towards me, but after ten minutes she's still lingering upstairs. Maybe she's waiting for me in her room. Normally, the routine has been that we watch some horrible TV show before making our way to her bedroom-or the nearest flat surface-to make love on. Ty's always saying, *"I like to make sure Wyatt's asleep before jumping you."* But maybe she's needy and ready now.

Making my way upstairs, turning off the lights as I go, I hear Tyler yelling from behind her closed door. "What the hell?" I say, under my breath. Did I miss someone coming in here? Is she still on the phone? As I reach her door, I hear a loud thud then pieces falling to the floor. Wyatt coming to her door and looking to the hall alarm written all over her face. "It's ok, Honey. Go back to bed. Your momma just dropped somethin'." Satisfied, Wyatt closes her door and returns to her bed.

Knocking lightly on the door, I open and peak my head around the corner. "Ty?" She doesn't answer, but as I step fully into her room I see her shaking body crumpled beside her bed. Her lithe body racked with tremors, as she cries into her pillow. I assume so that Wyatt doesn't hear her pain. But I do, I hear the pain through every sob as I move closer.

CHAPTER TWENTY-SIX

Tyler

As tears soak my pillow I feel a warmth encircle me. Zac's strong body comes around mine as if protecting me from some unseen danger. The sheer protectiveness of the position he has taken sends comfort coursing through my body. He doesn't say anything at first-just holds me. Just lets me know he is there and I'm safe. Something only he has been able to give over the time we've spent together. The comfort he brings from this simple contact is the only thing I need right now.

Turning in his caress, my sobs weakening to slight sniffles. I wrap myself around Zac like a monkey. Arms coming to rest against his ribs and my legs hooking at my ankles at his lower back. His warmth bringing my peace. "Tyler, what's goin' on?" he asks, placing sweet kisses against my temple and moving us to my bed.

I take a steady breath. "It was Kent. He called to say goodnight to Wyatt and she mentioned you being at dinner. Kent yelled at me and called me a whore for being with you. Yelling that he didn't want a deadbeat townie watching his daughter grow up. Saying we were no good, small town people and he was getting custody of Wyatt so we couldn't destroy her childhood." Hearing myself say Kent's hurtful words I can hear how ridiculous they sound. It doesn't make them hurt any less though. I know the courts wouldn't take Wyatt away from me, but the chance of Kent getting any custody of my daughter scares me. His words cut so deep and I don't want them defining my daughter.

"Shhh," Zac coos, rubbing circles into my back. "Turn over, sweet girl." Without hesitation I turn onto my stomach. Zac takes the hem of my shirt and lifts it until the fabric is over my head and drops it to the floor beside the bed. My breathing catches in my throat. Zac unhooks my bra. Placing a faint kiss to each shoulder as he pushes the straps down my arms. I'm practically mewling against the bed.

The bedside table drawer opens then closes and my eyes close as the warming lotion hits my skin. A thick line from the base of my spine to my neck undulating my body. A moan escaping my parted lips as Zac's strong hands massage the lotion into my skin. My body tingling with pleasure, calming my sore, stiff muscles.

Kent always leave me so tense. This is by far the best wind down since the divorce. Well, there could be one thing that made it better, but this is a sweet gesture. We'll have time for sex later. I want to talk tonight anyway. Zac and I have been getting closer over the past couple months and I'm picturing a future with him. Especially with Wyatt's blunder tonight, thinking of Zac in the male role to this family unit is becoming more and more a possibility.

"Hey." I turn my head to look over my shoulder at Zac as he continues rubbing my back. "You sure you're ok about earlier?"

Zac looks confused, fingers pausing momentarily. Then he smiles as realization dawns on him. "Of course. It was probably just a Freudian Slip, anyway, since Kent probably helped with homework while you made dinner."

"Actually, Kent would always tell Wyatt to 'figure it out.'" He was more the 'beer and football dad.'" I can hear the sadness in my own voice, but seeing it in Zac's eyes is almost too much. It's not pity, which is the plus side, since I get that from enough people. Instead, it's genuine sadness for what Wyatt had to grow up with.

Zac stops his roaming hands, wipes them on his pants, then twines his fingers in mine. "I never had a great role model in the dad department, you know this. But even with that sorry excuse for a man, I know what love is. Love is what you share with your daughter. What your parents share with you and Wyatt alike. Love is what I can give to Wyatt. She doesn't need Kent, I'll make sure of that."

Zac's lips fuse to mine and I melt. The way this man cares for my daughter is nothing like what I expected. I never thought when I moved here I'd not only find a way to heal my life, but also bring such a good man into Wyatt's life. I love that he loves Wyatt. I love that he cares for the two of us. I love-I love him.

God, do I love him.

Pulling back, I cup his cheek, "You're not the man I thought you'd be. You're better. You're a good man, Zachariah. I-I lo."

Zac interrupts me with another kiss. When he pulls away, he looks deeply into my eyes, "I love you, Tyler. I fell in love with a spunky high school, and nothin' has changed since then."

"When I was younger I thought I knew what love was. I thought I had it with Kent. But in the short time we've been doing, whatever it is we've got going, I've realized what I had with Kent was comfortable companionship compared to what you make me feel. I love you, too, Zachariah Jacobson and I only wish I'd realized it in high school."

CHAPTER TWENTY-SEVEN
ZAC

Walking through the doors of yet another new high school is no longer daunting. After three schools in six months, being the new guy is second nature. It's my fault after all. My last school had had enough of my "shenanigans" after the last prank landed twenty kids injured from the indoor slip and slide I organized down the main hallway.

So here I find myself at yet another school with yet another group of kids I don't care to introduce myself to. Walking towards the locker I was assigned, I find myself turned around. There's three hallways vertically and two hallways horizontal at the ends poorly labeled 100 thru 600. Except the 200 hallway is the office and the 700 hallway are the extracurriculares. This shit doesn't make any sense. I just need to find the L300 hallway.

Turning myself around for what feels like the tenth time, my backpack bumps something. Spinning on my heel I see the little thing I hit. The small girl is wearing shorts and a beaded tank top. Blonde hair flowing over her shoulders as she spins towards me. *"Sorry about that."* The girl's pixie sweet voice music to my ears. But that's not what has me captivated. The most beautiful blue gray eyes I've ever seen looking up at me has my breathing caught in my throat.

The sweet thing turns to look back at her friend before the other girl keeps moving along with the throngs of people surrounding us. *"Hey, I'm Tyler, are you new?"*

"Isn't Tyler a guys name?" I smirk finding my voice.

"Maybe so, but it's mine and if you want to continue being an ass you can find your class your damn self." She's fiery. I like it.

"You're right. I'm truly sorry," I say sarcastically. Fuck, I'm such a dick. *"So, Ty, where would I find the L300 hallway?"*

"I'm showing you only because my locker is down there and has nothing to do with that half-assed apology." With that Tyler starts walking and I'm more than happy to let her take the lead.

Her tight ass seems to dimple with each step in her tight shorts. Even if I wanted to look away, the pendulum motion of her hips has me hypnotized. Entranced by the gentle sway. A small strip of creamy skin on display between her shorts and teal tank top.

"Let me see your schedule." Tyler turns, holding out her hand as we take the steps down. Shit, I didn't even know there was another level. Now the L makes sense- lower 300 hallway.

Handing over the sheet of paper the office sent to my house last week, she smirks. She probably sees we have classes together. Hopefully we do, maybe I'll actually make it to class. *"See a class you like on there?"* I nod towards the sheet she's holding.

"Oh, we don't have any classes together, so I wouldn't know. But my boyfriend has three with you." The smirk widens and I have to physically will myself to keep in step with her. Of course she has a boyfriend.

Fuck!

Groaning low in my chest, I hold tight to the warm body in my arms. Tyler, the girl from last night's memory, is resting in my arms. She was Kent's girl then. She may have had passing flirtation with me. Maybe even a mild fascination with my bad boy tendencies, but she had always been his. But now, now the girl who didn't take any of my shit is naked and pressed against my body.

But the best part about this whole situation is not that for the past month I haven't had one damn flashback from my time deployed. No, the best part is that this perfect woman, sweet and kind, loves me. A part of me has loved her since that day in the hallway when I was so turned around I couldn't tell my head from my ass.

Then there's a noise coming from downstairs and I guess that must have been what woke me. Dislodging my arm from under Ty's neck as gently as I can, I stand and find a pair of basketball shorts to put on and see what the little morning person is up to.

Walking into the kitchen, the mess surrounding a little dirty blonde head is almost insurmountable. "Peanut, I think you're so messy we're just going to have to throw you away. There's no cleanin' you from here." I chuckle, moving in to kiss the top of her head.

"Haha, you're so funny, Zac." Wyatt doesn't even break a smile at my joke. "Now that you're up, why don't you just help me, Mr. Funnyman?" I look around and try to surmise what she's trying to make, but I keep coming up empty.

"Help you with what? What is it you're doin' here, darlin'?"

"Making Momma breakfast. I heard her crying last night and I want to make her feel better."

"Well, there's nothing funny about that, is there?" I beam at the kind soul Wyatt inherited from her mother. "Put me to work, Lieutenant. Where can I be the most useful?" I salute her before moving to wash my hands in the sink.

Fifteen minutes pass with Wyatt reading me step by step directions. Making sure I'm following her orders to a T. We've gone from working together to her yelling out orders and me following with baited breath. Something she's finding extremely entertaining. But who can complain when the final product will undoubtedly make Tyler happy. Thankfully, regardless of how it actually tastes.

As I'm placing the cookie sheet of pastries in the oven, a glimpse of blonde hair peeks around the corner. Tyler is sitting on the last step watching her daughter and I bicker over how everything should be done. Most of the time I know Wyatt is right, but what's the fun in letting a nine year old win?

While Wyatt continues ordering me around I bring her a cup of coffee, just the way she likes it. She joins us and puts the finishing touches on breakfast. "So, what's the plan today, guys?" Tyler asks, taking a bite of the whatever it is Wyatt had us make. Something sweet, sticky, and chocolaty.

"I have my game this afternoon," Wyatt offers.

"And I should probably stop by the office at some point," I add.

"Well, Judy and Ava have the store covered this morning and I don't need to go in until later to check on things for tomorrow. We have a big wedding cake to finish by ten tomorrow morning." Swiveling to look at the clock on the oven behind her, she says, "how about we go walk around the farmer's market for a little, then we can see if Grandma and Pop Pop can watch you while Zac and I go into work. I can meet all of you at the game."

"I can take Wyatt into work with me. I'll just be checking on restocking orders and admin work. We'll get lunch, go to the office, then you can meet us at the game," I offer.

Wyatt is jumping up and down before Tyler can even answer. "Yes, yes, Momma please. Can I go with Zac, I promise to be good?"

Tyler looks between her daughter and I, raising her eyebrows as if to say 'you sure you want to take that?' I shrug and smile. It seems to be enough to satisfy her because Tyler turns to Wyatt and says she better get dressed if she's going into work with me.

The farmer's market was great. I bought a rose for each of my best girls. It was gross and hot, but what else is new in Georgia. Though, every time we bobbed and weaved between the different vendors, I couldn't shake the feeling of being followed. It was the same feeling I got when Tyler and I were together at her opening months ago.

Casually checking over my shoulder and performing some stealthy diversion strategies I could see nothing amiss. No one was following us, but that didn't stop the shiver from rising up my spine with warning. I search each face we pass for anything suspicious, but nothing seems to point me toward the origin of my concerns.

"I need to head into the shop now." Ty leads Wyatt and I toward the parking lot. "You listen to Zac and I'll see you at your game." She pulls Wyatt into her arms and kisses her head.

"Yes, Momma. I'll keep an eye on him." The little runt thinks she's so funny.

"Haha," I wrap my arms around her and tickle her sides.

"Oh-kay. Ah, st-top. Unc-le Un-cle," Wyatt stutters between giggles.

Tyler is looking at us with a happy gleam in her purple eyes and I love that I can do that for her. After the years of torment, she's been through, I'm glad I can be the one to make things right-make her happy. "We'll be good. See you at the game." I keep Wyatt in my arms as I lean toward Tyler to kiss her goodbye. "Love you," I say, before kissing her cheek.

"I love you both, have a good lunch." Tyler moves toward her car. We took two cars so Wyatt and I could stay and eat lunch while Tyler rushed off to the shop. She's been doing great since the grand opening. She hired two new assistants a month after the opening, and they've been working out well, from what I gather. Tyler's been letting them manage the shop alone more and more. Now she's able to take weekend mornings off to spend with us.

Sitting at the game, I'm watching Wyatt warm up on the side of the field. The other mothers waving their hellos. They were very interested the first time I showed up here with Tyler and Wyatt, but after the four months we've been together they've gotten used to seeing me with my girls. I love the idea of that. The idea that Tyler and Wyatt are mine because they are. You won't be able to argue otherwise, Kent be damned.

Watching the referees show up and the other team take their positions on the field, Wyatt looks up at me, concern visible on her small face. "Where's Momma?" she mouths to me.

I shrug and reach for my cell. The game was supposed to start ten minutes ago. They're behind and clearly so is Tyler. I know she had a big wedding to prepare for, but I can't imagine she'd be late for this. It may not be a huge game, so to speak, but all games are overly important to Wyatt.

All my calls are going to voicemail and my texts are left unanswered. We're well into the second half and I know Tyler would never be this late without letting someone know. Without texting or calling me to let me know. Poor Wyatt keeps watching the parking lot and up at me to see if she missed her momma coming in. I'm having a hard time myself keeping my focus on the game when my thoughts are running wild with situations Tyler might be in.

Reaching for my phone again, I call Tyler's parents and ask if I can drop Wyatt off. I don't want to worry them so I say Tyler is working late and I want to bring her dinner and see if she needs any help. Fuck, I hope that's the case.

CHAPTER TWENTY-EIGHT

Tyler

Twisting the lock in the door, I race towards my car and break probably a dozen laws to make it to my house in enough time to change before meeting Zac at Wyatt's game. Thank God, he was able to take her. After single parenting- even while married- for so long, it's nice to have someone to share the responsibilities with. Not just help bring in a paycheck and assume that's contribution enough to the household.

Leaving my car door open and running while I take the front walk steps two at a time, I slip into the house and kick the door closed behind me. Except it doesn't close. It brushes past my leg and hits me square between my shoulder blades and the back part of my head. Bending forward, I'm momentarily confused and startled before the splitting pain radiates through my head.

What the hell happened? Turning to see how I

managed to hurt myself while closing the door I come face to face with a very drunk and very angry Kent. Backing away, I recognize the blurry vision and red blush as his tell that he's had well over his fair share of alcohol today. There's something else though. Kent has been an unhappy, resentful man for the majority of our marriage, but this. This is different. The look of pure distaste and malice in his stare stops be dead in my tracks.

"Kent, what are you doing here? You kn…"

"Where's my daughter, ho?" Kent cuts me off, beginning to look around the house.

"Kent, you shouldn't be here. You're drunk. I think it's best if you leave and sober up before you try to see Wyatt." I try to appease his want to see his daughter because it's not like I can say, 'Kent you're drunk, I'm going to make sure your daughter never sees you like this' to a drunk Kent.

"Didn't you get my letter? I'm not leaving here until I see my daughter. Fucking, Wyatt. You were always so set on giving her a boy's name? What you had it rough in life now you want our daughter to feel your pain. I never should have let you name her after a boy. It was probably someone you were fucking at the time." Kent spews his hate everywhere. Then, it hits me-his letter? It was him.

"Kent, I never cheated on you. You were the only man I've slept with and you know it." Trying to stand my ground while backing away. If I could just get to the phone I could call 911, but I left my damn cell in the car in my mad dash to get changed and to the field.

"Yeah, well you're sure as shit fucking people now. You and the fuckwad Zachariah. I knew he always had a thing for you. Always staring at you in school. Wanting what was mine. You're still mine, always will be. I popped that cherry. I fucked you so good." Kent's normally piercing blue eyes are almost black his pupils are so large. The short dark hair I'm so used to seeing frame his face has grown out and grown greasy with the booze. The man I walked down the aisle to and watched hold our baby so tenderly is long gone. The man in his place is a bitter, angry man.

Taking tentative steps back, bringing the phone nearer, Kent is advancing on me. "Kent, please don't do this. We'll talk to the courts and see about getting you visitation." Again, it's a bold faced lie. After this, I'm hoping I never have to see this man again. We're better off with his negativity out of our lives. "We don't need to rehash the past, I'm not yours anymore."

Clearly this was exactly the wrong thing to say, because in an instant Kent is on me. Both hands grabbing for me. Screw the phone, my entire body is set on fire with the need to escape. Vases and tables are knocked over in my effort to get away. But even with his beer gut he's fast. He has both my hands above my head and my front pressed against the nearest wall before I can reach the door.

With his left handing holding like a vice around my wrists, his right begins to roam. "Maybe I should just remind you how good it is with me. Remind you how I can make your body feel. Maybe put another baby inside you and force you to come back." Kent seethes into my ear. His hand moving under my shirt and pinching my nipples.

"Please, Kent, don't do this." I whimper, *"please."*

"What, baby? You don't like my touch anymore?"

Kent asks, lips against my neck. Fingers toying with the button on my shorts, diving into my panties.

I can't let this happen. I need to think. I cross my legs trying to block out Kent's touch. I scour the recesses of my brain to think of a way out of this. Then I remember one of the defense classes the wives put together. That's it.

Taking a deep breath, I muster all my strength and drive my hips backward against Kent in one sharp movement. The force throwing Kent over the back of the couch landing on his ass. Rushing to the nearest phone, I pick it up, but only get the 9 dialed.

"Ah, ah, ah. I wouldn't do that if I were you." Looking up I see Kent pointing his service pistol at me. Oh, God, he's really lost it this time. "I suggest you put the phone down and follow me to the car."

Out of options, I follow Kent to my car. Noticing for the first time Kent's beat up Chevy on the street. How could I have been so dumb to miss that on my way in? Kent motions for me to get in the driver's seat. Tears rolling down my face, Kent instructs me to drive to the warehouse district an hour away.

"I want to take my time with you before I see my daughter," he says, rubbing the barrel of his pistol up my inner thighs until he reaches my sex.

Tears blur my vision-this is it for me. Please, God, don't let Kent get his hands on Wyatt. Please, Zac, keep her safe. As I drive along the main highway, Kent's gun points to my stomach from his lap, I pray silently that Wyatt will be ok without me. I love her more than life and if I have to give mine to put Kent away and keep her safe once and for all, then that's what I have to do.

CHAPTER TWENTY-NINE
ZAC

Driving first to the Thomas' house to drop off Wyatt, I then head to the shopping center to see if Tyler got held up there. I don't see her car anywhere, but still hop out and recon the place just in case. Nothing seems out of order so it's to our houses next. Pulling onto our street, there's a random truck in front of Tyler's house, but her car is missing. Where are you, Tyler?

Parking in my drive, I make my way over to Tyler's. Walking up the front path I see Tyler's phone laying broken in the grass. Redirecting, I move to the side of the house, I look through the windows to see if anyone's still inside.

I see no movement, but see signs of a struggle. Everything is either upturned or broken. What the fuck? Pulling out my cell, I call up Peterson-I think he's still active-and make my way to the car.

"Hey, Corporal. I got a favor to ask you," I say after

he answers on the second ring.

"Sure, Serg. What can I do you for?" *Everything,* I think.

"I might have a situation on my hands, are you able to run a plate for me? It wouldn't really be on the right side of legal." I pray Peterson is willing to bend the law a little. Although, if I didn't think he'd do it I wouldn't have called him.

"Yeah, what's the number?" I rattle off the license plate and try the handle. The car's locked, but from what I can see there's a shit ton of beer bottles and cans littering the floorboards. Peterson hangs up to do the search, but I keep snooping.

Fuck, that's a pistol holster. Looking further I see no gun. "Fuck, fuck, fuck." Racing into my house, I move to my closet. Placing the fingers of my right hand against the scanner, my gun safe opens and I pull out a pistol and two spare mags. Placing the mags in my pocket, I shove the gun in the waistband of my jeans, against my back.

There's one last phone call I need to make, before I check back in with Peterson. After three rings, Trey answers the phone. "How soon can you get your scope ready for use?"

"Ah, shit. Someone's in a mood. Where we shootin'?" Trey chuckles. The fucker actually chuckles when my girl is missing.

Trying to remember he doesn't know the shit going on, I take a deep breath. "Tyler's missin'. She never met me at her daughter's game. There's a strange car in front of her house, littered with beer cans, and a gun holster minus the gun. I've got Peterson pullin' strings to check the plates, but I'd bet my left nut it's her scumbag of an ex. He's a cop in some shithole town up north." Grinding out the last part through clenched teeth. "Now I'm gunna ask you one last time, how soon can you get your shit ready?"

"Give me ten then text me an address." I can already hear Trey clearing out his shop and making moves.

"Ten-four." With my backup secured, I need to figure out where the hell that address is. "Peterson, tell me that car belongs to someone named Kent," I say after he answers the phone. If it's Kent at least I know what I'm dealing with.

"Yeah, Kent Williams. How'd you know? What's going on over there, Serg?"

"My girl's gone missin' and her ex's car is in front of our house. They must be in hers. She's got some fancy system in there. I need to know where that car is headin'. I need an address, Peterson." Hopping back in my Jeep, I make my way towards the main highway and give Peterson Ty's info to search.

"Alright, I hacked her navigation system," Peterson's voice comes through my speakers as I start up the Jeep. "It's headed north on nineteen."

"I need an address, Peterson. I got Hicks meetin' me," I say, taking the onramp to the highway.

"Ten-four. I'll let you know when it stops." As Peterson disconnects, I call up Trey and have him head south toward me. There's a lot of empty road between the two of us and it would be an easy stop for Kent to have Tyler pullover. Fuck, I can't believe he's come to this.

Ten minutes into the drive, my phone rings. "Yeah?"

"The car stopped. Serg, it's outside an abandoned warehouse. I have satellite eyes on it, but I won't be able to keep them there for long without red flags going off.

I sent the address to both you and Hicks." Peterson pauses as my phone dings with a text. "Careful, Serg."

"You know me."

"That's why I'm saying careful. You're reckless when you care about someone."

"I hear you, Peterson. Let me know if the car moves." I disconnect the phone, because Peterson knows me all too well. He was one of the men in my ear, through the coms system, as I made my way through the warehouse my last day on duty. I can't think about that now. I need to keep my head on to get to Ty.

"Hang on, darlin'. I'm comin' for you," I say to the empty interior of my Jeep.

CHAPTER THIRTY

Driving like a bat out of Hell, I get to the warehouse district in 38 minutes. Locating the correct building, I drive past it and park out of sight. Leaving my phone, I make my way back on foot. Trey was closer than I was starting out and he's already casing the place when I jog up.

"Alright, from what I can tell, this dude has her alone. I'm gonna warn you now, she's in bad shape. Mostly cosmetic, but it's there and I wanted you warned." Trey continues the rundown of what he thinks are our best options are. I pull my gun and check the chamber and mag. Both full and ready, I place it back into my waistband.

"I hear ya," I say, taking one last look at the building. "If you think the higher window is our best option then that's what we're doin'. We'll split and cover." I finalize the plan and we start to climb the transformers next to the warehouse.

Feeling adrenaline like I haven't felt in years, I hook my hands around the open windowsill and work my way through the opening as soundlessly as possible. Trey following close behind. We both pull our guns and start clearing room after room.

With the top floor clear, we separate and I move to the lower level. I can see Tyler now. She's tied to a chair in the middle of an open floor. There's only so many places to skirt around before I'll be out in the open with them. Tyler's bloodied face is puffy and her left eye looks like it may be swollen shut. And now, at this closer range, I can hear the venom Kent is spitting.

"You think he'll want you now that you look as ugly outside as you are inside?" Kent snarls into her ear from behind her body. I'm directly in front of Ty, but in the shadows of the floorplan, neither can see me. "You think he'll want your body after I'm done with you?" The asshole then takes his gun and brushes it against Tyler's inner thigh moving toward her core. The bastard has her legs tied to each chair leg, forcing them open. The fucker is toying with her.

Just like in the sandbox, I look up to make sure Trey has taken the high ground. Spotting his rifle barrel, I know he's in position if things go south. I'm not waiting any longer to get the asshat away from my girl. Stepping slightly out of the shadows, I use the face of my watch to attract Tyler's attention. She needs to play along. She needs to get his back to me before I can move farther out. The element of surprise is key.

She seems to understand what I'm gesturing as I point to Kent, then make a circle, point to my back, then to me. She closes her eyes, takes a deep breath then speaks, "Kent, you're right. Come here. Let me see you." Her speech slurred through ballooned lips.

"You were my first. It was so good. Let me remind you how good. I won't even use my hands, keep them tied up. Just come around and I'll open my mouth for you. You can gag me just the way you like." Tears stream down Tyler's bloody cheeks.

Steam rolls off my body. My muscles coiling tight at the words cooing out of Tyler's split and bloated lips. I can't listen to this anymore, forget surprise- I'm taking this bastard down. But as I'm about to move, Kent circles around Tyler, placing his back to me.

He's fucking petting her hair back, as if admiring his handy work. Admiring how he wore her down to nothing but wanting to please him. He's a fucking psychopath. But, he can potentially be talked down it appears. I think I can talk him down. He's on an ego trip, he just wants to prove his dominance. No one has to die today, but I'm not taking any chances. I cock my gun, then hide it behind my leg, finger inside the trigger guard-ready if things start to get hairy.

Kent must have heard the gun, because he turns then and see me stepping out of the shadows. "You fucking cunt," Kent yells at Tyler before smacking her with the butt of his pistol. Her head lists to the side, then stilling-a fresh cut against her temple. Gritting my teeth, I keep myself from pulling my gun and shooting the fucking prick. Turning back to me Kent spits, "she knew you were there, didn't she?" Kent's left hand toggles the gun like it's a pointer, moving it between Tyler and me.

I don't confirm, there's no point. He's already punished Tyler for it. "You here to rescue her?" I nod.

"You're a fucking pussy, you know that? You've wanted what was mine since high school. Don't think I didn't know how you looked at her. I bet you fuckin' shot your load to her alone in your bedroom. You're just getting my sloppy, loose ass seconds." He's proud as he talks. Thinking he's the bigger man because he had her first.

Trying to put a crack in his plan, I agree. "You're right. I wanted what you had in high school. Tyler was yours and I thought about her constantly." It's not a lie and it seems to be helping him loosen his guard- that's what I need. "I wanted her, and when she moved back I saw my openin'."

"And she wanted you? You deadbeat townie. What can you give her that I can't? You haven't even left the state probably, you, waste of space hick nobody." Interesting that he hasn't heard about my service. How did he think I found him? Or got all the way to the position we're in without him hearing me? He's a fucking tool that is dumber than a box of fuckin' rocks. He turns to Tyler, I assume to ask her the same questions, but it leaves him vulnerable. Just the opening I was waiting for.

I make my move. Dropping my gun- to ensure there's no 'accident'- I barrel into Kent, tackling him to the floor. With the surprise attack, Kent's grip loosens on the gun enough that I can knock it loose with my elbow and kick it across the room. With the threat of being shot eliminated I set to settle the score with Kent. I roll over him and straddle his waist with my hips. My knuckles beating down on his face. Blood trickling down his nose and from a small cut I've made along his left cheekbone. I see red. All noise has silenced and I'm unleashing pain on the sole man responsible for ruining the childhood of a nine year old girl and torturing the woman I love.

I'm still beating Kent when a hand settles on my back. Startled, I look up to see Trey, "That's enough. I think he's out. I called the cops and they're on their way with an ambulance. Although, it looks like we're going to need two." I look back down at the limp body below me, still not satisfied with the anger bombarding me. "Go get your girl, Serg." Those are the only words he could say to get me to forget the hatred coursing through my body.

Tyler.

She's ok, badly beaten, but she'll be ok and seems to have woken from Kent knocking her out. Kent will never be an issue for her anymore. Rushing to my feet I sprint the three feet to her and take her face in my hands. Moving my fingers over her bloodied skin I check to make sure nothing is broken or too badly injured. She's crying, "Baby, I'm here. He's not going to hurt you anymore. Can you stand?" I ask, lowering my hands to untie her, I can hear the faint sound of sirens in the distance.

"Zac, I was so s-scared. I-I didn't know if you'd b-be able to find me. He took m-my cell. How d-did you get h-here?" Tyler cries and slurs as she rises from the chair.

I pull her into my arms, loosening my grip when she winces from my touch. "It doesn't matter how I found you, only that you're safe. And you are now. I'm gunna keep you safe, darlin'."

"I know, I-I love you." Tyler, looks up at me, cups my cheeks, and presses her lips to mine. The kiss is chaste and I can taste the iron of blood, but it's perfect.

"I love you, too. Now, let's get you outside and checked out by the EMT."

Making our way to the front doors of the warehouse, we are met with cops trying to discern what had happened. Trey has taken off with his and my guns the way we came. Leaving a service pistol and an unconscious Kent the only things in the warehouse. Tyler begins to explain the man inside is her ex-husband who was angry about the custody arrangement. How he came to take his daughter away and was met with only Tyler. Drunk and desperate, he forced her into the car and brought her here.

The cops then asked my involvement. I explained that I had Wyatt and was tipped off that something was wrong when Tyler never made it to us. Finding the house a wreck and Kent's car still on our street I had to act. Explaining my military status was also a factor in how I was able to find and subdue Kent without police involvement. "I understand you may have more questions, but can they wait. I really want to get my girl checked out by the medics over there."

The cops nod and Tyler and I make our way to the ambulance hand in hand. About twenty feet from the truck, Tyler's grip on my hand weakens. I look over to see what's wrong just in time to see Tyler's eyes roll and her body go limp. Moving quickly, I reach for her, but I'm too late. Tyler's head hits the pavement before I can catch her. The only thing I could do to aid the impact was help break the force with which she hit. Medics run to us with a gurney and neck brace and whisk us both to the nearest hospital.

CHAPTER THIRTY-ONE

Tyler

Wet moisture licks up the side of my face. Kent's tongue tracing a line from my jaw to my temple. "You still taste so good." Kent moves to grind his bulging dick against my arm that's tied to a chair. Turning my head away, I cringe at the idea of touching Kent again- or him touching me. "Look at me when I'm talking to you, bitch," Kent yells, then cold metal connects with my face. Shocked, the pain doesn't register until I see blood splatter on Kent's left hand.

The pain radiates from the right side of my face and my vision begins to blur on the same side. I'm stunned into silence and afraid of what will come next. Unfortunately, next is Kent's lips against mine, his tongue trying to pry mine open. I bite his tongue and he pulls back to hit me again. This time with his fist. Not that the pain is any easier to manage.

"You want it rough, baby. I'll give it to you rough."

Kent moves his gun along my collarbone. Sliding it down over one breast, then circles the nipple. Peaks arise out of fear, but Kent is taking it as a sign of arousal. "You like it don't you, baby. Are you wet for me?" Kent moves the gun against my clit and tries to wiggle his other hand into my shorts.

Thanking God for the restrictive material since my legs are spread and tied to the chair so he can't get in. "Please don't do this, Kent. You don't have to do this." My pleas fall on deaf ears.

Then I hear it. A soft whisper. That's not right. Suddenly Kent disappears and the warehouse is gone from my vision. All I see is black, but I must still be tied to the chair- I can't move.

The whisper comes again and this time I recognize it. It's Zac, he's here. He's talking to someone about their head. Or someone else's head. Or about a head somewhere. I can't quite make it out. His voice keeps going in and out. I try to open my eyes. I try to move. To call out to him, but all my efforts are fruitless. Slowly a dark cloud rolls over my body and everything goes black.

CHAPTER THIRTY-TWO
ZAC

"Sir, you're going to have to stay here. We need to work fast and we can't do that with you hovering." A nurse stops the gurney at the emergency entrance of the hospital.

Lifting Tyler's hand to my lip, I kiss her palm. "I'll be right here, Tyler. Wake up for me." I say, as I place her hand at her side. The nurses rush Tyler's unconscious body past the doors and I'm left in the lobby staring after her.

A tear rolls down my cheek and I'm frozen in place. My breathing has become labored and I can't stop the worst case scenarios from flitting through my mind. I can't tell you how long I've been standing here looking at the doors, willing someone to come back and update me.

"Have you heard anything?" I turn to see Trey step up beside me. *When did he get here?* I shake my head and study the tiles at my feet. "Do you need anything?" I shake my head again as another tear rolls down my cheek.

"Actually, I need you to call Tyler's parents." I hand him my phone. "Her dad's in the contacts under Caleb." Trey takes my phone and disappears through the hospital main entrance.

I'm numb, I couldn't save her in time. All my training and I couldn't get to her before that asshole beat her unconscious. I should have been better. Pain rips at my insides and I turn to the nearest seat. Tucking my head between my knees I count my breathing. I can't fill my lungs and I feel like I'm looking in a tunnel.

"Zac," Treys voice pulls me from the seductive darkness. "You need to stay strong. Tyler's parents are coming and they're bringing Wyatt. You can't let her see you like this." He's right-Wyatt needs me. How am I going to be strong for her when my source of strength is lying on a table unresponsive?

"Trey, what am I gunna do? I can't lose her. Shit, I just got her back." Tears blur my vision. Fear lacerates my heart.

"Man, you can't think like that. You don't know what's goin' on back there. She could be waking up and everything's lookin' positive." Trey's always been my voice of reason, but I can't seem to pull myself out of the pit.

"I need an update. I need to know what's goin' on."

"Ten-four." Trey gets up and moves toward to registration desk. My head is throbbing and my chest hurts. The waiting is excruciating.

I drop my head into my hands and press the heels of my palms into my eyes. Trying to relieve the pressure inside my head. I focus on my breathing again and force the oxygen into my lungs. Where the hell is Trey, ten minutes pass and he's no longer at the desk. I stand to see if he's flagged down one of Tyler's doctors, but the lobby is empty.

As I move back to the seating area I notice my hands for the first time. My knuckles are beat to shit. Tiny cuts and the beginnings of bruises cover the backs of my hands. I'm not even sure if the blood is mine, Kents, or Tylers. It doesn't matter at this point, I guess. The pain is nothing compared to the lacerations in my chest worrying about Tyler. But Wyatt is on her way here. She doesn't need to see this. Walking to the bathroom I clean the battered skin and watch the blood disappear down the drain.

Making my way back toward the registration desk, I hear the main door slide open. "Zac," Wyatt's panicked voice yells behind me.

Turning I see Tyler's parents and Wyatt rushing through the doors. I crouch and open my arms just in time to catch Wyatt as she jumps into my arms. She buries her face in my chest. Her tears soak my shirt. My sweet baby girl was falling apart in my arms.

I tighten my hold around her and muster any strength I have, for this girl. I rise to my full height and pull Wyatt with me. She wraps her legs around me and clings to me for support. "Darlin', it's going to be ok. The doctors are workin' hard for your momma," I say stroking her hair.

Tyler's momma comes to hug Wyatt and I. Tears flowing down her cheeks, uncontrollably. Her baby girl is laying on a hospital bed and we don't know what's going to happen. Caleb places his hand on my shoulder.

Eyes red and puffy. He's trying to keep it together for the women. I know the feeling.

Trey returns and I look at him with questioning eyes. He shakes his head and I know he wasn't able to get any information. I cling tighter to Wyatt and try to take solace in the fact that I was able to keep her safe. I was there to make sure Kent didn't get both of my girls.

We move to sit and Wyatt sits on my lap. Her arms remain locked around my neck as her body slowly falls into an exhausted sleep. She has no more energy-no more tears to cry. I keep her close as Tyler's parents sit to one side and Trey sits to the other.

Hours pass like this and we're in a limbo. We still don't know anything other than they're trying to lessen the pressure on Tyler's brain. Trey has tried to keep my mind occupied, but nothing is working. All I see is Tyler's eyes before she went down in the parking lot of the warehouse. Her grip loosening until I lost her. I wasn't able to keep her safe.

"So, April is getting married," Trey blurts out. "Got the invitation last week."

"Tell her congrats for me." Why he's tellin' me about his sister's engagement while the woman I want to spend my life with is on an operating table-I don't know.

"She called and asked it is was ok to have Kenzie as her maid of honor." He hangs his head. Well, shit. Why would his sister think it was ok to have his ex-wife as her maid of honor?

"Man, I'm sorry. So, you told her no?" I ask. I hate to say it, but his sorrow is helping keep my mind off Tyler's situation.

"No, I couldn't do that to her. She's the reason I met Kenzie. It wouldn't be fair for me to not let her choose her best friend as her maid of honor. But I don't know how I'm gunna make it through this damn wedding. Good thing she said it's going to be a long fuckin' engagement. She wants a beach wedding and most things are booked already for the year."

"We'll think of-" I'm cut off as the Tyler's doctor comes into the lobby.

"Family of Tyler Thomas?" Caleb nudges his wife and I carry Wyatt to the doctor. The doctor looks at Wyatt in my arms and I motion for Trey to take the sleeping girl. She doesn't need to hear this. "Ms. Thomas has severe swelling in her brain. We're are working as quickly as possible, but because of her condition we have to be more careful. Who's the father?"

Caleb steps forward, "I am." Caleb grabs his wife's hand and squeezes. His lip trembling.

"The baby seems to be stable. We can't use some of the medications we normally would in order keep the baby from going into distress."

"Wait, I don't understand." Caleb waves his hands back and forth. I'm frozen trying to decipher the words the doctor just said. *Baby?* "Tyler is my daughter. I'm Caleb Thomas, her father."

"Mr. Thomas, I'm sorry for the confusion. Who is the baby's father? We need to know what your wishes are should the outcome be less than favorable." The doctor drones on, but I don't understand any of it. There's a baby?

"Zac, Zac." Mrs. Thomas has taken my hand and is trying to pull me back from the brink of devastation.

"How far along is Tyler?" I ask. It has to be mine, but I need the doctor to confirm it.

"Ms. Thomas is fifteen weeks pregnant. We need to

know what your wishes are for the fetus should Ms. Thomas' state worsen. We can perform a c-section, but it is much too early in the gestation for it to survive outside the womb. We could also leave the fetus and wait to see if it goes into distress."

I fall to my knees and collapse into myself. I'm going to be a dad. Tyler is pregnant with my child and I might lose them both. Tears stream down my cheeks and anger fills my soul. I want to kill Kent. I want to wrap my hands around his neck and watch the life leave his eyes. The pain of possibly losing Tyler and our unborn child is ripping at my sanity.

I need them to pull through.

"Oh, Zachariah," Mrs. Thomas pulls me into her arms and allows me to break down.

"I'll give you a few minutes to talk this over." The doctor leaves us to debate whose life is more important-the woman I love or the child we made together. There's no way in hell I can make that decision.

"Zac, I know you've just been given the best and worst news of your life, but you need to be strong. You have people counting on you-Wyatt, Tyler, and that baby." Caleb places his hand on my shoulder, but I can't bring myself to think about losing either one of them.

"Zac? Is Momma-" Trey is holding Wyatt's hand and she's looking at me with tear stained cheeks.

"No, no sweet girl." I hold my hands out to her and she settles in my arms. "I'm just sad that she's hurt. She's gunna be ok, peanut. We're all gunna be ok." In that moment I know what I'm going to do.

Tyler is strong. She's the strongest woman I know and if anyone can make it out of this with our baby it's going to be her. "We're gunna wait. I know Tyler can pull out of this. No, c-section. They're gunna make it."

"They?" Wyatt asks.

"I meant she. She's going to make it," I say, pulling her tight.

"I'll let the doctor know," Caleb says, patting my shoulder.

I hope I made the right choice. Please, God, let them make it through this. Holding Wyatt, we move back to the seating area and I rub her back until she falls into a deep sleep once again. "I love you, peanut," I whisper against the top of her head.

"I love you, too, Daddy," she mumbles in her sleep.

She may not know what she's saying in her sleep, but this moment will forever be my silver lining. Wyatt is my little girl whether she has my blood coursing through her veins or not. I'm gunna be her daddy-I *am* her daddy.

CHAPTER THIRTY-THREE

Tyler

Light streaming in from a nearby window wakes me in the most uncomfortable bed. Slowly swiveling my head to take in my surroundings I see I'm lying in a hospital bed. Zac is slumbering beside me holding my hand. Crumpled in an uncomfortable position in an armchair. As I try to smile, the pain radiating through my entire body shoots from all directions to the receptors in my brain. All firing at once and the memories of why I'm lying in the hospital come back in vivid detail.

Kent did this to me. He put me in the hospital like I always knew he would. I thought divorcing him meant I would escape this fate, but I was wrong. Kent made good on his promise to make me pay. I can only be happy I didn't pay the ultimate price and can spend another day with my daughter.

I gasp thinking of Wyatt. Is she alright? Did they

get Kent? I remember being abducted. I remember him beating me and trying to get into my pants. I remember Zac coming to save me. But that's it, that's all I remember. I'm replaying it in my mind, but it's like watching a movie and falling asleep before the ending. I don't know what happened to Kent or how the drama ended.

Zac must have heard me, because he's rushing to my side, taking my hand. "Wyatt?" Tears pool in my eyes.

"She's fine. She's with your parents. She's perfect," he says, placing my hand against his cheek. "God, you scared me. You hit your head and I thought," Zac pauses, swallowing. "It doesn't matter what I thought. You're back. You came back to me."

"Of course I did. You're my hero. You healed me when I thought I was unfixable. I love you, Zachariah." I brush my thumb over his cheek and trace his lower lip.

Zac turns to place a kiss against my wrist. "I love you, too, Tyler."

"Come here." I scoot over and pat the space next to me. Zac moves his large frame onto the bed and I snuggle into his side. Absorbing the sense of safety and security I feel when I'm close to him. "How long was I out?"

"Three days, but we'll talk later. You need to rest. I'm going to call the nurse and let her know you're awake."

There's a light knock on the door. I don't know how long I've been asleep or that I even fell asleep, but somewhere between the warmth of Zac's arms and the even rhythm of his breathing I dozed off.

"Ah, good. Your hulk of a man here tells me you're awake. I'm going to check your vitals, then I'll let all your doctors know." A thin nurse with short spunky hair glides into the room. "I'm nurse Jackie, I know just like the TV show- don't even get me started. Is there anything I can get for you?" I shake my head and Jackie moves a cart towards me. Proceeding to take my temperature, blood pressure, and check my monitors and lines. "Everything looks good on my end. How's your pain level?" she asks, pointing to a rating chart on the wall.

"I'd say about a nine. Pain, but no crying. My head is killing me."

"Alright, I'll see what I can do about getting you some pain meds." Zac and I both thank the nurse and she leaves assuring us a doctor will be in soon.

"Ty, there's something we need to talk about now that you're awake." Zac looks apprehensive and I raise an eyebrow in question.

A knock at the door pulls both our attention. "Come in," I say then look to Zac. "What was it you wanted to talk about?"

"It can wait till we're alone." Zac diverts his eyes to the ground and I'm starting to worry I missed something big while I was out.

A woman with graying hair and a white coat walks into the room and rests a hand on my leg. "How are you feeling, Ms. Thomas?"

"I'm ok. I'd be better if I got some pain meds," I try to joke, but it falls flat since laughing is majorly painful.

"Yes, I believe there are some coming. My name is Regina Vall and I was the OB/GYN doctor on call when you came in." My brain and heart stop momentarily. "I first want to say that everything looks fine, but we're going to bring in an ultrasound machine since the fetal monitor seems to show things went well while you were recovering."

"Oh my God, I thought my shorts were too restrictive. I remember him not fitting his hand in my shorts. He tried to. Oh, God." I try to hold it in, but red hot tears stream down my battered cheeks. Zac, tries to comfort me. Pulling me into his arms, shooting daggers at the doctor for causing me pain. I can't believe what Kent did to me. I can't even remember it. Will I be able to have more children? I don't feel pain down there, but that doesn't mean I'm not torn to shreds.

The doctor looks stunned and confused. "I'm sorry, Ms. Thomas, but I'm not sure you understand. The baby is fine from the initial fetal monitoring we did. We just want to check with an ultrasound that nothing has changed through the night. I'm sorry I worried you." Dr. Vall looks taken aback and contrite for causing such a reaction in me.

Then, as if my brain just switched to the on button, I register what the doctor told me. "What baby?" I ask.

"Umm," Dr. Vall looks at Zac then back to me. "Ms. Thomas, you're pregnant. About fifteen weeks, if the tests are accurate from two nights ago. Mr. Jacobson didn't tell you?"

I look at Zac and see the shocked smile on his face. He's happy, he wants a baby. "Fuck," Zac grunts. "I was gettin' there. You interrupted me as I was startin'." He traps the poor doctor in a steely gaze.

"Yes, well, we're just going to get some imaging to make sure nothing has changed. I don't suspect there has, we just need to make sure. The technician will be here soon to get started." Dr. Vall moves toward the door and as she reaches for the handle, she turns and smiles. "And congratulations."

"Thank you," Zac and I say in unison. I turn to Zac as he crushes his lips to mine. A soul searing kiss that leaves me tingling. Groaning at the twinge of pain that radiates from my wounded face, but not enough to stop the kiss.

"I love you so much, sweetheart." Zac says, pulling back and resting his forehead against mine. "You have no idea how scared I've been. When they came out and asked who the father was I was a mess. I thought I'd lose you both." Resting his hand on my stomach his eyes fill with unshed tears.

I laugh and curl into his lap and thank God that he put Zac in my life. That He sent him to heal me. To love me. To give me life again.

CHAPTER THIRTY-FOUR

Tyler

"Do you know what she'll think about it?" Zac asks, as we drive back home after I was discharged this morning. I'm still achy, but I feel so much better than when I walked out of that warehouse.

Kent tried to take me down and make me submit to his will again. I didn't let him win. While Zac may have helped take the majority of my weight, I walked out of that warehouse on my own two feet. Letting Kent know he hadn't succeeded in beating me down. Physically, yeah, I definitely needed a hospital, but Kent had still lost. I was walking out a stronger woman than the one he dragged in. I won and the bruises on my face and body were my medals of honor.

Now, we were on our way home to tell my daughter she is going to be a big sister. Uh, I'm not sure I'm ready for diapers again. But I have a feeling this is going to be a very different experience than it was the first time around. One, I'm older and wiser now; and two Zachariah is no Kent. He'll be there helping the whole way through. Poopy diapers and all.

"We should probably have a game plan though. Like logistics. Living next door to you has been great and if it's moving too fast, I can understand you keeping your place. We can make it work, I'm sure monitor signals can reach, it's not that far." I'm rambling and I know it. I can hear it, but I can't make my mouth stop moving long enough for my brain to catch up.

Zac, looks at me and smiles, "I do want to keep my place." A knot the size of Texas takes residence in my chest. "As much as I like staying over at your place, mine is much bigger. I have two more rooms than you and a pool. I think you and Wyatt should move into my place, make one of the spare rooms a nursery and the other a playroom for the kids."

I stare at the tattooed, war-hardened Army man and lose my breath at his love for me. "Oh," it's all I can get out. Zac has left me speechless.

"Is that something you would want?"

"Yes! God yes, Zac." I'm jumping in my seat as we pull into my driveway.

Zac reaches over and presses my upper body against his. My nipples tightening to attention as his hard chest meets mine. He moans at the nearness, "Darlin', that moan sounds oddly familiar. But I haven't touched you with my tongue yet, not like I did this mornin'."

I groan and melt into Zac as he kisses my neck. Remembering the orgasm he gave me just before a nurse came to check my vitals. I feel my arousal dampening my panties. "Shhh," I scold him. "You're going to get me all worked up before I have to tell my parents that I'm yet again pregnant and unwed. I'm sure I make them so proud," I joke.

"I know I'm proud of you." His earnest words melt me.

"You are a little bias. Now let's go. Can you get the packages?" Zac reaches for the two packages we put together over my week stay at the hospital, as gifts for my parents and Wyatt.

Wyatt comes barreling down the stairs to greet us only to slow down just before she jumps into my arms. My mother, of course, scolds her to be careful with me. Leave it to Grandma to baby me. Yes, I'm still in pain, but I'm sure as hell not going to complain about a hug from my daughter whom I haven't seen in days. She came to the hospital with my parents a couple times, but it wasn't the same and it scared her seeing me in that situation. This is a much more welcome greeting.

After we've eaten, Wyatt goes to pick a movie while we talk with my parents about Kent's trial and court date that has yet to be set. Then everyone moves to the living room. "Before we start the movie, Zac and I have a surprise for all of you."

Wyatt jumps up, bouncing on the balls of her feet ready for a present. Zac moves to the hall closet where he stashed the gifts and distributes them accordingly. Wyatt rips at the packaging and starts into hers while my mom daintily opens theirs.

Wyatt pulls out her loot. A shirt, that she doesn't read. A package of hot chocolate and marshmallows in a mug, that she doesn't read. A small box that she opens. As she peers in at the heart shaped locket that reads 'Big Sister,' she looks up at me then to Zac.

At the same time, my parents are pulling things out

of their box. A couple of mugs, that they don't read. A picture frame, that they don't read. And a bottle, that reads 'to keep at Grandma and Pop Pop's house.'

I smile at three sets of eyes and grab Zac's hand. "So, we have some news." My mother gasps and jumps up from her spot on the couch. Wyatt has tears in her eyes, but a smile on her face. "At the hospital, during all the testing, the doctors saw that I'm fifteen weeks pregnant. You're going to be a big sister, Bug. Are those happy tears?" I kneel and open my arms to my daughter. My parents knew about the pregnancy, but were afraid to ask what the outcome was after I woke up. After waiting a week, I can see the worry leave my momma as we tell her the baby will be fine.

Wyatt nods against my shoulder. "Yes, Momma. It's happy tears. I want to be a big sister so bad." She pulls away to jump into Zac's arm. He picks her up and the little girl wraps herself around Zac like there's no place she feels more safe than in his arms- I understand the feeling.

My parents come forward to hug and congratulate us. As we sit back down to watch the movie, Zac pauses it and stands. "I almost forgot, there are two more presents."

Confused, I cock my head and look at Zac, "I didn't make anymore presents."

"This is true, but that doesn't mean there aren't two more." Zac reaches in his pocket and pulls out two small jewelry boxes. "Tyler, one of these is for you and your answer will determine if the other present gets distributed." More confusion crosses my face. "I promise it'll all make sense in a second."

"Good, because right now I'm lost," I huff.

Realization hits as Zac lowers to one knee. Holding out a box with a beautifully simple solitaire diamond. "Tyler Thomas, girl with the purple eyes that captivated me into walkin' the almost straight and narrow through high school. When you went away to college I never thought I'd see you again. I never forgot about the girl that got me through school, but I understood you movin' on with your future and at the time, it was Kent. But now you're back and I'm not makin' the same mistake again. While I understood you bein' with Kent, I should have pushed to show you the real him even then. For that I missed out on ten years of a life with you. Not that I can be all that upset, because you brought Wyatt into my life. The two of you have completed me in ways I never realized were missin'.

"When we were in the hospital you mention me healin' you. But darlin', you healed me. Before you, I was walkin' around with scars on my back and scars on my soul. I lived in the memories of my fallen men. I lived in the flashbacks of the night I was rendered useless to the Army. But we've been together, I've only had one flashback of the night I got hurt. You call me hero and say I saved you. But Tyler, you've been savin' me since I was sixteen years old. And now I'd really like to make you my wife. Will you marry me?" Zac finishes and there's not a single dry eye around the peanut gallery from the couch. Including my hard-ass dad.

Looking to Wyatt, I know my answer. "Yes. Yes, I want to be your wife," I squeal as Zac picks me up and spins me twice before placing me on my feet to kiss me. "Now what's that one for? A consolation prize for if I said no?"

Zac laughs, "no, that is for my best girl." Leaving me

and movin' to the table to pick up the other box, Zac kneels in from of Wyatt. "Peanut, I know this has been a really confusing time for you and I know you might not understand everythin' that has been happenin', but know this. I love your Momma so much and I love you just as much. And even though I wasn't there to change your diaper or tuck you in when you had a bad dream, I will be there whenever you need me from here on out. If you'll have me?" Zac opens the box to show a beautiful silver bracelet with one 'I love you' charm dangling around it.

Wyatt nods her head and leaps at Zac. "Can I call you Daddy now?

I have to give the girl credit. Not many people can make a Ranger cry. But as Wyatt clings to Zac, asking if she can call him daddy, a tear slips from his eye. Zac looks to me and I nod, knowing this is right. This is how it always should have been. "Yeah, peanut. You can call me daddy now."

EPOLOGUE
ZAC

"Come on man, we don't have much time. I think they're lining us up." I grunt at Trey as he finishes the last letter on my finger.

"Dude, hold your balls. You're the groom they'll wait for you. Trust me." Trey rubs the A and D ointment on my finger and straightens. "Alright, you're done. How do I look?"

"Like a piece of shit looking to get laid by any and all of the single ladies here tonight. Just tell me you still have the rings."

Trey makes a show of looking for the rings. Patting his pockets in his pants then his jacket making my heart skip a beat. "Just fuckin' with you, they're right here," he says pulling the box from his back pocket.

"Hey, what did you decide to do about Alice's wedding? Isn't it in a couple months?" I ask Trey. We haven't really discussed it since the hospital. I assumed he'd bring it up if he needed to talk. Trey's a private person-I didn't want to push.

"Yeah, seven weeks, and I have no idea. Kenzie is for sure the maid of honor. I'm really kicking myself for not telling my family the truth. I should have just said she's a bitch who divorced me because she couldn't stand being alone while I was deployed. But no, I had to be the nice guy and tell my family the divorce was mutual." Trey shakes his head while he studies the ground.

"Call me when I get back from my honeymoon and we'll figure something out."

"Alright guys, it's showtime," the coordinator hollers. My limited groomsmen line up and proceed to take their positions at one end of the aisle under an arch covered in white roses and calla lilies. Trey stands next to me as my best man and he pats my shoulder as the first bridesmaid walks towards us.

The girls look great in their burnt pink tea length dresses. I know this because when I called it pink looking at the pictures Tyler about tore me a new one. I'm not forgetting that color anytime soon, but could they walk any fuckin' slower? I'm ready to pull the fire alarm just to speed them along. Then I see Wyatt. She looks so grown up. She's holding her baby brother, now six months old, as she walks down the aisle. Her eyes catch mine and I stick my tongue out at her and she giggles before handing Jack off to Tyler's mom.

Wyatt takes her position at the end of the line of bridesmaids as the music changes. I wink at her before turning my head to see Tyler. She's wearing a beautiful ivory dress. Her dainty shoulders uncovered in the strapless sweetheart neckline. Again, yet another fact

I know about women's clothing I didn't before this wedding.

Her breasts threatening to spill out over the material. She underestimated the changes her body would make after giving birth to Jack. While it went back to its normal size relatively quickly, her breasts have yet to bounce back. Not that I'm complaining. Watching her breastfeed my son has become a regular daytime special for me.

Taking her father's arm, they make their way to me. Tyler's eyes are more purple today than the blue-gray from when I first met her. When they lock on me, my mouth goes dry and Trey has to nudge me to close my mouth before Tyler reaches me.

Mr. Thomas shakes my hand acknowledging him giving her away then Tyler takes my hands and joins me under the arch. As the officiant starts the service, Tyler rubs her finger against my tender skin. We both look down and she sees for the first time the tattoo that Trey finished just moments before the ceremony. "ZTWJ" all the initials of our family tattooed across my finger where my wedding band will be placed.

I can hear the sharp intake of breath from Tyler and I'm validated in my need to surprise her. She loves it, I can already tell. The sparkling gleam in her eyes as she looks at the tattoo, then back to me says it for her. She looks past me and locks eyes with Trey and mouths, "I want one." I smile as she brings her attention back to me in time for our vows.

She goes first. "Zachariah, when I first met you I thought you were the most arrogant, most selfish person I had laid eyes on. I'm happy to say that the sixteen year old hooligan grew up to be one of the finest men I know. We had our passing flirtation and stolen moments throughout high school, but coming back to Dahlonega with Wyatt, you were the last thing I expected to find. You were the last person I expected to heal me, but you did. You put back the pieces of my life and reminded me of the girl you once knew. The me I longed to be again.

"And if that were all you had done for me that would have been enough. But it wasn't. You took one look at my daughter and saw her worth. Something that she had only heard from me for such a long time. You cared for Wyatt before you wanted to, even before you acknowledge your feelings for me. I couldn't ask for a better father for my children or a better man to share my life with."

Well, shit how do you go after that. I clear my throat "Thanks for makin' it easy for me. Who the hell wants to go after that?" I garnish a laugh from our family and friends and hope that's enough to get me through these words.

"Tyler, when I first met you I was a three-time-expelled nobody that was goin' nowhere as fast as I could. My dad had taught me early on that I wasn't goin' to amount to anythin' and that I needn't try. So, for years I lived my life as if that were the case. Then after a slip and slide accident my sophomore year I ended up at your school and bumpin' into you my first day. And for the first time I wanted somethin' for myself. I wanted to do well in school and make myself into somethin' so I had even a snowball's chance in hell of gettin' you.

"High school didn't work out for us, but I never forgot the girl with the blue-gray eyes the color of a thunder cloud on a stormy day, that turned the most beautiful shade of purple when she smiled. Especially when she smiled at me. You movin' back to Dahlonega was fate helpin' me out. My nightmares were eatin' me from the inside out. Marin' my thoughts more than the mangled skin on my back ever could.

"From the night I first kissed you my nightmares went away. You have saved me and healed me and gifted me so much that I feel I'll never be able to measure up. You have given me two beautiful children and I can only promise to be all the father and husband I can be." I smile as I work the Army slogan into my vows.

The officiant continues with the ceremony, but I'm not hearing him. His words are a drone as I look into the eyes of the only woman I've ever loved. Tears slowly trailing down her face, Tyler keeps dropping my hand to make sure her makeup isn't running. She looks beautiful. She is the most beautiful thing I've ever laid eyes on.

"I now pronounce you husband and wife." That I fuckin' heard and before he can give me permission, my lips are fused to Tyler's and our fate is sealed together. She's officially mine and I'm hers.

The way it was *always* supposed to be.

ACKNOWLEGMENT

I first want to thank the two people who read and edited this novel, Alli and Sevannah! You two have helped so much I can't begin to thank you for the work you put into helping my words mesh together better.

Then, there's Avery. I don't even know where to start. You have answered my countless questions, assuaged my endless fears, and been a true friend to me. Your guidance has been invaluable and I appreciate the time and care you took in helping me publish this and many more novels to come.

Rowena and Daniella, the work you two do in helping with my blurbs is remarkable. The ideas that ping between you two is a true masterpiece to watch.

The relationships I have made over the last year through social media have been some of the greatest I've ever known. The support and guidance everyone has given me as I made the transition from writer to author has been heartwarming. The writing community has welcomed me with open arms and I hope to one day help a young writer the way you all have helped me.

ABOUT
THE
AUTHOR

Audrey currently lies in Washington DC with her husband and three small children. She is a baseball fanatic that teaches ninth grade history when she's not playing chauffeur, maker of meals, keeper of the schedule, kisser of boo boos, or couch cuddler.

Audrey strives to add a laugh and a little lust to your day with her entertaining, slightly sad, stories and characters. Many of them have to adapt and overcome many challenges along the road to happiness- like who of us doesn't.

Love, Loss & Baseball, was Audrey's debut novel, available July 31, 2018 which is a twisty story of love, secrets, and of course baseball. I hope you enjoyed reading Healing Scars.

Keep a look out for Trey's rough vacation at his sisters wedding. Will he be able to overcome the pain of seeing his ex-wife?

Made in the USA
Middletown, DE
31 July 2020